W9-AHH-717

Praise for

WE ARE GATHERED

LONG-LISTED FOR THE 2019 JQ WINGATE
LITERARY PRIZE

"Skillfully told through multiple first-person narratives, *We Are Gathered* portrays not only the couple's story, but also — or rather, primarily — the stories of their friends and family . . . Jamie Weisman adroitly constructs a community of characters, each created with a private network of thoughts and feelings, hopes and dreams . . . a masterful portrait of both sharp and delicate beauty."

— *Jewish Book Council*

"As sparkling as a glass of champagne, and as moving as a wedding kiss, Weisman deconstructs the novel — and the nuptial — to tell a story about the guests, all of whom are bound to their pasts, created by their pain and elevated by their passions, set against the blazing hope of happily ever after. 'You can't know who you are until the end of the story,' says one character, but in this novel, it's clear who Weisman is from the first sentence: a writer to watch."

— Caroline Leavitt, best-selling author of
Pictures of You and *Cruel Beautiful World*

"Unique . . . compelling . . . creatively put together."

— *Book Riot*, "All the Books"

"*We Are Gathered* is suffused with insight and warmth, interweaving the voices of vastly different characters in a big-hearted and clear-eyed story of life's biggest choices: who to love and how best to love them. The fast-moving, playful intelligence Jamie Weisman brings to this book makes it both compulsively readable and oh so worth the read."

— Heather Harpham, author of *Happiness: The Crooked Little Road to Semi-Ever After*

"With dazzling storytelling and a stunning eye for truth, Jamie Weisman gives voice to the never-heard in *We Are Gathered,* revealing the interior lives of wedding guests as they reckon with paths taken — and not. An amazing book."

— Randy Susan Meyers, author of *The Widow of Wall Street*

"Jamie Weisman's debut novel, *We Are Gathered,* is a pleasure. Like the best kind of party, it has an engaging, energetic mood, lots of captivating people to get to know, and no one wants to leave at the end."

— Tova Mirvis, author of *The Book of Separation* and *The Ladies Auxiliary*

"Weisman glides through several points of view with a graceful fluidity, illuminating the complex interior lives of her characters, and in doing so creates a poignant slice of life much greater than the sum of its eloquent parts."

— Kris D'Agostino, author of *The Antiques*

"A multifaceted story of the difficulties people face."

—*Library Journal*

WE ARE GATHERED

WE ARE GATHERED

JAMIE WEISMAN

MARINER BOOKS
HOUGHTON MIFFLIN HARCOURT
Boston   New York

First Mariner Books edition 2019
Copyright © 2018 by Jamie Weisman
Reading Group Guide copyright © 2019 by Houghton Mifflin Harcourt
Q&A with the Author © 2019 by Jamie Weisman

All rights reserved

For information about permission to reproduce selections
from this book, write to trade.permissions@hmhco.com or to
Permissions, Houghton Mifflin Harcourt Publishing Company,
3 Park Avenue, 19th Floor, New York, New York 10016.

hmhco.com

Library of Congress Cataloging-in-Publication Data
Names: Weisman, Jamie, author.
Title: We are gathered / Jamie Weisman.
Description: Boston : Houghton Mifflin Harcourt, 2018.
Identifiers: LCCN 2017056987 (print) | LCCN 2017046218 (ebook) |
ISBN 9781328793270 (ebook) | ISBN 9781328793294 (hardcover) |
ISBN 978-1-328-58518-9 (paperback)
Subjects: LCSH: Jewish women—Fiction. | Weddings—Fiction. |
Domestic fiction. | BISAC: FICTION / Contemporary Women. |
FICTION / Jewish. |FAMILY & RELATIONSHIPS / Love & Romance. |
GSAFD: Humorous fiction.
Classification: LCC PS3623.E45 (print) | LCC PS3623.E45 W4 2018
(ebook) | DDC 813/.6—dc23
LC record available at https://lccn.loc.gov/2017056987

Book design by Martha Kennedy

Printed in the United States of America
DOC 10 9 8 7 6 5 4 3 2 1

To Victor

CONTENTS

WE ARE GATHERED

The malformed and the moth-eaten

THERE IS NO JUSTICE in this world, and you can start with the simple fact that some people look like Elizabeth Gottlieb. That some people have high cheekbones, wide eyes, long lashes, and look better than the rest of us even after they've just come back from running the six miles that they claim exhilarates them. That those people will never sit alone at snack time, will always have a partner for the art project, will turn down at least two dates for prom before going with the person they really want to go with, that they will be given the option of extra credit if they fare poorly on chemistry exams, will be invited to parties, will have youthful flings with movie stars and at least one semifamous drummer in a band, and then marry a good-looking guy who wants nothing more than to provide for her into her old age. No justice. None.

Stories since the first image was scratched onto the side of a cave have started with the beauty of women and the courage of men. No amount of surgery, gym time, makeup, or designer clothing could ever make me look like my friend Elizabeth, and although you might argue that I contribute to the world in different ways, even more important ways because my SAT scores are higher and the screenplay I will someday write will teach the world about the tragedies of American imperialism or create a radical empathy for the mentally ill, Elizabeth doesn't have to hit the books, study poetry, save orphans — in other words, all she has to do to match my contributions is raise me one eyelash, and I'd have to fold. She is better in all ways than I, and there is nothing I can do to change that simple fact.

But let me start at the beginning, before we got to this, Elizabeth's wedding day, when guests are streaming up the driveway, friends of the Gottlieb family in pastel dresses and suits, all too warm for what will be summer weather in springtime. How fitting, though, for spring to bend to summer in honor of the bride, the summer's day that Elizabeth can be compared to and be found more lovely and more temperate. The scene is not sullied by the sudden honk of a beige van snorting up the driveway and forcing guests onto the freshly cut grass. Rather, the guests float aside and the van chuffs to a stop, a gentle giant, come to bow his knee to the princess.

The van door opens and Elizabeth's grandma, Bubbie Ida, steps out. She was always the prettiest grandmother, and I see she is rocking a periwinkle suit and a diamond brooch. She steps forward to receive a kiss from a guest. Bubbie Ida told us to sit with our ankles crossed, not our thighs, to prevent varicose veins. She also said to cover half our plate with a piece of bread and eat only what we could see. That would keep us from getting fat. The side of the van opens, and there is that beeping sound that trucks make backing up as a man in a wheelchair is lowered to the ground on a hydraulic ledge. Ida takes the reins of the chair to push. Propped in the chair is what is left of Elizabeth's once fearsome and terrifying *zayde*,

Albert Gottlieb, once one of the richest men in Atlanta before he was far eclipsed by the founders of Home Depot. Bubbie Ida is stopped every few inches by well-wishers. Then she comes face-to-face with Zayde Albert's doppelgänger, a tiny thread of a boy curled into a wheelchair, whom I at first take for Stephen Hawking before recognizing Jeffrey Wolf, who I did not know was still alive.

I heard that Elizabeth's grandfather had had a stroke. I was always scared of Zayde Albert growing up. They had an overly chlorinated swimming pool, the only one we had access to before the neighborhood ones opened up, so we would congregate there in May and swim until our eyes turned red. Bubbie Ida had installed a slide, obviously for the use of children, and she made us sandwiches with the crusts cut off, but if you dripped water into the house or splashed the plants in the planters, Zayde Albert would yell. Now he is confined to a wheelchair, his skin ashen and his eyes bruised. I feel pity for him and want to look away, and with the quick drop of my head, eyes shifted to the side with a sudden fascination for something on the ground, I recognize a move people have made in response to my appearance.

My mother once called him a small-time despot who ruled over the synagogue and his business — I actually never knew what business he had, just that he was a businessman and rich. Now look at him, boneless, almost skinless, he should be wrapped in cellophane and Styrofoam, and put in a refrigerated case. So sad and pathetic, the remains of him. I feel pity, and a bit of revulsion and fascination, but then the light flashes off the white stubble of his beard and it glistens like spun glass. There is a silk spiderweb line of drool from the corner of his mouth to his shoulder. He is magnificent, this empty conch of a man, fossilized, museumworthy, propped in a wheelchair that should be a marble stand. Move over Michelangelo's *David*, I give you *Decrepitude*.

Let me run into the house now, find a bathroom and a mirror. Stare at my own face and title it *Not Decrepitude*. Let me think. Is there an equally weighty word for "not quite right"? Not so obviously wrong as a human being with three eyes or one, not a cyclopean monster but a mistake. I give you *Abnormality. Anomaly. Deviance. Oddity.*

Portrait of the artist as a high school loser. I had a port-wine stain covering half of my left cheek, encircling my left eye like a claw, extending down my neck, and, no, to all the people who have asked or imagined, not touching the breast. Because of the port-wine stain, I had a limp. The blood vessels erupting on my face were buried in my leg, but they made the right leg fatter and longer than the left. It was corrected in childhood with a surgery that involved breaking and fusing my femur. I spent the summer between first and second grade recovering from the surgery. The legs are the same length now, but the limp is incurable. Despite years of braces and orthopedic shoes, it cannot be fixed. Since infancy, I have worn glasses, though they have corrective lenses for the right eye only. The veins have smudged my vision in that eye, though my parents reminded me it could be worse. The first specialists told them I would be blind and have seizures and perhaps mental retardation. It was a good thing my father was a doctor. He took me to Boston Children's, and we met Dr. Lloyd Hartman. He should have been a cardiologist with that name, my dad never tired of saying. Dr. Hartman told my parents I would not be retarded and I would not be blind, but there was no fixing the port-wine stain. It went too deep.

My baby pictures are hideous. I was a fat, multicolored gargoyle with an eye patch and a swollen cheek. One day, I tore the pictures out of the photo album, ripped them to shreds, and threw them away. When my mother found them, she showed the confetti to my father, and my father knocked softly on my open door and came into my room. I was ten years old. I was reading a book, book reading being the refuge of many of the deformed and untouchable. He put his hand on my cheek. He said, beauty is as beauty does. He told me I was beautiful and that one day everyone else in the world would see what he could see. For his sake, I did not cry. I stared at the pages of my book. Marcia Brady is the pretty one. Cindy is cute. Everyone finds Jan, with her glasses and big teeth, annoying. At ten, I knew how the world worked.

In middle school, seventh grade to be exact, Sheila Bradford, who took ballet and was obsessed with all things dance — she had ballet slippers on her backpack, her lunch box; she walked like a penguin with her toes permanently askew — had the sudden revelation that the port-wine stain made her classmate — the author, me — look like a harlequin. Look, she said, pulling out a notebook with a picture of a black-and-white harlequin face on it. It's you. From seventh grade on, that was my nickname, the Harlequin, and I embraced it, the character who could be both jester and victim, *comedia* and *tragedia*, laughing on the outside and crying on the inside. I hated the nickname, so I exulted in it, introduced myself that way, used it as my moniker in the yearbook.

I had no one to sit with at lunch, so I ate a sandwich in a far corner of the library since food was not allowed among the sacred plastic-covered books. The librarian, Mrs. Coolick, was perfectly aware that I was eating lunch and pitied me. Watch as the artist wipes the crumbs of her sandwich into her hands and pours them back into the plastic bag and takes them home to be thrown away. If there was justice in the world — justice, a concept no less magical than immortality and human flight — those crumbs would blossom into a miraculous plant that would cure the cursed beast, or better yet, would turn into a giant dandelion. When the artist blows on it, all the frothy seeds snow over the land and turn everyone they touch into a harlequin like her. She runs outside and witnesses the transformation, a land of beasts, equality. A far shot: the cursed princess extends her arms out and lifts her chin to the sky. Someone takes her right hand, then her left; the beasts join together into a ring and dance. Cut to: Tokyo, under a pagoda, Japanese beasts. London, Big Ben; Russia, the onion domes in Red Square; Paris, the Eiffel Tower; a Masai village on the Serengeti — all transformed in her image.

I limped down the hall clutching my books to my chest. I was very smart. I was valedictorian. I applied to all the Ivies and blamed the port-wine stain when the big three rejected me. I was sure I saw Ms. Naomi Carlton, the admissions director at Yale, wince, stare, then recompose herself to act as if she had never noticed the purple carpet on my face. Naomi Carlton: I cast you as the wicked witch, stick a wart with a dark hair on your nose. Of course, having reached the ripe old age of twenty-eight now, I might remove poor Ms. Carlton's wart and let her defend herself. No one from Mansfield got into Yale the year I applied, a fact my guidance counselor blamed on the unprecedented acceptance of four Mansfield students the prior year. But still, I saw the look on her face. Keep the wart, Ms. Carlton. Have people ask you what's on your nose and try to pluck it away.

I was accepted to my fourth choice, the University of Pennsylvania, and had to inform people back in Atlanta that it was not a state school despite its name. When I got the courage to ask Evan Elkins, baseball star and four-year unrequited crush, to sign my yearbook, he said his pen was out of ink, laughed, turned away, signed someone else's yearbook. There was a graduation party. I was not invited. Everyone in the school except for me and the three other bottom-rung students (Roger Petrovniak, calculus genius and victim of cystic acne; Henrietta Schlossberg, who is later diagnosed with schizophrenia so the Mansfield High students who called her crazy were right in a way; and morbidly obese Paula Godwin) was invited. In the movie, Roger, Henrietta, Paula, and I would throw an alternative party. The audience's sympathy starts in act one as the four of us spend graduation night eating greasy popcorn and watching an old movie, let's say, *Dr. Strangelove*. In act three, a decade has passed. The world has become a dangerous place. Nuclear war with North Korea and Russia has left most of the country uninhabitable. Our future rests in the hands of one man and one woman, Roger Petrovniak, who has discovered a new planet with blue seas and grassy plains, and Carla Lefkowitz, the only one who has been able to decode the language of the planet's seemingly friendly, albeit wary, inhabitants. The Mansfield High ten-year reunion is held underground in a dimly lit bunker with plastic flowers rescued from the last surviving Walmart for decorations. Henrietta has become a warrior woman. Paula, having lost all her excess weight through the meager rations we are allowed, is now stunning and unrecognizable in the skintight gray jumpsuit that everyone wears in the apocalyptic future. Evan Elkins, not looking so handsome without a tan, gets up the nerve to ask Paula to dance. He says, "Did you go to Mansfield? I don't know how I wouldn't remember someone as beautiful as you." Suddenly, the whole room shakes. Paula stumbles into Evan's chest. Roger pulls Henrietta and me out of the crowd. Bare lightbulbs swing. Circuits fizzle and pop. There are screams and bodies litter the floor, frothing at the mouth, bleeding. Another attack, the big one we have feared. Roger has a spaceship. It can hold only four people plus a hundred million test tubes of DNA that will be used to turn this new planet into a replica of Earth. Paula pushes Evan away from her, runs into Roger's arms. We step into a glass tube while the rest of Mansfield's desperate alumni throw themselves up against the exterior, their nails tear off as they try to claw their way in. As the tube rises, they drop away like bugs. The last thing we see, from the safety of our spaceship, is the blindingly bright explosion of what was Earth. We are not blinded. Roger has given us protective eyewear.

Of course, this would not happen. Paula, Henrietta, Roger, and I are not friends. The stain of our rejection would only grow brighter in one another's company. We give one another no solace. If the world ended, we would die alone.

In college, the cold Philadelphia winters allowed me to wear turtlenecks that covered 50 percent of my port-wine stain. I was admired for my writing skills; people fell in love with me before they met me after reading my poems and stories. Some of what my father (who had just been diagnosed with lung cancer despite never smoking) told me seemed to be true. Some people valued intelligence as much as beauty. Though I knew that most of my classmates were as superficial as anyone, they usually edited their impulses to get to a higher level of thought, and they tried to see past the port-wine stain, the awkward gait, the wide-set eyes, the weak chin. I made friends who read one another's poems and short stories, talked about James Joyce and Flannery O'Connor, who also had a limp. At a visiting writer's workshop, Toni Morrison singled out one of my stories for its wit and empathy. When she pulled me aside after class to praise the story, I was sure that the famous writer had confused me with someone else until she produced the pages themselves with "by Carla Lefkowitz" at the bottom and the title "The Pun(ishment) of Clara(plegia)" at the top.

Marco Hunter, an aspiring writer himself, watched the exchange and became my first boyfriend. He took me out for coffee and forced me to read his short stories. Because he had curly hair and long eyelashes, and actually seemed to like me, I ignored the fact that Raymond Carver had already written these short stories. I gushed that they were amazing, insightful, the work of a great talent. I praised them and scrawled *brilliant* in the margins. Marco, of the curly dark hair, the gapped front teeth, the hairless chest. He was a thing to behold. Marco kissed me on the quad. When he kissed me, he kissed the red lid of my right eye and told me that the flames of my face ignited my words. He called the mark on my face a gift. When I told him my nickname, he adopted it immediately, lovingly. He called me *hermosa arlequín*. His mother was from Honduras. He was a bilingual miracle to me. Marco wanted to see all of me. We went back to his room, and I made every effort to keep my clothes on. I obliged him in every way that allowed me to keep my shirt buttoned because I half suspected he just wanted to see if I was purple all the way down, purple breasts, nipples, thighs. I had been asked before — more than once — if I had a purple pussy, and I was certain Marco had imagined this himself. Months passed this way. When we finally made love — my first time, but I didn't tell him that — all the lights were off. He whispered that my skin was soft and smooth, and I thought I could hear the surprise in his voice — what was he expecting? Jelly? An exoskeleton? When I thought he was sleeping and I tried to sneak into the bathroom, he flipped on his reading lamp to look at me. "It's only on your face," he said, and he sounded disappointed. Then I realized, men must have "sleep with freak" on their bucket list, and this was not going to count for Marco.

Inevitably, Marco fell in love with someone else, someone blond with a little nose and perfect skin. We never broke up. He just disappeared. I waited for him outside his senior Victorian literature seminar to ask him what I did wrong, though, of course, I knew the answer. He told me to stop stalking him. In the screenplay, the audience is now hating Marco. In act three, he will get what he deserves. He stupidly goes into the basement when he hears a thump; the deranged woman cuts off his head with an axe. Okay, ten years have passed. I am twenty-eight. Marco can keep his head. First college relationships have a short half-life. I know that now, but it wasn't as easy for me to replace Marco as it was for him to replace me.

After Marco, I had sex several more times. I liked sex, but I never really had another boyfriend. I just thought, Hey, you want to fuck the purple girl, I'm good with that as long as you are okay with extended foreplay.

I graduated Phi Beta Kappa and wanted to go as far from the University of Pennsylvania and Atlanta as I could, but what could you do with an English degree? I considered graduate school, a dissertation on the deformed in literature from Medusa to Mary Wollstonecraft. I couldn't get past the title. The ugly did not do well in literature. In the movie version of my life, our heroine gets a degree in anthropology and finds a tribe in Papua New Guinea where port-wine stains are considered the highest form of beauty. She and her colleagues are trekking in the jungle, looking for a lost tribe rumored to have floated on the shards of Noah's Ark over the oceans to the Coral Sea, washing up at last on a tiny island along the archipelago that collectively forms New Guinea. As they trek, Matthew Willingham, an esteemed British cartographer, burns with fever and finally succumbs along the swampy shores at the mouth of an underground river. The next to fall is Vanessa Lopez, an Argentinian primatologist who has mistakenly eaten a poisonous mushroom. As she writhes in pain and vomits, she hallucinates a vision of the tribe. They are purple, she cries, her engorged face and bloodshot eyes straining to see her vision. She reaches her hands out; *"Hermosa, hermosa"* are her last words. Alone now, our heroine, drinking water from cupped leaves and sleeping under the stars, unable to close her eyes, haunted by the last words of her friends and the indecipherable sounds of the jungle, presses on in search of the tribe. She is riddled with

mosquito bites, almost starving; her hiking boots are in tat-
ters. Perhaps she has gone mad herself. She parts the dense
growth of the forest, barely flinches at the snake hissing at her
from the vines. There it is: a waterfall, pink and orange flowers the size of dinner plates, drumbeats. She sees the back of a
small child running from her. "Wait!" she calls out. The child
turns to her. Big black eyes rimmed with lashes, long dark
hair, and a purple face. The child smiles at her beatifically,
says something in a foreign language; now other children appear, then adults. They fall to their knees and bow. They have
been waiting for her, the half-white, half-purple woman who
can bridge both the magical and the mundane worlds. She
becomes their queen. In real life, she winds up with an entry-
level job in publishing in New York.

I vowed never to return to Atlanta, Georgia, where Scarlett O'Hara's descendants are alive and well, and still making
life miserable for the flawed and the outcast and the down-
trodden. But I had to go back. A lot. Because my father,
Marty, who I loved, got sicker and sicker. I sat with him while
he wasted away in the hospital bed, hooked to oxygen. We
watched lots of TV; the Braves lost in postseason again. My
dad stopped liking the Dodgers when they moved to Los Angeles and the Yankees after Joe DiMaggio retired. I remembered Joe DiMaggio from the Mr. Coffee commercials; when
I was little, I once asked my dad who he was, and he said,
Only one of the greatest ballplayers of all time. Oh, and Mr.
Marilyn Monroe. Despite all that time at my father's bedside,
I was in New York when he died.

I came back for the funeral and to help my mom pack up
his suits and shoes and books. My father liked to dress well,

and he had a collection of ties, from the thin black ties of the sixties to the fat wide stripes of the seventies to the present. I chose one skinny baby-blue tie for myself. I used to think I would give it one day to a man I love who loves me back if there ever is a man I love who loves me back. I have packed and moved that baby-blue tie from a series of shitty apartments in New York to my current shitty apartment in Los Angeles. It's all I have of my dad, the only man who ever really loved me. Four years have passed with almost no visits to Atlanta, and now I am back because Elizabeth is getting married. This might be the last time I ever come to this city. My mother has retired to Hilton Head, South Carolina, to turn leathery there while watching the Atlantic from her balcony. There is nothing but bad memories left in Atlanta.

I can cover this birthmark. I could go to my friend Elizabeth's wedding and present an entirely different face to the people who were so brutal to me in high school. Ta-da — I am the Harlequin no more. I am just a regular person who survived Mansfield High and went on to greater glory. I was working on a film set when Kelsey Porter, makeup artist extraordinaire, noticed me. She said I could easily cover my stain if I wanted to. These days, according to Kelsey, there is no reason for anyone to have less than perfect skin. With the wonders of a good dermatologist, and failing that, makeup, we can all look as dewy and flawless as a silent-film star. She said no one in Hollywood would be beautiful without help. Hollywood, she said, is a mess of pockmarks, scars, and disfigurement. If a tsunami washed over LA, she insisted, we'd be standing in a freak show. Kelsey assumed that I already knew this, so she asked if there was a political reason I left my birthmark visible — was I taking a stand? Was it important to me in perfect Hollywood to be so demonstrably imperfect? I assured her I was apolitical and that I had tried every form of makeup in the department store, even paint, to cover the stain, and nothing had ever worked. The paint chipped and cracked; the makeup caked and peeled. It was an unfixable flaw. Kelsey sat me in her chair, and with a few dabs of a foam triangle, the mark that followed me, shaped me, and cast me in the movie biopic of my life in the roles of Kid Kicked Out of Sandbox, Morose Middle Schooler #2, Outcast of Eleventh Grade, and Girl with No Date for Prom — the stain that I first noticed at the age of three and tried to wash away and cried and cried when it wouldn't come off until I noticed my mother crying with me — had vanished. I pressed my face closer to the mirror. I could see the makeup, but it was not obvious, and when I touched my face, it felt like skin. I stared and stared and refused to cry. It was so easy. It took only seconds.

"You look beautiful," Kelsey said.

"I wouldn't go that far."

"You do," she insisted.

"I look almost normal," I said. "And that's good enough."

Kelsey gave me the makeup. It could be ordered only by a professional, so she also gave me a card and told me to call her whenever I needed more. I never used it again, and Kelsey called me three months later and asked if I had lost her phone number, since by now I would surely need more makeup. She got my number from my boss, Carter Graham, yes, that Carter Graham, the movie star and Academy Award nominee; two-time Golden Globe winner; Hollywood bad

boy, twice engaged but never married. I told her I wasn't using the makeup, and she said, "I thought so. I pegged you as a
political one. Good for you."

"It isn't political," I said.

"Then why aren't you using it?"

I didn't have a good reason. "I don't know," I said. I thought
about it later, and I guess the reason was that if you aren't going to be beautiful you might as well be ugly. What am I without my birthmark? Everyone in the village knew Franken-
stein's name. And Dracula. And wasn't the portrait so much
more interesting than preening, foppish Dorian Gray himself? From the day in first grade when Todd Coleman called
me a freak and mimicked barfing at the sight of my face, that
stain has gotten me noticed.

My parents used to tell me that you could barely see my
port-wine stain. They were more concerned about the fact
that my right leg was longer than my left, and though I had
already had one surgery, the pediatric orthopedist said future surgeries might be needed throughout my life. I arrived
at First Montessori with a purple face, a brace on my leg, and
heavy black orthopedic shoes I have seen only on old men
with tremendous amounts of dandruff. In a screenplay, this
is when you start to fall in love with our heroine, watching
her suffer as an innocent child, but in real life, you recoil at
her difference, avert your eyes, or pretend not to notice at
best and laugh, mock her, or call her names at worst. I get it.
My mother needed to believe that the port-wine stain didn't
matter. Since they call it a birthmark and she's the one who
gave birth, she has always felt responsible for my disfigurement, as if it were some punishment for her visited on her

daughter because the gods could think of nothing crueler. I am not sure what sin she could have committed to merit the punishment, but as we age, I see the list of reasons to incur deity-driven wrath growing longer and that we are constantly making deals with the devil. Many people — who knows, even I — might agree to mar their children in a disfiguring but fundamentally harmless way in order to sell a screenplay or marry the man of their dreams. Satan would never show up in a red jumpsuit and horns, holding a trident and breathing fire out of his nostrils. He would show up in the form of a diet pill, a glass of white wine, and a false-negative pregnancy test. He would show up as a movie star, devastatingly handsome albeit unwashed and unshaven, who says, Work for me for a few years and I'll introduce you to agents and producers, guide you through the war zone that is Hollywood, get your career started.

By elementary school, I knew my father was a liar and that the red mark on my face was not beautiful. In art class in fifth grade, I painted my cheek white, and Mrs. McMillan, my teacher, scolded me and sent me to the principal's office. The school nurse cleaned the paint off with paper towels, rubbing so hard it turned the port-wine stain a livid purple, and then she sent me back to class, but I didn't go. I hid in the AV room until the end of the day and walked home long after the bell had rung so I would be alone. Eventually, I accepted defeat. I became the Harlequin. I even introduced myself that way to those too polite to ask what happened, to let them know that I know my face is two different colors. In case you were wondering, I have a mirror. It's not news to me. I was born this way. Self-inflicted pain is so much easier to bear than the slings and arrows that others deliver. I suspect this truth was known to the monks in hair shirts. Hyperbole, I know, but what are movies if not hyperbole, and what are movie stars if not hyperbole incarnate? And I, for some reason not even clear to me, have chosen to make my home among the movie stars. I am even in love with one.

As ridiculous and unrequited as my four-year-long high school longing for Evan Elkins was, my current one-sided love affair is even more absurd. I yearn, I ache, I pine for my boss, Carter Graham — yes, that Carter Graham, who, despite what Kelsey and other makeup artists might imagine, is physically flawless, dazzling, even when unwashed, reeking of body odor. Movie stars really are different from you and me, even from Elizabeth, so healthy and happy. Everyone stops and stares at Carter; the assemblage of his features as show-stoppingly abnormal as a Cyclops only they stir desire rather than revulsion. I know because I have seen him naked. I have not seen him naked in any kind of romantic tryst. It wouldn't occur to Carter that his personal assistant who always knows when to refill his herpes medicine and keeps track of the constantly changing cell phone numbers necessitated by the broken hearts he leaves behind is someone he could have sex with. Carter undresses in front of me the way someone undresses in front of a dog. He doesn't care what I think of him, and though, like a dog, I may gaze adoringly at him, I do not linger on any one part more than any other, from eyes, to hands, to knees, to the tangle of hair between his legs, while he changes pants in his trailer or gets ready for a date with some knockout. I am embarrassed by this ardor, and in the screenplay that I write of my life, I root against this romance. The whip-smart homely assistant must fall in love with the kindhearted and secretly ultrawealthy chauffeur or the "just returned from a Haitian mission trip" doctor or the public defender getting the innocent man off death row; and when she takes off her glasses or finds the right laser treatment, she will turn out to be stunning, and the coldhearted, shallow, oversexed movie star will grow old alone, bloated with alcohol and regret. That's how it works in the movies, but not in real life, where the coldhearted, narcissistic, oversexed movie star reaps all the rewards that this world has to offer and keeps trading in brilliant, talented, beautiful lovers for younger, more brilliant, more talented, and more beautiful lovers and spends not one minute alone and experiences not one moment of doubt or regret.

Carter pretends that it is stupid to be beautiful. Only beautiful people say things like that, just like only rich people say money can't buy happiness. The ugly and the poor know the truth. Make *me* beautiful and rich, and I promise I will rejoice. Of all his attributes, Carter will tell you, his looks are the most useless, and what matters is really what you think about William Faulkner and whether the French Revolution was about money or citizenship and if you are lucky enough to have a green thumb and are able to grow heirloom tomatoes. Any of these talents, Carter Graham will tell you, far outweighs beauty, but I know a shitload about William Faulkner, have memorized approximately a hundred poems from Shakespeare to Auden, can grow a mean tomato, wrote a critique in French of *Citizens* that my professor mailed to the author of the book, Simon Schama himself, and I would trade it all to go through life with the ease that has been granted to Carter Graham and, to a lesser degree, my friend Elizabeth Gottlieb.

I briefly considered asking Carter to come to this wedding with me although it would be a disaster even if Elizabeth hadn't slept with him, the guest of the lowly bridesmaid upstaging the bride. Carter definitely sucks the air out of the room, and in far, far from Hollywood Atlanta, all eyes would be on him even if he showed up, as is entirely possible, unwashed in jeans and a sweatshirt, especially if he showed up unwashed in jeans and a sweatshirt. For a week, he let me think that he might do it. We are close, Carter and I. I am his personal assistant. I read all his scripts. I read and summarize books he might want to option for his production company, and then Carter talks about them as if he has read them, and he thinks he actually has. When Carter voices an opinion, even though it is mine, he does so with complete conviction, as if years of thought have led him to this conclusion: Alyosha is not the hero of *The Brothers Karamazov*. Ivan is. To talk to him is to feel completely understood, known, and cherished; though after years of observation, I am now aware that he has forgotten about you the moment the basketball game comes on and that you are not his soulmate; you momentarily fill the emptiness that every actor has. Only empty people can assume so many identities. You have to be naked, after all, between each costume change. Most of us are too implacably ourselves to ever convincingly be someone else. We're cooked, hardened; we can only change by breaking. Actors have a hollow core and can become whatever you fill them with, wine, milk, water, sewage, starlight.

When Carter asked me whose wedding it was, I said, "Elizabeth. My best friend from kindergarten." He looked at me blankly.

"You met her," I said. Still no glimmer of recognition. "She was in law school in Virginia. Really pretty, tall, curly black hair. Freckles." Still nothing. "Carter," I said. "You slept with her."

"Oh," he said finally. "The one from Virginia." He acted like he remembered. "She was really sweet."

I hadn't been in touch with Elizabeth for at least a year or two when I moved to LA, but six weeks after I arrived there, I got a call out of the blue from her — she was going to be in Los Angeles and couldn't wait to catch up with me. I'm sure it never occurred to Elizabeth that she wasn't the first acquaintance who suddenly developed a burning desire to reaffirm our deep friendship now that I was working for a movie star. When she arrived, I suggested we visit the La Brea Tar Pits. I took a bit of perverse pleasure in taking people who came to visit me to a science museum since I knew they wouldn't actually come out and say that the reason they had come to see me was to (a) meet the gorgeous movie star I worked for and (b) see other movie stars. As it happened, Carter came to the museum too.

Carter only ever asked me about my social life when he was between women, which meant he was on the hunt. There is one thing I can say about every actor I have ever met: they can't stand to be alone. What would Freud say about my inability to lie when Carter asked me what I was doing on Saturday, my rightful day off? On almost every other Saturday, I could have said that I was sleeping late, catching up on reading, maybe hitting the gym, going to a movie with one of my friends who Carter had met and didn't care for, and he would have waved me off and gone to the Bel-Air where he would undoubtedly find someone to go home with him. I could have lied. I knew what to say to be dismissed, but instead I said, "My friend Elizabeth is in town."

"Oh yeah?" Carter raised an eyebrow.

"We were thinking of going to the La Brea Tar Pits."

"What's that? Is that the new soccer team?"

"No, it's a science museum. Thousands of years ago there were these tar pits and all these ancient animals like giant sloths and mastodons fell in and their bones were preserved there. It's really cool, and it's right on Wilshire. They have all these models of what prehistoric Los Angeles looked like. People think it's brutal now. Before there were agents, there were saber-toothed tigers."

"It's cool, really?"

"Yeah, you'd like it."

"You sure you wouldn't mind?" he asked, accepting.

"No, I'm sure my friend would love to meet you."

"What's she doing in LA?"

"Visiting. She just finished her first year from law school and she needed a vacation."

"Law school? Cool. What time are you going?"

It never occurred to me that Carter would actually come to the museum. Elizabeth and I were standing in the dim light of the pits, looking down at a diorama of a giant ground sloth caught in the black tar that would both kill it and immortalize it. The artist who made the model had captured its agony and fear; its eyes rolled back in its head, paws reached uselessly up to us, but 20,000 years ago, we weren't here, and the mastodon standing in the safety of the tall grass couldn't have helped if it had wanted to. Elizabeth was fidgeting, but I painstakingly read every plaque in the museum. She was dressed for Rodeo Drive, in a romper and sandals. I was wearing a U Penn T-shirt and leggings.

"This place is really cool," Carter said. Elizabeth and I both jumped in surprise. "I love science. Mastodons are so much cooler than elephants." Carter assessed Elizabeth and glanced at me with a smile. "I'm Carter Graham," he said, as if she wouldn't know. "Carla and I work together."

"Hi," Elizabeth said. Even in the dark light, with the soundtrack of braying animals in their death throes, you could see the flush and glow of Elizabeth's face and hear her quick inhale. I thought about shooing out the Boy Scout troop that had just entered, shutting the doors, and telling them to get on with it, I'd be back in an hour.

"Elizabeth Gottlieb, Carter Graham," I said.

"Thanks for letting me crash," Carter said. "I love this place. It makes me feel better about my life. People think LA is brutal now, but they should see how it used to be. I think my agent is bad, but at least he's not a saber-toothed tiger." He smiled, and both she and I were dazzled. As many times as I have seen it, I still melt when he smiles even though it isn't meant for me.

And then he turned on the charm. One of Carter's gifts is the ability to convince you that he is suffering in his Hollywood Hills mansion with the infinity pool and the six-car garage. *He is suffering.* Ridiculously overpaid for trivial work, forced to have lunch with people engaged in the bloodthirsty power struggle that is the movie business, these Los Angeles philistines who care nothing for — Where is the worst current global crisis? he asks me, and I tell him the civil war in South Sudan. He's forced to have lunch with people who do not even *know* about the war in South Sudan, he parrots. No one *understands* him. They are all using him except for (fill in the blank here), though, of course, you are using him, maybe not for his movie star status but for his astonishing good looks and charm, his you-are-the-center-of-the-universeness that you feel when he turns his gaze on you and declares you the epitome of a Scorpio, fierce, brilliant, and passionate, or a Pisces, gentle, wise, and romantic, or (fill in the blank with whatever you want to believe yourself to be). He hasn't tried that charm on me because he knows I think astrology is idiotic (as opposed to astronomy, which is the actual study of the geophysics of the universe — Carter often confuses the words), but I love him nonetheless since he is all the unrequited crushes I have had since kindergarten to college rolled into one Übermensch package of charisma and beauty.

We walked to the next room. A dire wolf was drooling over an ancient horse the size of a zebra but with a lovely tawny color instead of black-and-white stripes while a giant ground sloth lumbered in the background. There we all are, I thought. Poor Elizabeth, the graceful *Equus occidentalis,* is about to be the dire wolf's lunch. What does the sloth care? What can Harlan's ground sloth — *Paramylodon harlani* — do about it?

Such are the ways of the world, then and now. And who was Harlan? Elizabeth and Carter drifted off, leaning into each other, whispering. After that room, we had the option of going to look at the site of ongoing excavations, which I would have liked, but Carter said, "I know this awesome place for sushi near here. Wanna go?"

Elizabeth glanced at me, and I shrugged. "Sure." We got into Carter's car. He had driven the BMW so as not to be too flashy for the law student. I sat in the backseat, and since the top was down, my hair was destroyed and I could barely hear the conversation; but I caught a passing line in which he said he was tired of actresses. He wanted someone with a real job. In Hollywood, it was impossible to meet someone like her. I hate sushi, but I didn't say anything. Carter ordered expansively, and we couldn't eat it all. I watched the tray of colorful raw fish congeal and rot while my movie-star boss seduced my friend. He started off with generic questions. She mentioned that her father was a lawyer, and he said, "Tell me about a time you were proud of your father." He stuffed sashimi in his mouth. "Or ashamed."

Elizabeth furrowed her brow and thought hard about the question. I wanted to shout, Oh, for God's sake, make something up; he doesn't care. It doesn't matter. He asks every girl that question. If I was writing the script, I would make Elizabeth smarter; my heroine of the dystopian future would be onto him. She would say, "He took down a Russian mobster who was smuggling heroin in baby formula. A thousand babies died until my father threw him in jail and tossed away the key." Her dad is a fucking tax attorney. His moments of heroism involve not inflating his billable hours and getting a friend's kid out of a DUI pro bono.

When the check came, Carter said, "What are you doing later? I've got an extra ticket to the Lakers game. It's kind of a cool thing to do when you visit LA. Courtside Lakers game. I know Carla hates sports, and I wouldn't want to interfere in your plans."

"We were going to go to Santa Monica and see the pier."

"You can do that tomorrow," Carter said.

I said, "If you want to go, it's fine with me. I have work I could do."

"You sure?"

"You should go. Even if you don't like sports, it's a great experience."

She turned to Carter. "You don't have anyone else you'd rather take?"

"I promise you," he said, half smiling in a way that showed his dimple. "There is no one else in the world I would rather take."

I picked Elizabeth up from Carter's house two days later when she was to fly back east. They were out by the pool. Elizabeth was wearing khaki shorts and a sleeveless button-down knotted at the waist. Carter was shirtless and wearing pajama bottoms. Her hair was freshly washed and dried, still damp at the tips. As was often his habit, he had not showered in days. I could smell him from the other side of the pool. His hair hung greasy and uncombed, and still both Elizabeth and I wanted him.

There was a half-empty bottle of expensive wine on the patio table. He stood to hug her and then kissed her forehead. I waited a polite distance away while they said their goodbyes. She held on to his hand as she turned away and didn't drop it until she had to.

"You ready?" I asked her. There were tears in her eyes.

"Hey, Carla," Carter called out to me.

"Hello, Carter," I said, trying to sound weary.

"Did you read that book that Scott sent over?"

"I did."

"And?"

"I think we should do an updated version of *The Tempest*."

"You know I don't want to do any horror films."

The tear was starting to trickle down her cheek. "Are you okay?" I asked.

Elizabeth nodded, sniffled. Carter walked with us up the stairs into the hallway. He said, "Sorry. I can't go to the door. Paparazzi. Long lenses."

In the car on the way to the airport, she said, "I think I am in love with him. He told me things he's never told anyone else."

"About his cousin's suicide?"

Her mouth unhinged. "Well, of course, *you* know. You've known him for two years."

"Please tell me you used a condom, Elizabeth."

"He said he is in love with me too. He's tired of dating movie stars. He wants someone smart and real. He's going to come to Atlanta next month. He's up for a movie that might shoot there, but it's probably easier for me to transfer schools, like to UCLA Law. Wouldn't that be awesome? We could see each other all the time."

"Don't change your life for him, Elizabeth," I begged her. "He isn't worth it."

"And no. I didn't." She wiped her nose on the back of her hand. "Use a condom."

For a month after meeting Carter, Elizabeth considered coming back to see him since he apparently had mentioned something about wanting to get to know her better. Once she realized that Carter was not in love with her and six months later was 100 percent sure that she did not have a sexually transmitted disease, she never spoke of him again. That is Elizabeth's gift. She decided that the whole thing was a mistake, and so it never happened, just like that. Once, about a year later when I was home visiting my dad, Elizabeth insisted I join her and Debbie Shapiro on a girls' night out. When the subject of Carter came up, Elizabeth's only comment was, "I don't actually think he's that talented."

Debbie said, "Are you kidding? He's amazing." To me, she said, "You're so lucky to work for him." Carter is very good at his job, and everyone, Debbie Shapiro, Elizabeth, the world at large, assumes he is the people he plays. He is a suicidal teenager brought back from the brink by the high school nerd; he is Mr. Darcy; he is Gregory Filipovich, the reluctant asthmatic hero who ingeniously saves a bunch of kids from a band of Chechen terrorists; and he is Moishe Gold, a Jewish orphan who is cloned by Dr. Mengele and survives only by murdering the successive clones of himself. All these women are in love with Carter, the self-effacing hero. That's why their love is fake and only mine is real.

• • •

27

I am fifteen minutes late arriving for prewedding photos, and the wedding planner, Carol Silverman, is in a tizzy. She practically yanks me out of the car. She is barking orders into a walkie-talkie as if we were headed into combat.

"Don't you look lovely," Mrs. Silverman says to me, without actually looking at me.

It's surprising Carter hired me in the first place. In general, he doesn't like ugly people. I guess he couldn't resist my pedigree. Cute assistants are a dime a dozen in Hollywood, but there aren't as many Ivy League grads. Plus, I'd worked for a few years. I was the assistant to the head of acquisitions at William Morris in New York. Ah, New York. I miss New York, where it is almost a virtue to be ugly. A hundred years from now, there will be no one in Hollywood who does not look like a clone of Scarlett Johansson or Channing Tatum, but people in New York will be moving in the opposite direction, having their ears enlarged, getting tattoos of birthmarks, figuring out what to eat to make your head swell out like an alien's. When that happens, I will be the queen of New York City, but when I lived there, I found that a limited amount of ugliness might have been acceptable, like Adrien Brody's big nose, but deformity was as ostracized as it is everywhere else.

Brad Kerker, my boss at William Morris, knew that Carter needed an assistant. To this day, I don't know if he suggested me as a joke, because he seemed shocked when I told him Carter had hired me and that I was moving to California. Brad was New York, fat, with perpetual tomato-sauce stains on his tie, but publishers loved him, and he had a way of getting the earliest copies of future bestsellers and optioning them on the cheap. There is one thing Hollywood loves more than beauty, and that's money, and Brad Kerker knows how to make it for them. When I quit, he said, "But I need you here."

"Then why did you put me up for the job?"

"I thought you'd want to meet Carter Graham."

"I did. I liked him. He hired me."

"You're going to hate LA," he told me.

"Probably," I said. "But I kind of hate New York. And he's paying me the same salary and I only have to work twenty hours, so I can do some writing myself."

Brad snorted. "You'd better find out which twenty hours, Carla. And what exactly is your job description?

"Director of development and acquisitions for Vertigo Productions. He just formed his own production company so he can make movies outside the Hollywood mold. He's tired of just getting action flicks. He's really smart, and he thinks you're amazing. It's a great opportunity for me, Brad."

"Every actor has his own production company. Scott fucking Baio has his own production company. The guy who played Squiggy on *Laverne & Shirley* has his own production company. This is not a good career move for you, Carla."

"I can't get you coffee and bagels for the rest of my life."

"What do you think you're going to do for him?"

"Read scripts and galleys, background research for roles. I know there will be some scut work in there, but that's okay. It's only twenty hours a week."

"Fine, fine." He waved me away. "You're replaceable, Carla. Everyone is. Before you go, make sure there's another Carla sitting in that chair. Maybe one a little taller."

My friend Elizabeth Gottlieb has avoided all this humilia-

tion. She has a gift that I hope the fairies will bestow on my
child if I ever have one. They gave Sleeping Beauty beauty
and song, and then kept her from dying from poison. I used
to wonder what the third gift would have been if it hadn't
been used to mitigate Maleficent's curse — probably grace.
No need for brains in a Disney princess. Elizabeth's gift is
contentment. She used to tell people she wanted to go to Yale.
She didn't have the grades for it, but the world had always
given her whatever she wanted up to that point. I am not sure
she even applied. Mr. Perry, the Mansfield guidance counselor, was pretty blunt about your options. At some point senior year, she acted like she had never heard of Yale. After
she was accepted at the University of Virginia, she made it
clear that it had always been her first choice. Whatever she
has is exactly what she wants. I have reached the ripe old
age of twenty-eight, and here is the wisdom I can bestow:
there is no greater gift than that. If all you've got is a double-
wide trailer but all you *want* is a double-wide trailer: ta-da!
You win. Elizabeth has never set her aspirations at anything
higher than reasonably achievable. College, law school, marriage, house in the nicer part of town, vacations to Paris and
the Caribbean, 2.2 kids, designer dog. I am sure Elizabeth will
not be barren, but if, God forbid, she cannot have children,
she will never have wanted them in the first place. Note to
self: someone with these qualities will be the heroine of my
future dystopian world. She will look exactly the way Elizabeth looks today, bursting with health, long wavy black hair, a
spray of freckles on the nose, freshly tanned, makeup so sub-
tle it looks like she's not wearing makeup. Surround her with

giant-headed, tattooed minions in yellow chiffon dresses and let her accept them and love them.

"Carla!" Mrs. Silverman is shouting my name. The bridesmaids are lining up for the procession. I have always known that Elizabeth meant more to me than I to her. I kind of think she likes it that way. She is used to being admired, and it is easy for her to give of herself since others so willingly give to her. After the rehearsal dinner in which seventeen out of eighteen of the bridesmaids got up and told charming stories about Elizabeth, all of which concluded with how she had helped them through something really difficult, I tried and failed to come up with a list of eighteen friends, much less best friends. In the screenplay, I am the last one at the podium. I turn to Elizabeth, and after the dull stories, I eloquently start to sum up all the qualities that make her so special. Her eyes shine. The audience suddenly realizes that though she is beautiful I am something more. I have a soul. I am the one deserving of love. Without my noticing, someone slips in the back door and listens, nodding with each word; his eyes fill with tears. It is Carter, who has learned too late that he loves me. He pushes through the crowd to get to me, but before he reaches me, he sees me passionately kiss Harry Silverman, who has returned from saving gorillas in Africa to find me. I am going to leave with Harry Silverman, and we are going to spend the rest of our lives in a remote Rwandan village fighting poachers and surrounded by rescued chimpanzees and silverbacks. Carter will drown his sorrows at the open bar. "I am so sorry," he will call as I pass by him. He swirls the cheap vodka in his glass, and we see his bloodshot eyes.

I can't remember the names of all of Elizabeth's brides-maids, but there is a swirl of them, two baseball teams' worth, all in pale yellow, a color that only looks good on people with a deeper tan than I have. Debbie Shapiro, whose older brother, Steven, once called me a dog, is here. Two of Eliza-beth's college roommates, one of whom is the heir to some kind of big money and a champion equestrienne, are here. There's a girl from France and one with an accent I can't quite place, Germanic but not German, I think. Three from law school, two from summer camp in North Carolina. Mrs. Sil-verman is flapping her arms to herd us together. She needs a lasso and maybe a barking dog. In the movie version of this day, I trot over to the general scrum, not sure where to stand. I trip over an out-of-place chair and stumble into Debbie Shapiro, look up — something's not right. Her head is inflat-ing, first one cheek bulging out like the gullet of a bullfrog, then the other. Before my eyes, she expands, her head now the size of a large watermelon, though mercifully the updo is staying in place, the rhinestone barrette still sparkles in the sunlight. The expansion shows no sign of stopping; she has passed beach ball and is on her way to hot-air balloon. Her eyes are stretching out and bulging. Somehow, she hasn't noticed. She glances down at me and smiles in the way she has always smiled at me, pity and arrogance combined into a bleached, toothy grin. She drapes an arm — not an arm, a tentacle — around Elizabeth; coyly cocks another tentacle, this one shoed in a golden sandal, in the air; and smiles for the photographer. Another young woman, a redhead who I

32

think Elizabeth knows from college, lumbers over to join the picture. Her head is more elephantine, neckless, planted on her shoulders with large fleshy Buddha ears flapping in the wind. No one shows any sign that they can see what is happening. Elizabeth brushes her bangs to the side. In thanks, the elephant girl nods her head. She has no trunk, just a regular pert little nose, slightly upturned, minuscule in the middle of her enormous head. The wedding photographer motions his hands to get them to stand closer together. "Beautiful," he calls.

The wedding planner whistles us together — yes, Mrs. Silverman has obtained a whistle; now all she wants for is a whip — and here the bridesmaids come, trotting obediently to join octopus and elephant.

"Carla." Mrs. Silverman blows her whistle until she is red in the face, but it is set to a pitch I can't hear. She stomps over and drags me into my place at the end of the line.

The guests are hastily taking their places. Hundreds of white chairs have been assembled on the lawn of the Gottliebs' house, and it's hard for the high-heeled and the hobbled to make their way. The two wheelchairs come bumping along and almost collide. There is a standoff between the crippled, Zayde Albert, ancient, and Jeffrey Wolf, young, both shriveled. It's a tie.

We are supposed to be hardwired to decide what is beautiful and what is ugly. I read a study somewhere that even infants responded more happily to pictures of what we consider beautiful faces than to ugly ones; they cooed and clapped and smiled for Angelina Jolie and burped and wailed and farted for the Elephant Man. But as I force myself to look at Zayde

Albert and Jeffrey, admitting to myself that I don't want to really see them any more than Carter Graham or Evan Elkins or Marco Hunter really wanted to see me, because in those two are all the mistakes of the universe, all the wars we lose, all the deaths, all the rot, the seaweed that strangles the mermaid, the crusted semen on the thigh, Venus squatting on the toilet — the longer I look the more they seem to sparkle and glow — I think the time may come that my dystopian future may turn out to be utopian when we evolve to see the beauty in the stroked-out and the misshapen, the one-eyed and the cleft-lipped, the swollen and the stained. Innocent babies will smile at what was once considered hideous; electrodes will record their joy. I dream that it will be empathy, not beauty, that will stir our souls and make us fall stupidly in love. After all, there is much more that is imperfect than is perfect in this old world.

The two wheelchairs face off for a moment before the women behind them lean forward, air-kiss cheeks, and weave to the side, one right, one left, pushing their respective albatrosses (albatri?) ahead of them. Onward.

The summer between junior and senior year of high school, Elizabeth and I volunteered for a week at a camp for disabled children. Larry Wolf, the other Jewish guy in the quad at the University of North Carolina when our dads went to college, had a son with muscular dystrophy. Jeffrey. We all knew Jeffrey. We saw him at synagogue on High Holy Days. His wheelchair blocked the aisle. His mother always sat next to him, sharing her prayer book with him and running her finger over the Hebrew, ignoring anyone who seemed annoyed by the inconvenience of the wheelchair in the narrow aisle. My dad used to go over to their house in the middle of the night to help with emergencies. I didn't know the details of these emergencies, but I used to imagine them, my dad reaching into Jeffrey's chest to restart his heart, attaching electrodes to his brain, fishing things out of his throat with his bare hands. After my week at that camp, I knew better what he was doing, changing a catheter, bandaging a bed sore, suctioning yellow-green mucus from the dark cavern of his throat. I was a terrible sleeper, so I always heard him go and heard him return, and I listened hard to hear the things my parents said to each other, that there was no greater tsuris than a sick child, nothing worse than watching your child suffer. I used to think they were talking about me, and I would stare at the dark dots that danced around my room at night and wonder what they weren't telling me until one day I realized they were talking about Jeffrey Wolf, not me.

"The mountains of North Carolina take your breath away. In the morning, clouds float waist-high over the emerald-green fields; black-eyed Susans and violets grow wild around turquoise-blue lakes. It is here that the disabled children come to feel a soft breeze on their faces." That was how my earnest and exploitative college application essay started, for what high school senior volunteers at a camp for the disabled without intending to put this horizon-expanding experience on the application? Prose too purple for Harvard. Maybe I would have done better with realism: for example, I could have described the red draining sores that developed on the limbs of the kids who, having lost their motor skills, were a smorgasbord for the horseflies and mosquitoes. The camp was equipped with special swings, but we were so graceless loading the kids in, hauling up their stiff limbs, and clamping each leg into place that I doubted the feel of the wind on their faces could make up for the discomfort of getting there, and then swinging lopsided and crooked because we could never get the balance right. The kids grimaced and moaned, but they grimaced and moaned even sitting still, so it was impossible to know if we were hurting them. I was assigned to a little girl named Janie. I say little, but she was actually only a year younger than I. Janie was only four feet tall, eighty pounds, and scrunched up like a wadded tissue. My job was to try to stretch out her contracted limbs, and I would hold her in the swimming pool under the merciless southern summer sun, balancing her on my thigh and tugging at the stiff rubber of her fingers that were clamped shut as if she were holding the secret of the universe in her sweaty palms. I didn't make much progress with her, but the doctor told me there wasn't much progress to be made. The concept of progress with these kids was all wrong. Stasis was the only goal, she said.

The last night at Camp High Mountain, I woke in the middle of the night. It was hot and the fans must have shorted. Elizabeth was sleeping in the bunk above me. She and the other counselors combined to make the quiet hum of the sleep of the just and youthful. I tossed around for a while before giving up and leaving the cabin. The cabin where the crippled kids slept was air-conditioned and electrified since many of them could not control their body temperatures and could die from overheating. I wasn't planning to go there. I walked around the lake in the moonlight. We could not understand the things the campers said to us, though sometimes the nurses got it, and their parents could translate their rumblings into whole sentences, lectures even. The cabin for the campers had a faint glow, red and blue, from the instruments that sustained their lives. Moths papered the screens on the windows. I stood on the stairs and listened to the technology.

The doctor had also told me that the camp wasn't really for the kids; it was for their exhausted parents. Sometimes the kids smiled, but that could be a reflex. So too their frowns. They were locked in their bodies and who they were, who they were becoming as they grew up — well, not grew *up* but grew older, aged, and advanced through time — no one could ever know. I went into the cabin where it was blissfully cool. I could tell that a lot of the kids were not sleeping, and when I stopped at the first bed, I saw Jeffrey. He had curly hair, almost white blond like you see only in little kids; his skin was burned red, and his nose was peeling. He stared right at me with the bluest eyes, bluer even than Carter Graham's. His lips were parted, and the inside of his mouth was black and deep and dark, bottomless. His arm trailed on the floor, and a fuzzy green caterpillar was inching across his hand. I brushed it away and picked up his hand and held it. If I could love this boy, I could love everyone. It could be universal, general, a love freely given, born whole and fully formed with no expectation of return, a love that could perfect the achingly imperfect world. I kneeled and looked into his eyes; he stared back at me, unblinking. I asked, "Can I touch you?"

He shifted, and I think he nodded. I touched his cheek, the curve of his neck. What is it that makes us want to kiss — not just things of beauty but also the vulnerable, puppies, children, the ones we love? To touch our mouth to their skin? The caterpillar returned. I brushed it away again and kissed his hand, his warm and human hand. Then I tucked it next to him under the covers. He was so beautiful that I thought my heart would explode with empathy and sorrow. I stayed next to him and we looked at each other for a while. Then his eyes started to slowly close, then open, then close again, giving into sleep. The doctor told me that they felt pain; every day of their lives they felt pain, but they could also learn and imagine and dream like all the rest of us. In the semidarkness, I couldn't make out the faces of the other children; there were moans but also sighs, grunts but also songs. The nurses slept there, and I thought I would be in trouble if I was discovered. At my foot, I saw the green caterpillar, and though I do not like bugs, I scooped it up in a fit of exuberant goodness and carried it outside to release it.

The wedding is starting. I must line up with the seventeen other bridesmaids. If I stare at them long enough, I think I might be able to see the future, when they have double chins, saggy breasts, twenty unlosable pounds around the middle, disappointment creased into their foreheads. I can see their husbands, chosen from among the handsome groomsmen, gone bald, atherosclerotic with broken blood vessels on their coarse faces, bunions on their feet. We will walk down the garden path — it's literally a garden path, with gardenias and rosebushes lining the aisle — and with each step, we will be carried into the future, closer to decay. Debbie Shapiro steps forward, and she marries, divorces; halfway down the aisle she loses her left breast to cancer; her second child hates her, but her grandchildren give her joy until she slowly expires in her nineties. The college roommate, there she goes, steps out bravely. She will have true love all her days. Her husband will adore her through the thyroid condition that makes her gain thirty pounds and lose most of her hair; he will love her C-section scar and tolerate her bitterness at not getting the respect she deserves as a second-grade teacher. The lovely girl from France — I remember her name, Therèse, one dainty foot forward, and all that time in the sun in Marseille begins to wrinkle her skin. Eighty steps to the front, and by the time she gets there and turns to face us, her skin has turned to leather and her cheeks are cavernous, sunken. When she smiles, yellow teeth and bleeding gums fill her mouth. She has never married. She ends her days in a nursing home where she receives no visitors. But the law school roommate, she becomes a judge. She has four children, and one goes to the Olympics, wins a silver medal for the heptathlon. We're going to walk through life with a soundtrack, Pachelbel's Canon. I might have picked something else, Beethoven's Fifth or maybe something by the Sex Pistols. It's my turn now, and seeing what has happened to the seventeen that have gone before me — the groomsmen not excepted; they are all up there, decrepit, leaning on canes, one in a motor scooter, in varying stages of baldness, with scars, stooped, half blind — I should be scared, but if anything, I am thrilled. The road indeed rises to meet you and smacks you in the face, and the end for all of us is the same whether sudden or a quiet erosion. Squinting again, I see that there are now actually gaps in the line of bridesmaids and groomsmen. In the minutes that have passed, a few have died and been borne away, and one or two didn't make it at all.

I, the bottom-rung bridesmaid, link hands with the bottom-rung groomsman. We will stand at the end of the entourage, the last stragglers in the parade, and if everyone wasn't waiting for Santa Claus to come, they would have left long ago. He doesn't look at me. I accept that. By the time we reach the end of this garden path, he will be ugly too.

I step forward and resolve to quit my ridiculous job and do something, anything else, leave LA, abandon the screenplay, and write a novel or go to medical school or convert to Catholicism and die defending the rain forest. To my great shame, I am in love with a movie star. I have been enchanted by his eyes, spellbound by his body, and though he is not good, I love him simply because he is beautiful. I am shallow and vain; the reflection of his beauty will not bring me light. I walk forward, resolved. I must leave Los Angeles and change my life. I will never be Elizabeth Gottlieb. Even if I never have a day like this or marry a man like Hank or assemble two hundred people in one place to wish for my happiness, I will try for something different. I will try to make people see the world — and all the people in it — in all their tragic ugliness and pain, see them and love them. I will dedicate my life to creating something that will inspire us all to touch our lips to the crippled and the maimed and the sad and the cynical and the malformed and the moth-eaten.

I reach the end of the path and walk all the way down the line to take my place and turn to face the guests. The music switches to Mendelssohn. Everyone rises. Elizabeth appears out of nowhere, as bright as the sun, pristine in white, the colorless color. I am standing here, a hundred years old, remembering this day.

To be a king, you have to be born a prince

WHAT IS THE NAME of that girl standing there? What is her name? The ugly one, Elizabeth's friend who used to come and swim at our house. You'd think medical science would have figured out a way to treat that birthmark by now. But then they haven't figured out a way to fix my brain, so doctors aren't so smart after all. Don't deserve all the money they make. It's a sham, medical science; they give us pills — how do we know they work? I can tell you what doesn't work. Everything they've tried on me. Now they've left me here, parked under a Japanese maple that is doing nothing to keep me cool, and I'm staring at that girl, the ugly one with the purple face.

This morning, my wife dressed me in one of my best summer suits, an expensive tan linen from Italy. Ida knotted a green and white silk tie around my neck, pulling it a little too tightly, as usual, and hammered my feet into a pair of new leather shoes. She wet the brush under the faucet and combed what is left of my hair directly off my face. The brush was too wet, and drops of water slipped down my cheeks and fell onto the lapel of my coat where they left dark spots like teardrops. I could see the spots, but I could do nothing about them. I could not point them out to my wife, nor could I complain that the tie was choking me and that the sock on my left foot had fallen down and was folded uncomfortably inside the shoe. Some time ago, months, years, days, I had a stroke and lost the power of movement and the power of speech. No one but me knows that none of my mind was lost. None. Not knowing what is left of my mind, the same people will treat me, at various times, like an imbecile, like the man I was, like a fragile child, or like an insensible lump of flesh. When my wife dressed me this morning, she was silent until she had finished the task. Then she stepped back to examine me. Almost done. The catheter bag was full of urine; she clamped the tubing, detached the bag, and seconds later, I heard the toilet flush. She left me there, trousers around my knees, limp penis, useless now though once it gave her pleasure; now it flopped against my thigh, boneless, a dog's ear, a dead eel. Ida returned with the bag, hooked it up, pulled up my trousers, zipped the zipper, wiped off imaginary lint, and folded my hands in my lap. Then she sighed and declared, overarticulating, "Albert, we are going to Elizabeth's wedding today."

My wife is still an attractive woman. She was a beauty when I married her, and I won her over the efforts of almost every other Jewish man in town. When she was younger, she had long blond hair that she piled up on her head in ringlets. I loved to watch her take it down a curl at a time. She was slender, like a young tree, and her body was smooth and cool to the touch. Not many people knew I was unfaithful to her, but all those who did, at one time or another, expressed their dismay. There is no such thing as a woman who is prettier than my wife when she was young, but only simple men are driven to infidelity by lust. As she stands before me now, only slightly heavier than the day I married her, her hair still blond but dyed now to an unnatural margarine yellow and her eyes framed with puffs of pinkish-gray skin, I try to assess whether I love her, whether I have ever loved her. I provided for her; I protected her. She has never known fear or want or hunger. It would have been my job, in the event of war or famine, to sacrifice myself for her, but love? Love, to me, belongs in the realm of the philosophical where pale, weak men contemplate their navels and other things that never change the world. This is the reason that I have declared my love for my wife only a few times in the sixty years that we have been married. I almost never spoke those words to my two sons. Thinking about it now, as my wife balances with one hand on my wheelchair and adjusts the strap on her high heel, I think it is possible that I never said it to them at all.

Our colored gardener, Mitchell, has to help load me into the van that Ida uses to shuttle me back and forth to the hospital and family events. More than anyone, Mitchell treats me like a child, and I cannot help thinking that this is a form of revenge and that he is having fun at my expense. Good for him. I would like to ask him if this is his intention, but, of course, I cannot speak. Mitchell is always cutting flowers from the garden and bringing them into my room in over-filled vases, splashing water. As he sets them down, checking to see if they are in my line of vision, he declares, "There, Mr. Gottlieb. I brought you some roses. Aren't they pretty?" Mitchell has worked for me for more than twenty-five years. I am not a prejudiced man, never have been. A few years ago, I decided that he knew me well enough to call me by my first name, but since the illness, he has returned to a formality that has not existed since the earliest days of our association. Why, I do not know, and I suppose I never will. Considering all the things I will never know is one of my primary occupations as I sit here, very still, waiting to die. Mitchell snaps my wheelchair into place, talking while he works. "I'm going to get you locked in here, Mr. Gottlieb. Good and safe so you won't slip around." I am facing forward, and Mitchell is working behind me. Occasionally, his hand brushes my face, and he apologizes. Ida climbs into the driver's seat. Driving makes her tense, and I am amazed and impressed that she can maneuver this large van. Before the stroke, I always drove, even when my eyesight began to fail and my reflexes slowed. Mitchell sits up front in the passenger seat. My wife finds me in the rearview mirror, and I hear Mitchell murmur, "He's okay. He's not going anywhere."

Elizabeth is my oldest son's youngest daughter. She is a pretty, intelligent girl, and I suppose she is my favorite grandchild, though she doesn't have much competition. Her older sister, Katie, is a lesbian. She never wears dresses, and her hair is cut shorter than a sailor's. Katie has called me, at various times, a reactionary, a chauvinist, a bigot, and even a Nazi. We do not like each other. Ben is the only boy, a son like everyone wants. I am fond of him, though I do not think he is as bright as Elizabeth. When he was younger, he was a fine athlete, and I had a few proud moments watching him on the baseball diamond and the tennis court. At some point, however, he decided that he did not like competitive sports, and he took up jogging and cross-country skiing. He tried to explain his reasoning to me once, but it struck me that he was investing too much meaning in what are essentially games. I believe he gave up competitive sports for the same reason that I did: because he reached a point where he began to lose. My younger son, Eddie, has only now started a family, though he is on his fourth marriage. His wife, Sharon, is a cold woman with the long face and wide-set eyes of a horse, but she is strong, and she keeps Eddie in line, something that his previous three wives, all more attractive and weaker willed, were unable to do. They have one child, Matthew, a hyperactive little boy who tries my patience. Even Ida finds him exasperating, and she loves almost all children. Sharon is pregnant with another child, a girl, and we are all hoping that she will have Eddie's face and Sharon's mind. This will not make her beautiful or brilliant, but the reverse combination would be worse.

There are hundreds of people at the wedding. We drive past rows and rows of shiny automobiles: Mercedes, BMWs, even one boxy black Rolls-Royce. Josh, my oldest, is a lawyer, and he has done well for himself. I was disappointed when he chose law school over medicine. He was a bright kid, and he could have gone to any professional school he chose, but he was shy and sometimes inarticulate, and I thought he lacked the social skills to prosper in a world where charm is as precious a commodity as intelligence. I tried to steer him away from business; he didn't seem tough enough. Corporate law seemed to offer the same pitfalls, but he insisted on going that route, and given the results, I suppose I was wrong to discourage him. I do not know what he does that is so valuable, but he is paid well, and his house is large, and his friends are wealthy.

There is a parade of women in floral dresses and dark-suited men puffing their way up the driveway. They step onto the grass when they see the van coming and look a little disgruntled. At the top of the driveway, Ida stops the van, and Mitchell walks, hunched over, to where I am strapped in and unbuckles me. A crowd gathers around the van, and Ida embraces people I've never met. Eddie's face appears when the door slides open, and he steps up to help Mitchell with my wheelchair. "How ya doing, Pop?" he asks. If I could, I would grimace. Eddie never called me Pop when he was growing up. I was Dad under normal circumstances and Father when he was hurt or angry. When he went off to college — the first attempt — he had a fair-haired, all-American, tennis-playing roommate who called his father Pop. Among other things that Eddie picked up from that boy — drinking gin and tonics, using the word *summer* as a verb, playing golf — he picked up that name. It sounds false on his lips, and I have been waiting twenty years for him to stop using it. Eddie is wearing cheap cologne, and he smells like Pine-Sol. He swoops over me, and I see that one of the middle buttons on his shirt has come undone. Together, he and Mitchell lower me from the van. Eddie tells Mitchell that he can take care of me, and he calls out, "Mom, I'm going to take Dad somewhere shady." He parks me in back of the chairs, alone, then leaves me. I hope he is enjoying his revenge.

There are flowers all around the courtyard of my son's house, big bursting yellow tulips and roses. White-jacketed caterers slip among the crowd carrying empty silver trays. A semicircle of plastic chairs has been arranged around a lace chuppah. No one is sitting down yet and, thank God, the ugly girl has moved away. I am stuck facing forward, staring at the white columns of the front of my son's house. Eddie returns and squats down in front of me. He searches my eyes, and I try to convey through them that I am alive and cognizant. This takes a great deal of effort, but I might as well try to push the Empire State Building over with my bare hands. "Elizabeth is getting married today," Eddie tells me. It is the umpteenth time I have heard this news. "I wonder if you know that," Eddie says. There is a bit of cotton stuck to his face, and I imagine he nicked himself shaving. When Eddie was a boy, he never emerged from an encounter with a razor with fewer than three wounds. Mornings, we sent him off to high school with flesh-toned Band-Aids pasted all over his cheeks and neck. Eddie scans the crowd behind me. His hand shoots up, and a moment later, Sharon is with us.

"Hello, Albert," she says. "That's a very nice suit." She turns to Eddie and tells him, "I'm going to sit in the back row with Matt. He'll never be able to sit through the whole ceremony, and I want to be able to make a discreet getaway."

"Okay," Eddie concedes. He and Sharon almost never touch, and Matthew is the only thing I have ever heard them discuss. Sharon is overdressed in a frilly blue outfit, and I think of the praise that Eddie has heaped on her family and consider that it must be ill deserved. Eddie does not know how to praise. All compliments bestowed on others are really backhanded insults meant for me.

Eddie stands suddenly, and I hear him call, "Thank goodness. Can you stay with him for a while?" I recognize my wife's perfume, and then her hurried geisha walk. Eddie and Sharon disappear, and Ida sits beside me, a yellow rose corsage sprouting from her wrist, her fingers curled around her pocketbook. Out of the corner of my eye, I can see that she is frowning. I want to tell her to go and leave me alone. Ida loves to socialize; she puts people at ease, and by the end of any party, there are at least two women who consider themselves her new best friend. I have watched her across many crowded rooms. She tilts her head when she is listening, and she never laughs but rather smiles inwardly to herself as if she knows the true meaning of whatever joke or story has been told. This leads people to credit her with a degree of understanding that she does not really have.

Wedding guests begin to shuffle into their seats, and Ida lifts her hand frequently to wave. I see I am not the only poor schlub in a wheelchair; that kid is here, the crippled one we used to always see at the synagogue on High Holy Days with his mother parading him around like she was such a saint. I thought he'd died, but maybe he's like me, stuck between life and death, staring at the sky. Josh finds us, kisses Ida, says nothing to me. He says, "You're sitting in the front row." Behind me, I hear him say, "Let me do it." He grabs the handles of my wheelchair and pushes me over the grass, jostling me back and forth. People stare at me, my head bobbling, my pants leg caught in the wheel, freed, caught again, freed. "Maybe you should have left him at home," Josh says.

When my boys were young, I was just starting out in business for myself. My father had left three grocery stores to my older brother with the understanding that when I finished college I was to enter the business as an equal partner. This never came to pass. My brother and I differed on almost every count, and I spent two frustrating years arguing with him before he finally wrote me a check for a lump sum and told me to leave. I was nervous at first. Josh was four, and Eddie was less than a year, and Ida had expensive taste. I wanted Ida to worry with me, but she blithely assured me that she knew I would succeed at anything I tried, and she continued to eat lunch at the country club and make weekly daylong trips to the beauty parlor. I considered my next move very carefully. I did not have enough money to fail. My brother probably would have taken me back into the business as an employee, not as a partner, but I would rather we starved before that happened. Ultimately, I took a leap of faith. For no reason stronger than a hunch, I used the money I had as a down payment and took out a loan to buy a fleet of twelve Mack trucks and started a produce-shipping business. I paid my drivers well, and they worked hard, but I accepted no excuses. If a shipment was late, I docked their pay 10 percent for every hour overtime. We moved oranges, peaches, tomatoes, and onions all around the Southeast, and the business grew quickly. The more it grew, the more time I had to spend working, the more I worried, the more I yelled. Ida used to tell me that we had enough money. When I would consider a new venture — a canning factory, some retail stores of my own, a fleet of airplanes — she would answer: Why? Don't we have enough? I could not make her understand that standing still was not an option. In business, you have to be a shark. The minute you stop swimming, you start dying.

I'll admit that I enjoyed watching my brother's house fall into disrepair as we moved up into bigger homes, fancier neighborhoods. It was a sweet moment when my brother finally had to come to me for a loan because the banks had refused him. I wrote him the check, and we did not discuss the terms of repayment because we both knew that was something that was never going to happen. I was magnanimous, and I refrained from pointing out that in all the issues over which we had disagreed I had turned out to be right and he wrong. I gave him the check and did not force him to look me in the eye, and then I never mentioned it again. I know now, and I think I probably knew at the time, that this magnanimity hurt him worse than if I had squeezed him, gloated, and nagged. From a position of need, grace seems almost impossible to attain, though, of course, it comes quite easily when you have power. It was the grace that I wore as carelessly as my own skin that hurt him most.

The three stores that bore our last name gradually crumbled, so by the time my brother finally gave up and sold the property, they looked as if they had survived a war. Before the last store was torn down, I walked through it with my brother. It happened to be the first store my father had built, and I remembered running up and down the aisles chasing my brother among stacks of cheeky apples and navel oranges that seemed to stretch higher than the Tower of Babel. My father played classical music in the store, and the shoppers, wheeling their gleaming silver carts over the snow-white polished floor, all seemed to be participating in some kind of ballet that my brother and I interrupted with the shriek of our rubber-soled shoes. By the time my brother conceded defeat, the floors had faded to a putty gray, flat and streaked with black skid marks. The shelves were empty except for a few random bags of potato chips and boxes of cereal gnawed open by mice and spilling their innards. The store smelled sweet and rotten, and in the cases that used to hold generous slices of fresh meat, there were bloodstains that seemed malevolent and foreboding, as if something vicious had happened there. The stated purpose of that final walk was to make sure that we had made the right decision; that the building was not worth saving, but by then, the decision was irreversible. The property had been sold. My brother asked me to walk through the store to prove that he could muster grace when necessary. Before we locked the front doors, the glass of which had long since been shattered and then covered with strips of graffiti-marred plywood, my brother told me, "I guess you were right all along."

There were times, as my empire grew, that I feared I would lose it all and that Ida and the boys and I would be reduced to poverty. I had money saved, but I also had debts. Everything was liquid, and it was a cruel game, where the winner is not announced until the very end. So there were these factors driving me: vengeance, righteousness, fear; but when I put those all together, they do not amount to anything like the momentum I had in business. It was something greater than money that drove me; it was creative, artful. I realize this now, and I hate to admit it, for I have always been indifferent to art, and I considered this indifference an advantage, one that would ensure my survival over those lesser creatures who stop to dawdle and dream and do not see the pouncing lion until it is too late. Were it not for indulgent husbands and fathers, I am sure the art lover would have long since been bred out of existence. Art inspires us to foolish things, and it was the artist in me, not the businessman, who let my company grow and distend until it became as unwieldy as the *Hindenburg*. It was the artist who would not admit that there was no heir apparent and that I was becoming too old to steer the ship. When the stroke came, there was not a single other person who knew the extent of my business; there was no way to carry on in my absence. Ida has tried to hide from me the fact that, bit by bit, she has sold off my empire, what part of it that did not actually dissolve in her hands, for far less than it was worth.

Ida does not think I can understand her, and she generally behaves as if I am not in the room. Since the stroke, I have belatedly discovered the true nature of the woman I married: she is sloppy and sensual and even brave, all qualities she never before revealed to me. I have discovered this only through her absent-minded behavior; she is more natural in front of me, in my supposed stupor, than she ever was when I was conscious. But she must feel that if there is any part of me left with cognition it would be the part of me that ran the business. Thus, while she walks in front of me in her bra and panties and distractedly touches her own breasts, she is fastidious about ushering people away when the subject turns to the business. Nonetheless, I have overheard my share of phone conversations; and others, especially Eddie, are not as careful. I know what is happening, but I am amazed that I do not care. Maybe the stroke destroyed my emotions or tilted the balance. In my frozen state, I find myself affected by little things, most of which I probably would not have even noticed before, and completely unmoved by the few issues that I was passionate about. My business is crumbling; it will not survive me. I used to dream of stores bearing my name far into the future, when men traveled highways in the air and Mars was a vacation spot. It is clear that this is not going to happen, but then, most of the things that we predict for the future do not come to pass. What does it matter? I am going to die soon. My granddaughter is marrying a Christian boy, and no one seems disturbed, not even Ida, who still lights the candles on Friday nights and prays with her fists tucked into her eyes; not for my benefit, I now know, because she has continued the ritual as I sit immobile in my wheelchair, fascinated by the dripping of the wax. I told my sons I would disown them if they married outside of the faith. They obeyed me, even Eddie, every time. Perhaps I should have told them it was okay to fuck outside of the faith. Maybe that would have allowed them happier lives. In any event, they have probably figured that out.

Eddie wasn't quite right from the moment he was born. It was obvious to me, and I said as much to Ida, but she denied it. "Every baby is different," she said, as if she knew. Women often speak with unearned authority on the subject of child-rearing. He cried furiously all the time, soiled his diapers in rapid succession, and refused to accept a bottle from anyone but his mother well into his twelfth month of life. He walked late, and then clumsily, falling often and wailing each time.

This was all the more difficult to bear since Josh had been an easy child, slow to cry, adept and quick to learn. He spoke early, and then almost immediately in complete sentences. He learned to walk, and before we knew it, he was propelling himself around the room, holding on to coffee tables and bookshelves. He was eager to please us, and when I brought out the old movie cameras, he turned toward me gleefully and clapped his hands and waved. He was three when Eddie was born, and he treated the baby as if he were a toy. He referred to Eddie as "my baby," and he came to fetch his mother whenever he cried. "My baby is hungry," he would say. Or "My baby needs a new diaper." Josh was protective of Eddie, probably because Ida used him as if he were a third nanny. Ida had plenty of help. Her mother was over at our house constantly, and we had a full-time maid, Jessica, Mitchell's mother. Jessica loved babies, and both my children, I must admit, seemed happiest in her arms. She would sing and waltz them around the kitchen, holding them one-handed while she polished the counters with Comet. But when Jessica left at the end of the day, Ida would frequently dispatch Josh to care for the baby. This practice did not please me. Often, when I returned from the office tired and wound up, I was greeted by Josh and the baby in the playpen and Ida on the telephone. After dinner, when all I wanted was some peace and quiet, Josh entertained the baby with hide-and-go-seek punctuated by shouts of "Boo!" and "Surprise!" I tolerated it as long as I could, but eventually I would have to put a stop to it, and whenever I did, the baby began to cry. Ida rushed in from the kitchen, and Josh sat crestfallen in the center of the room, his whole face sliding into his lap.

As Eddie grew, his problems worsened. He was temperamental and disobedient. He refused to put away his toys or share or clear his plate after dinner. Any attempts at discipline resulted in a tantrum. When he was six years old, he began to run away, and one night I had to call the police to search for him. They found him in the woods behind our house, and I do not think I was being excessive when I spanked him hard that night. He cried, but then he cried if I looked at him the wrong way, so there was no way for me to really judge the pain he was in. In any event, he survived, but he did not learn, and there were spankings that followed that one, some with a belt. I'm not sure they accomplished anything, but I do not regret them. If Eddie had been changed by those punishments, transformed into the boy I wanted, he would be happier and more prosperous today.

People are taking their seats. Women whose faces I remember but whose names I have forgotten stop by to tell Ida how pretty she looks. I may have slept with some of them, but they don't even glance my way. Maybe they want to remember me the way I was; maybe, like Mitchell, they're in on the joke. A rabbi and a minister are conferring at the altar. If I was still a presence, they would not have dared to affront me in this way. In fact, if it was up to me, I would not be here at all. I have made a policy of rejecting interfaith marriage, and I do not intend to change that policy. It's not so much that I believe in God, but people need rules. If we start to compromise our principles, our lives are meaningless. Elizabeth is a sweet girl. She is pretty and compliant. In fact, aside from her dark hair, she resembles her grandmother more than her mother. Not that my daughter-in-law is unattractive, but compared to Ida, most women come up short. I would like my granddaughter to be happy, and it is for this reason that had I the wherewithal I would have protested this union. I have indulged her. She needs rules. Ida used to say it was because I had no daughters of my own. Elizabeth would sit in my lap when she was little and read quietly while I balanced the books. Later, her friends would come and swim at the pool. Some of them were disrespectful, loud, and abrasive, but never Elizabeth. She cleaned up after herself and her friends, put the lawn chairs in order, always remembered to thank Ida and me. Who do you think paid for summer camp in Maine? When the children were little and before Josh made partner, I offered before he had to ask. Riding lessons, even her own horse at the barn until she discovered boys. Extra money in college that summer when she wanted to go to Los Angeles to see her friend and suddenly needed a thousand dollars. That was me. But not without conditions. Good grades and the right aspirations, marriage, a family, no traipsing around Africa or finding yourself in India, no teaching the poor inner-city kids — as if that's what they need.

The bridesmaids and groomsmen are taking pictures. From somewhere comes the hesitant sound of an unprofessional flutist. The girls are self-conscious, their narrow arms tucked into the arms of the groomsmen. The sight of a girl's arm, thin with the slight tracing of veins and a few glossy golden hairs, has always aroused me. There is no reason to lie just because I am near death. I am attracted only to young women; this is another survival skill. In the area of sexuality, I don't mind admitting I am primitive. Young women are capable of bearing children; that's why men want them. Simple as it may be, the attraction is powerful and pointless to fight and joyful to indulge in. Some of Elizabeth's friends are very pretty. A red-haired girl in a sheer pink dress passes by me. Her waist is winnowed, and her long legs are visible as enticing shadows through the fabric. When she turns to face the crowd, she reveals a lovely face, a bewitching smile. Some of

Elizabeth's friends used to flirt with me. Not seriously; I know none of them actually considered going to bed with me, but they would place their hands on my shoulders and lean in to hear me whisper a slightly scandalous story about one of their teachers or employers. They would laugh, some uncomfortably, some wickedly, at the implications of the story and playfully reprimand me. "Mr. Gottlieb!" they would exclaim.

"Call me Albert," I would instruct.

"Mr. Gottlieb," they would repeat.

I never pushed them or chased them, though I liked to have them near.

It was a different story with Eddie's and Josh's girlfriends. I was a young man when I had my family, and I was far from old when the boys started dating. I did not need them to meet women. Women are attracted to power and success. Opportunities appeared before me almost everywhere I went, lonely women in airport lounges and hotel bars, the wives of less successful men, secretaries. I had more than one opportunity to go to bed with girls younger and prettier than the ones my sons brought home from school, so their girlfriends did not tempt me until Eddie arrived with Caroline. To this day, I don't know what the girl saw in my son. She was beautiful. That adjective is overused by most people. I bestow it rarely. There are probably only five or six women I have encountered in person who earn that praise. My wife was one of them. My first affair was another. The wife of the founding partner of the law firm where my son works — he was not a man you would want as an enemy. A Russian émigré I met at a reception twenty years ago. Those are all who come to mind. And Caroline. Eddie talked about her for weeks before he brought her home. He met her at the yacht club where he was working as a lifeguard after abandoning college for the second time. Despite his clumsiness on land, Eddie turned out to be agile in the water, and he won a few swim meets in high school before learning that he was not qualified to compete at college level. This came as a crushing blow to him because some foolish coach in high school had told him that with practice he might be good enough to go to the Olympics. Eddie believed anything anyone ever said when it was praise. That is why he found himself married three times. All his swimming could earn him was a job as a lifeguard and instructor at the East Point Yacht Club. Caroline was a waitress there; she came from a poor family and was migrating from village to town, town to city, city to metropolis. Last I heard, she was in New York, so I guess she got as far as she could go. Poverty could not have been an obstacle for a girl like her, a head turner with ice-blue eyes and the kind of body that inspires physical pain in men. I am sure more than one wealthy member of the yacht club had made a play for her, but she liked Eddie. When his job ended in September, he brought her home with him to meet the family. I suppose he intended to marry her, though he never outright said it.

As soon as she stepped out of Eddie's beat-up old green Dodge, one long leg at a time unfurling, I knew there was going to be something between us. I was standing in the doorway, having been instructed by my wife to greet them enthusiastically, and the moment I saw Caroline, I realized why they use lightning bolts and fireworks to depict sexual attraction. There was some electric force between us; she recognized it too, and she stared at me for a minute, not surprised, before turning to allow Eddie to take her hand.

I did nothing to encourage her, though I will admit I spent more than one dinner in a trancelike state imagining her without any clothes on. Eddie was a slave at her feet. He had gone off to the yacht club with James Dean hair, long and swept over his eyes, and he returned with a crew cut. When I commented on his hair, Eddie grinned and shrugged and confessed, "Caroline likes it short." He had also taken to dressing neatly and wearing cologne and polished shoes. Ida was pleased with his transformation, though I recognized it as superficial and transitory. After dinner, Ida would instruct Eddie to take Caroline for a walk, or she would suggest that they go watch TV while the "old folks" turned in. I bristled when she referred to us that way. I know she meant it lightly, but neither of us was old. Ida could have passed for Caroline's older sister, and I still had all my hair, a flat stomach, and the strong arms of a tennis player.

Nothing would have happened if Eddie had only been a little more responsible, but then I have wished for Eddie to be a little more responsible all his life.

He and Caroline got drunk one night. I did not know why they were drinking, but I could hear them downstairs in the punctuated silences from the television set, giggling and slurping at each other. It was late, and I had a long day of work ahead of me the next morning. Eddie had shown no signs of looking for a new job, and he had flatly refused to go back to college. He was sleeping in and staying out late, and I was already contemplating the talk I was going to have to have with him. Ida had read my mind earlier that evening, and just before she went to bed, she said quietly, "Let him rest awhile. He's in love."

Ida was sleeping on the other side of the bed, curled up with her back to me. Her nightgown had slipped down her arm, and I stared at her shoulder, as smooth as an egg in the moonlight. I reached out to touch her, but I stopped myself. I did not want her to wake up. I did not want to see her open eyes and hear her voice. I wanted to make love, but not to her. I heard the back door open, and suddenly there was a flood of light in the backyard. The trees stepped forward out of the darkness. I crossed over to the window to see what was happening, standing there in only my pajama bottoms. The light was strong, and it turned the backyard into a murky green sea. I heard Eddie's voice, but I could not see him. Then Caroline stepped over to the swimming pool. She was wearing white shorts that cupped her ass like a closed flower. She dipped her foot into the water, then pulled her shirt over her head and dropped her shorts, wriggled out of her panties. At first, she stood with her back to me. She let her hair down, and her arms, in the floodlights, seemed to glow like X-rays. I was staring at her ass, praying for her to turn around. I knew I should stop them; they were probably drunk, and they should not be swimming, and they were making far too much noise for 2 a.m. in our neighborhood, but I was waiting for Caroline to turn around. I heard Eddie shout, "Here I come!" And then Caroline turned around, and I saw her breasts, ripe and full, and the small triangle of hair where her legs met, and then I was longing for something more, for her to part her

legs as if a tremendous amount of heat were steaming between them. Eddie came running out and dove into the pool.
He surfaced a moment later and grabbed Caroline's ankle and
tried to pull her into the water. She resisted, and he got out
of the water, dripping wet. I hadn't seen my son naked since
he was a child, and I was a little amazed to see him covered
in hair. He scooped her up into his arms and marched toward
the pool, but he did not see one of the deck chairs in his way.
He tripped, and Caroline flew from his arms, and a moment
later, there was screaming, and Ida and I were both running
downstairs.

It's funny how most of the time you can trip and get up,
and then there are those times when you actually break something. Ida and I found our son and his girlfriend completely
naked. I pretended to be as surprised as Ida was. Ida went to
Eddie, and I went to Caroline. The first thing I did was cover
her with a towel. She was holding her arm and sobbing. Even
sobbing, she was enchanting; the tears made her eyes shine
and her lips tremble. She reached for me with her good arm
and buried her face in my chest. I put my arms around her;
the skin of her back was like velvet, and I let her cry, soothing
her. Eddie calmed down quickly, and he came over to Caroline, apologizing. He seemed oblivious to the fact that he was
naked. I could smell the vodka on his breath. He tried to replace me, and I swear I tried to let him in, but Caroline clung
to me. I could see her arm was swelling, and I was pretty sure
it was broken. Eventually, I whispered, "We should take you
to the hospital, sweetheart." She nodded into my shoulder.
Ida brought her a bathrobe, and we wrapped her in it. I was

careful not to touch her, though I was aching to. Eddie rode with me to the hospital, the two of them in the backseat and me driving. Eddie tried to comfort Caroline, but she stared out the window, whimpering occasionally.

She had fractured her wrist, and it had to be set in a clumsy white plaster-of-paris cast that her fingers protruded from like moles. Eddie apologized to her again and again, but she set her face as firmly as the cast and would not listen. Finally, she sent him out of the room and told him that she wanted to speak to me. When she said this, she interrupted one of his apologies. At first, he did not appear to understand what she had asked for. He looked from her to me and back again, his mouth half-open with that stupid expression he has had since infancy. She repeated her request, and he stammered, "Okay," and backed out the door, not taking his eyes off her, as if he were never going to see her again.

Caroline leveled her gaze at me. She had a scratch over her left eyebrow, but otherwise her face was flawless and composed although I sensed she was calculating her next move. "This thing has to stay on six weeks," she told me, though she knew I was aware of that. I had been in the room when the doctor put the cast on. "I won't be able to work during that time." She shifted her eyes to the corner of the room and raised one eyebrow and almost smiled. "What do you think I should do about that?" she asked, adding, "About the fact that I broke my wrist in your backyard, Mr. Gottlieb?"

"I'll give you some money," I said immediately.

"That's very kind of you," she answered. Then she thought a minute, and she asked, "How much?"

Her robe was loose, and I could see the shadows of her

breasts and the bones of her clavicle. "Exactly as much as you need," I said.

Annette comes flurrying up. "Ida, we need you for pictures." I cannot turn my head, so I don't see Elizabeth coming until she swoops into view and one of the flowers from her hair drops in my lap. "Zayde," she says, beaming. "I am getting married." I'm relieved I cannot speak because I do not know what to say. To a goy, I think. It's not right. The girl is so pretty, blank skin, sparkling eyes, a face as small as a memory. If I could speak, I would have to lie and promise her she was going to be very happy. When Elizabeth was a child, I gave her silver dollars whenever she visited, and she told me once that I was the richest man in the world. I told her that I was not, and she thought a moment, and asked, "Are kings richer?"

"Yes, they are," I said.

"When are you going to get to be a king?" she asked me.

"I'm never going to be a king," I said. "To be a king, you have to be born a prince."

"I have to have a picture with Zayde," Elizabeth says. For some reason, her mother acts like this is an outlandish request. She stands up, looks around, flails her arms.

"We can't move him. We'll have to bring the photographer here."

The photographer, a perfectly able-bodied if absurdly skinny man with a ridiculous goatee, comes trotting over, laden down with three cameras as if he's documenting World War Three. Elizabeth squats down next to the wheelchair and gazes up at me. She is beaming; she has yellow flowers in her dark hair, and the veil swirls around her. She is smiling so hard she looks like she might explode. She looks like a little girl, too young to be getting married, but she is older by eleven years than Ida was when I married her.

I am amazed that the institution of marriage has persisted so long. Through the sexual revolution, women's lib, gay pride, AIDS, still people want to stand up and swear that they are going to love only one man or one woman for the rest of their lives. They want to do this in the face of overwhelming evidence that it is not in most people to remain monogamous. Indeed, it may not even be natural, and it may not favor the preservation of the species. I understand why women want to get married. Once they have children, I am convinced, their ability to love men is diminished; the full force of their love is directed toward their offspring, and husbands cannot compete. This was certainly true for Ida and me. Once Josh and Eddie were born, she proved herself a fierce protector, a lioness, who saw me not as an ally but as a potential threat. She interrupted many spankings with her sudden cries, throwing her body over the child and glaring at me, proclaiming bravely, "You'll have to hit me first." These were the only occasions when I saw her courage: when it was directed against me. When she had a car accident or when the house was robbed or one of the boys hurt himself, I was called home from the office and always found her inert on the sofa with her curled hands pressed to her lips. She would turn her eyes, as big as billiard balls, up to me and wait to be told that everything was all right.

On our wedding day, we weren't thinking about children. At least I wasn't. I had waited for her. I did not care about the ceremony. Though Ida comes from a large family, I had only my brother. I invited him only because she insisted. It was not lavish, nothing like this event with flowers and caterers. We went to the synagogue, we got married, we had a lunch afterward. I was twenty-one years old; she was seventeen. We were children. I know that now, but that's how old people were when they got married. Elizabeth is twenty-eight. She would have been considered an old maid. No one told us that marriage would be hard. There were no therapists or counselors. You got married, maybe for love, for lust, for comfort, because it was time and you didn't want to die alone. You had children. You didn't think about what you wanted. Ida was gorgeous, yes, and when she walked down the aisle all in white and lifted the long white veil to show her face, her red lips, her sweet eyes, everyone gasped. She took my breath away too. Every man wanted Ida, but I was the one who got her. When I carried her across the threshold that night, I could barely feel her in my arms. If it wasn't for her perfume and her twinkly laugh, I would have thought I held nothing more than a dress, just yards of silk and ribbon.

Ida would have loved to put on a show for a wedding if she'd had a daughter, but Josh got married in Birmingham. It was Annette's mother who was in charge, and all we did was pay the rabbi and send them on a honeymoon. Eddie's had three weddings, and we haven't been at a single one. This last one, to Sharon, was at a city hall in California where they met. Eddie manages a seafood restaurant. Sharon is a computer programmer. She makes twice as much money as Eddie, and I overheard Eddie tell Ida that after the next baby is born he may give up his job at the restaurant to stay home with the kids. It is a good thing I cannot talk, or I would have to voice my opinion of that arrangement. I suppose I should be grateful that Eddie has finally found someone who can take care of him. Before Sharon, he bounced around from job to job and called me when his funds were depleted, which was about every other month. Sometimes I refused to send him money, but then he would wait until I had left for work, and he would call his mother. Ida wrote him huge checks that she kept concealed from me until they had cleared. Often, this led me to bounce checks of my own, a terrible embarrassment as some of them were made out to business colleagues. I could never make Ida understand that it was hard to trust a businessman who was incapable of balancing his checkbook.

Eddie's second marriage was over before I heard about it, a wealthy girl of limited intelligence whose father stepped in to have the marriage legally declared null and void. The first wife had been about a year after Caroline, a shy, dowdy girl he met at the yacht club the following summer. Alice or Alison was her name, something with an A. He married her at the end of the summer, and he stayed at the shore, working in her father's business for another month or two. He called me in October and told me that he could not work for his father-in-law any longer, that he had quit his job, and that he wanted to come home and help me run my business. I told him he could come home for a while but the business was stagnant. I was cutting back staff, and I was not sure I would have a position for him. "I'm not running a charity," I said. I told him he should think about going back to college.

When they walked in the door, the girl looked about six months pregnant. Eddie told me he wanted to surprise us. I, of course, understood immediately why he could no longer work for his father-in-law. The man, no doubt, found it galling to employ the boy who had taken advantage of his daughter. Eddie was a good-looking boy, he had that, and let no one tell you that women are any less superficial than men. Dull, humorless, unambitious, but almost movie-star attractive, my son never went without women. I could see it as clearly as if I had been there: the good-looking, broad-shouldered, slap-smiled boy reporting to work, flirting with the secretaries while the executives whispered among themselves about the boss's daughter. That would be too much for any self-respecting man to bear. The girl's father had sent them away, but he'd given them money. The first few weeks Eddie was home, he and the girl went out every night. They bought presents for Ida and boxes full of baby clothes, pink and blue, but then the girl decided she needed to rest. She became embedded in the couch in front of the television set, and then Eddie went out alone, stayed out all night sometimes. When he was home, they closed the door to the television room and yelled at each other. I told Ida that they would have to leave, but she said, "It's hard when you're just starting out. We fought too."

After a few more weeks, the girl's father came and got her. I wasn't there when it happened. Ida told me a stout man in a blue Lincoln had arrived and rung the doorbell. Ida opened the door, and he introduced himself politely. He asked where his daughter was. Ida led him to the television room, where he asked if they could have some time alone. A few minutes later, he emerged, with his daughter following meekly behind him. They left everything, all her clothes, all the baby clothes, the soft blue blankets with ABCs and teddy bears stitched in. After they left, Ida went to find Eddie. He was in the backyard by the pool, drinking a beer and lying back on a lounge chair. Ida was not sure he knew what had happened. She told him, and he said, with his eyes closed, "I know."

So Eddie has another child out there somewhere, which means I have another grandchild. I never asked him if he heard from that girl, if she had a boy or a girl. Ida used to wonder about it sometimes, but I would say, What does it matter? Josh has given you three beautiful grandchildren to love — you think something about that one would be special? It's just another kid, you can love one, you can love a hundred, it's all the same. They grow up and leave you. They don't stay babies. When she would moan about it, I would flip on the television, find a show, and point to a girl. There, there she is. Now are you happy?

I only really lost my temper with Eddie once, though there were hundreds of times when he brought me close. He got drunk at his own bar mitzvah and vomited on the dance floor. He skipped school and forged his mother's signature on the excuses. Once, when the neighbors were out of town, he and some friends climbed their fence, swam in their pool, and then attempted to take their car for a joyride. They rolled it out of the driveway in neutral but were unable to get it started. When I came home from work, it was sitting perpendicular in the middle of the road. I'm sure there are other things he did that were concealed from me by his mother or his brother. Josh's only transgressions came in defense of Eddie. He remained protective of him all his life, even as Eddie grew bigger and stronger than his older brother. Josh looks like Ida, wiry and wide-eyed and fragile. This is appealing in a woman but not in a man, and he dated little in high school. His date for the senior prom, I learned years later, was arranged by Eddie.

I returned from the office late one night to find Eddie and Ida engaged in a minor argument. I could hear their discussion when I walked in the kitchen door, but as soon as they heard the door slam, they clammed up. I followed their voices into the living room. They both glanced guiltily at me and then away. Ida was wearing a short white tennis skirt and a white polo shirt. She must have just returned from the courts because there was a narrow pencil line of sweat down the center of her back. "What's going on?" I asked into the air.

"Nothing," Eddie said.

Ida looked at him and then at the front lawn. I saw the red lawn mower there and a single lane of cut grass.

"Why didn't you finish cutting the grass?" I asked.

"I'm going to do it tomorrow," Eddie said. He jammed his hands in his pockets.

"Do it now," I said. I turned to walk back into the kitchen. I could smell my dinner there, and I was hungry. Ida followed me, and after I sat down at the table, she delivered a tinfoil-wrapped plate. She unveiled a neat partitioning of chicken and potatoes and green beans. I stared at the food. Steam was rising off the plate. I waited for the sound of the lawn mower starting. It did not come. I tilted my head. I heard Ida suck in her breath. A moment later, I heard the garage door lifting and a car starting. I pushed back from the table and ran out to the garage just in time to see Eddie backing out of the driveway in Ida's white station wagon. I ran after him; I know he saw me. I was still holding my napkin and waving it in the air. It must have looked like I was trying to surrender. The station wagon screeched as Eddie peeled away.

I don't know why it was just too much to bear that night. I refused to eat my dinner, and Ida wrapped it up in the same foil and put it in the refrigerator. I was determined to stay awake until Eddie came home. Ida took a shower and came downstairs in her bathrobe, the same one that would later show up on Caroline. It was pink velour with a hood. She smelled of apples and baby oil, and when she touched my neck, her skin was moist and a little slippery. "Aren't you tired?" she asked me.

"No," I responded truthfully.

"Hungry?"

"No."

"Do you want to watch television?" She stepped forward and punched on the TV. Her robe was tied tightly around her waist, and it showed the top curves of her hips. She turned the dial, announcing the programs to me. I let her go on for a while before I said, "I didn't say I wanted to watch television." She turned around to face me with the TV glowing behind her.

"Albert," she said. "He's young."

"I know," I said. "I was young once too."

She scrutinized me. She obviously did not expect that response. "Would you like to come to bed?" she asked. It was early, so I assumed that was an invitation to make love, though I am not sure. In sixty years of marriage, Ida never once initiated sex.

"No," I said. I was staring at her midsection. "I'm going to wait for him."

Ida took a hesitant step forward and tried to smile. "I'm sure anything you have to say can wait until morning."

"I don't think it can," I said in a monotone.

Ida puttered around in the kitchen for a while. She checked on me once more when she was done and announced that she was going to sleep. I nodded and remembered to say "Good night." I was not even sure Eddie would be coming home that night. As far as I knew, he had never spent a whole night away, but it was certainly not beyond him. After the eleven o'clock news, I turned off the television and turned on the front lights. They revealed the abandoned lawn mower, its silver handle jutting up and the body hunched forward like a dog sniffing the ground. I stepped out into the front yard. Little bugs were swarming around the floodlight; I could smell the freshly cut grass, what little of it there was. I crossed over to the lawn mower and seized its handle. I pushed it into the garage, and standing there in the space where Ida's car was supposed to be, smelling oil and paint thinner, I felt something shift and yaw in me, the beginning of a new kind of anger: furious and consuming. It filled my whole body until it pressed against the back of my eyes and made my fingers and toes throb. I balled up my fist to hit something, but there was nothing to hit. I let my fist fall into my empty hand. I went back to the living room and waited. At 2 a.m., Eddie came home.

The living room filled with the light from the high beams, spotlighting some of Ida's little possessions: a brass clock, a crystal candy dish, a small porcelain ballerina. They all looked pathetic and embarrassed in the harsh light. Eddie parked in the driveway. He was probably avoiding the noise of the garage door opening, hoping not to wake me. I stood at the front window and watched him trudge up the driveway. He trailed his large feet behind him as if they were flippers. His shoulders were hunched and his hands were sunk so deep in his pockets that it looked as if he could scratch his knees. He stopped to look at the house for a minute. I had turned off the light in the living room, and I am certain he could not have seen me, but it seemed as if he were staring at exactly the spot where I stood. He fixed me with a look of scorn and derision, then shifted his shoulders, one at a time, back into place and walked upright to the house.

When he walked in the front door, I was standing there in the full light of the hallway, waiting for him. I knew I would have to speak first, but I enjoyed holding him there for a minute, with the door still open behind him and moths and silver gnats streaming over his shoulder into Ida's neat and orderly house. He would have to push past me to get inside, and part of me wanted to wait and see if he had the guts to try that, but I could not hold out after storing my anger all night.

"You deliberately disobeyed me," I said.

Eddie locked his eyes with mine. There were pink pimples on his cheeks, and they disgusted me. I waited for him to respond. The house settled in creaks and sighs behind me, and I could almost hear Ida asleep upstairs, a light whistle of breath.

"I'll cut the lawn tomorrow," he said.

"No," I said. "You'll do it now." I stepped forward to give him a light push out the door.

"The fuck I will," he said. He said that after my hands had risen to give him the light push. By the time I made contact, those words had unleashed my anger, and I shoved him hard with both hands out the door. He stumbled backward but managed to stay balanced. Then I saw the silver car keys flash in his hands. He darted away from me, and taunted, "I'm leaving and I'm never coming back," but he moved too slowly. I was not going to let him get away again, and I sprung out of the doorway and grabbed him around the neck and turned him to face me. He was surprised, and instead of the defiant look he'd worn a moment ago, he had that stupid baby-drool face, hurt and uncomprehending, as if he had just arrived at this confrontation, not provoked it.

"You live here," I told him. "You're not going anywhere."

At the sound of my voice, the hurt look disappeared, replaced by malice, and he lifted his hand and slapped me on the back of my head. That was too much. I still had a hold on him, and I slapped him back and shook him hard, and then I caught a hand that was curled into a fist and I twisted it and threw it away like the worthless piece of garbage it was turning out to be. He fell then, I'm not sure how, and I found myself on top of him with my arms pinning his shoulders, the weakling. He didn't even fight back; he opened his tender pink mouth, and bawled, "Mommy." A square of light showed up on the dark green grass. All I was doing was holding him still, but he cried and gasped for breath and pleaded. "Don't hurt me," he screamed, which was ridiculous. I had no intention of hurting him. His eyes were closed, and he had long girlish lashes. His body was thinner and less substantial than I had expected it to be. It was easy to hold him there, and then I heard Ida cry, "Oh, my God, Albert."

I felt her hands on my shoulders, sharp birdlike claws digging into my white shirt. "Get off of him!" she shrieked.

I was under attack, and I had an instinct to defend myself. I lifted a hand and tossed her away. Then she was in my face, her hands splayed against my nose. "Get off of him," she screamed. "Get off of him." One finger pressed into my eye, and a nail caught in my neck. It wasn't that she was stronger than I; it was that something — I think it was the smell of her — brought me back to where I was: in the middle of a starless night on my front lawn with both my wife and my son turned against me. I sat back on my haunches, then let Ida push me over so I lay on my back a moment. I saw Eddie scramble away and then stop and turn back to his mother. Ida held Eddie; she was facing away from me, toward the street, but she spoke clearly, "You are an animal."

The car keys gleamed like dropped treasure. I picked them up, and I ran for the car. I slammed the door when I got inside, and I made the tires screech as I pulled away.

Who has a wedding outside? A young dark-haired man in a morning suit, a man who looks like he's never worked a day in his life, is posing for pictures with other young men. They do not seem bothered by the heat in the slightest. It must be the stroke. Everything wrong in the world is blamed on the stroke. Sweat drops into my eyes and burns. It's an inferno under this sun. I wouldn't be surprised if this whole place went up in flames. Again, the tragedy of not being able to move my neck. I have no warning that Eddie has returned. He says, "Dad's getting overheated. I should take him inside."

Ida says, "He's fine. Don't make a scene. Besides, he wouldn't miss Elizabeth's wedding."

"He looks like he is going to have a stroke."

"He's already had one."

"Elizabeth loves him," Eddie mutters. "He was nice to her."

Ida picks up my hand. She whispers, "It seems like just yesterday I was the bride." I cannot see her face, but I know the expression she is wearing: distant and dreamy, her lips barely curled into a smile, as if the beauty of whatever she is remembering is greater than joy.

For a few days after Caroline broke her wrist, the tension between us was palpable, swampy and dense, but we were never alone. Eddie hovered around her, waiting on her hand and foot. At dinner, he cut up her food into little pieces and fed her. At night, I might see them sitting by the pool with him rubbing her back or brushing her hair. I even once found him ironing one of her dresses. He was embarrassed when I walked in, and he set the hissing iron away from him, but the pull of her was strong. I gave him an incredulous look, but he fingered the fabric of the dress and refused to meet my gaze. Finally, I said, "Can't your mother do that?"

"She's shopping," he said. "And Caroline wants to wear it now."

I walked away, leaving him in the laundry room with the faint smell of singed cotton and the blue scent of detergent; his perfume, I thought.

We were not alone for days until one Saturday when Caroline dispatched Eddie to buy her some special shampoo from a store downtown and Ida went to the hairdresser. I had decided I should close the pool. It was late September, and though it was still hot, I thought closing the pool might signal to Eddie that the summer was over. I was just pacing up and down the patio when I heard Caroline slide the glass door open, and announce, somewhat conspiratorially, "It is so quiet." I squinted up at her and the sky. Clouds were forming, dense and heavy, a late afternoon thunderstorm. We both heard the ominous rumble.

She crossed over to me, supporting her broken wrist with her good arm. The heavy cast only served to underscore how delicate the rest of her body was. She stood beside me and sucked in her breath. "It's going to rain," she said. A thick curtain was dragged across the sky. The bright blue pool water turned gray, and we stood together with the sky closing in around us. It was suddenly oppressively hot, recycled air, her breath, my breath. What she breathed out, I breathed in. She tilted her head, closed her eyes, parted her lips, waited. I kissed her. She pressed against me, unwinding in my arms. When the kiss ended, she dropped her head back, supported by my hands, and opened her mouth to accept a raindrop. Then she smiled at me and watched, amused, as if she was trying not to laugh, as I slivered my hand between the buttons of her dress and caressed her breasts. We went upstairs to fuck. She's the only one I ever screwed in my own bed. I had intended to go into Josh's old room, but she led me into the master bedroom, and we did it there. Twice more before I sent her away.

After Caroline left Eddie, he moped. Strange as it may sound, it was probably for the best that he found out that I had screwed her, written her a check, and told her to leave. It jolted him out of his lethargy, and if fury with me was the price I had to pay to get him moving again, it was cheaper than doctors. I never intended for him to find out. It was she who called one day while I was at work, sobbing, to tell him that she was in love with me. Ridiculous. Making love to her turned out not to be as pleasurable as I had expected.

Eddie waited until Ida had gone to bed to say anything to me. He found me in my office paying some bills, one of which I remember, oddly enough, was from Dr. Robert Goldberg for Eddie's annual teeth cleaning. Eddie came into the office without knocking. He stood far from the desk, and said, with his eyes closed, in a flat, emotionless voice, "I know about you and Caroline." He swallowed. "She called today and told me she's in love with you. I hate you," he said. "You're lucky I love Mom more than I hate you, or I'd tell her." He turned his face to the side, and I noticed that his jaw, like mine, formed a perfect right angle. "I'm leaving," he said, "and I never want to see you again." He turned and left the room. I wasn't scared he'd tell Ida. I wasn't angry. I was proud of him.

Elizabeth and a blond-haired girl are standing together, arms around each other. I remember this girl; I remember she was cruel and rude. If she dropped a potato chip, she wouldn't pick it up. She'd watch while Ida bent over to get it. This one used to come over to our house and lie on her stomach, her bikini top undone. She has a lovely pointed chin and full lips, and with the sun behind her, I can see the outline of her breasts and thighs through her dress. If I were a younger man, I might have felt something for her, but as pretty as that girl in that dress looks, Ida was prettier by far. Every party I went to, every business affair, I would look at the wives of my friends and colleagues, and think, Ida is prettier. A man is judged by the woman with him, and Ida's beauty made me more powerful.

The girl briefly looks over the rows of chairs at me, then away. No one looks at me for very long anymore. Staring out like a zombie, I remind them how thin the line is between life and death. Plus, I imagine I am rather grotesque, though Ida takes pains not to let me see myself in the mirror. There is laughter at something I didn't catch. The sun is high overhead, streaming down in braids and cones, and the yellow tulips look golden. For a moment, all the sounds in the world separate. The girl's words break down into letters. I can hear each bird alone, the shifting of legs in chairs, the gurgle of stomachs. The girl shimmies.

Eddie says, "Shouldn't they have started already?"

Ida murmurs back, "It starts when it starts, sweetheart."

Children go to their mothers for hugs and forgiveness and to their fathers for discipline and protection. I know everyone is talking about a new kind of father: gentle yet stern, kind yet strong. No one wants to accept that some rules are difficult and unpleasant but necessary. We live in a world of sharp delineations, and the greatest efforts of humans will not be able to change that. Everything splinters: day and night, light and dark, living and dead, heaven and hell. Efforts to change this, I cannot help believing, are motivated by weakness, by people who are afraid to face life as it is: a brutal and exhausting gallop through a desert populated by predators and parasites. I wish sometimes that this truth would have left me for a minute: though seeing the world for what it is has made me a success in business, I am aware that it has also denied me some foolish pleasures.

A horde of girls in yellow dresses swarms in front of me. One turns quickly to the side, and for a moment, I think, There is Caroline. Caroline — I would like to tell you about the damage you caused, though maybe it wasn't all bad. It helped my son grow up. I still think about you sometimes. She is gone in a flash. And then there is Ida, young again, nuzzling her head into the neck of another man, not me. I blink my eyes. It's all I can do. Maybe Eddie's right; I am having another stroke. The first one caught me unaware, but I've been waiting for this one, the one that will take me away once and for all. Of course, that girl isn't Caroline. Caroline would be older if she was here, the same age as the mother of the bride. She would be middle-aged, and if she was still thin, then her face would be narrow, creases at the corners of her eyes, lipstick bleeding into her skin. And that isn't Ida. Ida is old, approaching ancient, and me, well, I'm dead.

A woman comes stomping to the altar, pushes the rabbi and the minister aside, and shouts over a walkie-talkie. "Places everyone. It's time to start the show."

The world is big for those who can imagine

ELIZABETH GOTTLIEB WAS BORN four years before Jeffrey. It is hard to believe that that was twenty-eight years ago and that now we are attending her wedding. We've known the Gottliebs for years, but we've never known them well. Still, twenty-five years or more of superficial knowledge can accumulate to something approaching depth. I've seen their children grow up, and they've seen mine — well, my two youngest at least — grow up too. What they've watched happen with Jeffrey is different. He has grown up more quickly than the others, blooming in seconds like one of those time-lapse flowers in a science movie and then beginning his retreat, folding back into himself, shedding petals and leaves until eventually — Soon! Soon! — he will be nothing more than a bulb, as small as a fist.

Twenty-four years ago, I gave birth to the most perfect baby boy. He came out without a cry, greeted the world with a smile. The doctor said he was beautiful. A little baby boy with a full head of downy dark hair and blue-black eyes. They gave him to me to hold, and he squinted up at me, his fuzzy wet head and his mouth gaping open like a caught fish, and I thanked God for him. I remembered to thank God, and while the nurses and doctors buzzed around me and said that he was beautiful and healthy and they needed to weigh him and do some tests, I swallowed his head with my hand, and whispered, "Thank you, God," because I know that everything in this world, every petal on every flower and every feather on every bird and every second of every day, is nothing less than a gift from God.

My mother and father came the day after Jeffrey was born, and it was the greatest happiness, peering through the shiny glass windows of the nursery to the third crib from the left in the second-to-last row where a black-haired baby was sleeping, his little mushroom of a fist curled up under his chin. No matter what happened later, and what I have endured since then, we had that moment of joy, that moment a gift from God.

It took us several days to decide what to call him. Before he was born, we had determined that if it was a boy we would name him Isaac Joseph, but when we actually saw the child, that name seemed wrong, too weighty and historical for one little baby, and so, after several days of deliberation, with the bris looming over our heads, when the decision had to be made, we called him Jeffrey Brian Wolf, names that seemed to give him room to grow. In light of subsequent events, I've thought a few times that perhaps Isaac was the name he was meant to have, the bewildered child, unaware of what God has asked of him.

Once we got him home, all his black hair fell out, and a week after the bris, he was as bald as a Chinese monk. I was careful of that little pink head, and Jeffrey had a variety of hats to wear whenever we went outside, broad-brimmed sun hats with his name stitched in that kept the sun from his face and his face from the sun. I was like a superstitious old lady, afraid to let anyone, even the sun, see what a beautiful baby I had. What a naïve hope it is: to expect to keep your child safe. All we really ever have to go on is faith and superstition.

Jeffrey was bald for six months, but he gained weight and was healthy, even chubby. At eight weeks, he could grasp my fingers in his hand. He loved to use his hands then. When Larry came home from the office, he would dangle a pen in front of the baby, and Jeffrey would grab it and try to tug it away. Larry said that was a sure sign that Jeffrey was destined to be rich. I told him there were more important things in life than money. Jeffrey, I expected, could be anything he wanted to be: a musician, an artist, a rabbi, an astronaut. Larry liked to tease me, and he would answer, "You can get rich doing any of those things except being a rabbi. Try not to mention rabbis to him." Jeffrey was a talker back then too, gurgles and squeals mostly; he was a happy child, given to express his joy with a skewed-up face and two randomly paddling fists.

His hair grew in at six months, almost white blond, which was strange since both Larry and I are dark. We expected it to grow darker later, and it has mellowed to an ashen color, but for the first five years of his life, he carried around that colorless hair, as if he had been somewhere and seen something horrible. The superstitious old lady in me has made up stories around that hair. I don't allow myself to believe them, but I can't control my mind enough not to wonder. The jealous sun caught a glimpse of my beautiful boy before I had a chance to hide him and first pulled out all of his jet-black hair. Not content with that, she stole him from his crib one night and led him through the darkest parts of the world, forced him to witness and imagine all sorts of horrors, maybe even whispered his fate in his ear or forced him to choose his fate over another tragedy, my death or his father's death. When he came back, his mind may not have remembered what he had seen, but it was imprinted on his soul, and his hair, when it finally shook itself free and began to grow, couldn't muster the faith to have color. That story sprang up in my head one day, more like a lost memory than something made-up, and there are things about it, especially the idea that Jeffrey made a bargain, sold his body but not his soul, that make more sense to me than they ought to. It is strange, after all, that while Jeffrey has decayed, crumbled, contracted, and contorted, his father and I have passed through the years with only a few gray hairs and no illnesses greater than worry.

As for Jeffrey, well, the only word for what has happened to Jeffrey is that he has become. He has lived much longer than anyone expected him to, and though they say sometimes muscular dystrophy affects the mind, it has not affected Jeffrey's, though at this point he can barely speak. Once in a while, he can squeeze out a few words, and sometimes I can actually understand him, and it is amazing what he is saying. Usually, he is telling me to look up at the stars.

For Jeffrey's sixteenth birthday, Larry bought him a powerful telescope. I don't know how Larry knew to get him that telescope. Jeffrey had never before expressed an interest in astronomy, but he loved the telescope immediately, and he loves it still. He spends hours at it, propped in his wheelchair, his head fallen over to the side. I bring the telescope up to his eye, and he stares at the heavens. When he was sixteen, it was already difficult for most people, even Larry, to understand Jeffrey when he spoke, but I have to admit there was something wonderful about his words in those days. It was like he had become a baby again. I understood everything he said, just as I had when he was two and a half years old and blathering away without the help of *R*s and *S*s. I was always at his side, translating for Larry or Amelia and Will, his younger sister and brother. We learned about the constellations and the movement of the planets. We had a *Farmers' Almanac* to tell us which days were clear, and we strained to see the moons of Jupiter or the rings of Saturn.

One night, we stayed up late to watch a meteor shower. Amelia and Will wanted to stay up too, but they had school the next day, and I sent them to bed. Larry waited with us for about an hour, but there were no shooting stars during that time, and he got bored and went inside. After a while, he called to me that he was going to sleep, and he clicked off the lights in the living room and the kitchen. The house was dark and quiet enough to hear the hum of the refrigerator. There was only the porch light on, and Jeffrey, angling his head up to the eye of the telescope, told me to turn it off. I did, and then it was completely dark except for the night sky and the not-quite-full moon buoyed in the treetops and the pale gray scar of the Milky Way. Jeffrey told me we would not see shooting stars until after midnight. I do not know how he knew that. We sat there silently, and I could swear I heard my children, the two healthy ones, sighing in their beds upstairs. The clock in the hall chimed twelve times. Jeffrey cocked his head and counted out loud with each chime. Then he smiled. He could still smile then, though it was a loose and reckless thing, an avalanche sliding across his face. He let his head fall straight back. It fell heavily and stopped abruptly. There was a cat meowing in the neighborhood somewhere, and Jeffrey said, "Kitty, *shh*," as if the stars needed quiet to perform.

I didn't see the first meteor. I was busy watching Jeffrey. His neck by then was thin and twisted like a candy cane. He had no shoulders. It was like a children's drawing where the arms attach straight into the back, more like wings. His hands, of course, were always knotted, but people didn't know how soft they were, like pillows, his twisted arms and legs too, stuffed with cotton. "I saw one!" he exclaimed when the first meteor fell. His left hand rose an inch from the wheelchair. "Did you see?" he asked. I told him that I had not. "You have to look," he told me.

I looked up, but I wasn't concentrating. I was thinking I should have let Amelia and Will stay up. It would have been nice for them to have something to share with their brother. One time, I overheard Amelia tell a friend that her older brother was a cripple. I thought to correct her, but it was true. What could I tell her to say? Amelia was always direct. The year before Larry bought the telescope, when she was thirteen years old, Amelia came home from school and informed me that she knew Jeffrey was going to die soon. She had looked muscular dystrophy up in the encyclopedia, and it said most people died before the age of twenty. She seemed dispassionate when she said it. Her hair was cut short then, because she didn't like to comb it. She must have been playing soccer that day, because it was dirty and sweaty and sticking straight up off her forehead. I said, "Honey, only God knows when someone is going to die."

"That's what the book said," she countered.

"Books aren't always right."

She decided not to argue with me. She fixed her face into something private and turned away, but since that day, I could not help wondering if she chose not to love Jeffrey as much as she would have if she didn't know he was going to die.

"There's another one," Jeffrey exclaimed. "Did you see it?"

"No, honey," I admitted. Jeffrey's eyes rolled in his head.

"You weren't watching," he accused.

I closed my eyes and tried to clear my head, but there were always too many thoughts crowded in my mind. I wondered if I had signed Will's permission slip for his school field trip. "Stars are much bigger than planets," Jeffrey said. "Those aren't stars we're seeing." It always seemed like such an exhausting effort for him to talk, but at sixteen, he still liked to lecture me. "Those are meteors," he said. "Or comets. They're just pieces of stars."

We waited awhile before the next one came, and I saw it. I shouted out even before Jeffrey could make a sound, and I think he was pleased. He really wanted me to see one. It was so fast, and as soon as I started to think about it, I wasn't sure I had actually seen it, but Jeffrey confirmed the sighting. "That was a big one," he said. I touched his hair, his mysterious hair that didn't look like anyone's in the family. Will and Amelia were both dark, an obvious mix of Larry and me, but sometimes I'm not sure where Jeffrey came from.

"Are you tired?" I asked him. "Ready for bed?"

"Let me see another one," he begged.

We waited. The next one was a long time coming. The tips of the trees scratched at the sky. It was October, and the backyard was brimming with leaves, all sifted together. There wasn't much of a wind, but when it blew, you could hear the leaves lift and fall, sigh. I switched my eyes from the sky to Jeffrey, and I said, "Isn't God amazing, Jeffrey?"

He didn't answer me. A few minutes later, he shouted, "There's another one! Another one. Did you see it?" He laughed.

Just before I put him to bed that night, he told me that when he grew up he wanted to be an astronaut. I don't know how much Jeffrey believed in his own dreams. I never discouraged him, but I also tried not to encourage him too much. I did not ask him why he wanted to be an astronaut, as I'm sure I would have asked Amelia or Will. He told me anyway. "Astronauts don't have to know how to walk," he said. "They float."

We took Jeffrey to muscular dystrophy camp one year. I was reluctant at first, but Larry thought it would be good for him, and for us. Since Jeffrey was born, I had not spent one day away from him. Larry worked it out and made all the arrangements. He timed the week so that Amelia and Will would also be away at camp, and Larry and I intended to take our first vacation alone since the children were born. As it turned out, Elizabeth Gottlieb was Jeffrey's counselor. She was seventeen, and he was thirteen. She was growing, and he was shrinking. The day we dropped him off was hot and fiercely sunny, with threads of ocean wind in the air. Elizabeth had requested Jeffrey as one of her campers, and she had decorated his bed with streamers and Tootsie Rolls. Carla Lefkowitz was there too, poor thing, always trailing next to Elizabeth, trying to hide her birthmark. I should have told her, Be happy it's just a birthmark; look at how much worse things can be. The two of them stood in front of the cabin, shaded by pine trees, Elizabeth with her hands on her hips, nodding intently as Larry rattled off the minutiae of Jeffrey's care, and Carla looking embarrassed. At home, I am the one who attends to Jeffrey's whims, and I am the one who keeps a careful catalogue of his idiosyncrasies, but when we go out in public, Larry takes over. I am perfectly capable of maneuvering Jeffrey in his wheelchair. I bathe him every day by myself, locking his arms in the straps we've installed in the bathtub and lifting him out, as slippery as a fish, my hands under his arms and my feet braced against the toilet and the sink. When he was a baby, with no idea of his impending doom, I would linger over his bath, run the warm water through my fingers, caress the velvety softness of his brand-new skin, sneak my fingers under his chin and around the back of his round head. After he got sick, but when he was still small, bathing wasn't so difficult. He slowly lost his ability to get in and out of things — chairs, beds, bathtubs — but as he weakened, I couldn't leave him alone for fear the day would come without my knowing it when he would sink under the soapy water of the tub and be unable to lift himself out. I bathed him with his brother for years until Will started to complain that Jeffrey was too big. When he lay down in the tub, he took up all the space, and Will switched to showers. Now, if I am too tired to think about bathing him, I can strap him into a chair and shower him off, but, of course, I get wet too. We make such a funny couple, me in a bathing suit and Jeffrey under the artificial rain, his hair sudsy; me kneeling at his feet to clean between his toes and, as quickly as I can, his buttocks, between his legs where now he has hair, and in that small section of his body that looks like an adult even though the rest of him is a shrunken man—strange and mythical, grotesque even, I will grant you—or an overgrown twisted version of a boy, also grotesque to those who have never seen a child with muscular dystrophy.

Larry did not want Elizabeth and Carla taking care of Jeffrey. When I told him she would be at the camp and had requested to help care for Jeffrey, he rolled his eyes and asked rhetorically, "Is that appropriate?" I did not see the problem at first. Elizabeth's father, Josh, and Carla's father, Marty, and Larry had been college roommates. Josh and Larry weren't terribly close. I don't know what we would have done without Marty's help—everyone needs a doctor for a close friend—though his skill set did not translate to his daughter, who was just a kid, and Carla had never shown any interest in Jeffrey before, though she saw us often at synagogue. Elizabeth, on the other hand, always made a point of stopping by and trying to talk to Jeffrey, albeit in too loud of a voice despite the many times I have told her that his hearing is unaffected by his muscular dystrophy. I didn't see any reason why they shouldn't care for Jeffrey. In fact, it seemed better to have him assigned to someone who already knew him, even if only superficially. I told Larry I thought it would be nice for Jeffrey. He had known Elizabeth since he was a child; he used to go to her birthday parties—before and after he got sick—and he always seemed to like her. I asked Larry what the matter was.

He just frowned and said he did not think Elizabeth and Carla were old enough to be taking care of Jeffrey. He reminded me that Jeffrey was a boy, and Elizabeth or Carla might have to bathe him or change his clothes.

"I am sure they'll leave that to the nurses," I said. "Besides, I don't think there's a risk of one of them falling in love with him."

He seemed shocked to hear me say that and turned away.

Larry would never admit it, but I know he is a little ashamed of Jeffrey. It is a combination of emotions: shame, sorrow, self-pity, and bitterness. There have been times when I have seen him looking at other people's families, and I know he is thinking, Why me? Josh Gottlieb never seemed to have anything go wrong in his life: three healthy children, all college bound. I realized as he turned away that this shame was the reason he did not want Elizabeth taking care of Jeffrey, reporting back to her parents the details of his limitations. Carla wouldn't have anything to report. Her father often came to the house to help us when things happened late at night, a clogged catheter, a slight fever. But Josh Gottlieb and Larry were colleagues, even competitors, and Larry always kept score. It was better, in his mind, for Josh Gottlieb to have only a vague idea of what we went through. For his colleague to know the full extent of our struggle was to Larry somehow humiliating. I have never looked at it that way. We are neither heroic nor condemned. We are just playing the role that God wants us to play. There is no need to sugarcoat it. God's world, including Jeffrey, especially Jeffrey, is beautiful exactly the way it is.

It did bother me a little bit when Elizabeth crouched in front of Jeffrey's wheelchair, cocked her head, and sang, "We're going to have a lot of fun, Jeffrey."

"He's not a baby," Larry said to her, a little more sternly than he should have. "He's not retarded."

I winced for Jeffrey when Larry said that because Jeffrey probably did not realize until that moment that that is what he looked like to other people. After that day, Jeffrey would correct people. "I'm not retarded," he would say when he sensed they were talking down to him. They could not understand what he was saying, and they would look behind the wheelchair to me.

"He says he's not retarded," I would translate.

We left Jeffrey in Elizabeth's care. Carla must have been assigned to another child, because we didn't see her with him again, just Elizabeth and Jeffrey. I remember her standing underneath the flagpole; there wasn't enough wind to lift the flag, and it hung, limp and sad, its stripes twisted inward. When we were almost to the car, I turned to look back again and wave. Elizabeth waved, then lifted Jeffrey's hand to make him wave, the way children lift the hands of their dolls. I almost turned around and got him when I saw that. "What is she doing?" I asked Larry, unwilling to believe what I had seen. I knew Larry would share my anger, and a wave of disgust came over his face. He stared at Elizabeth, a pretty girl. Slender, high cheekbones, and enchanting. I thought of that Frank Sinatra song, *"When I was seventeen, it was a very good year."* Jeffrey would never know that joy, summer days, pretty girls, first kisses. I started to go back to save my son, but Larry took hold of my arm.

"You need to rest," he stated.

"No, I don't," I answered.

"I need to rest," he said. I examined him to see if he was lying. His eyes did look a little red. Larry has a long, thin, aristocratic face, the kind of face that looks funny when it assumes any emotion: joy, sorrow, or anger. People consider him attractive, but he is only truly handsome when his face is blank. When he smiles, he looks endearingly goofy, and when he frowns, he is ugly. Usually, he is able to maintain the blank repose that suits him best, and this can make him very difficult to read. He touched his finger to a drop of sweat on his temple, and I decided he was telling the truth. The camp was in North Carolina, and we had planned to spend a week at the beach. Larry put his arm around me. "He'll be fine," he said.

We were back to pick Jeffrey up the next Saturday. I could not believe a week had passed. I felt I had wasted it. It took me three days just to get used to the fact that I was not needed every second of the day. Larry had to practically restrain me to stay in bed in the mornings, but it wasn't relaxing for me, lying there. The energy was there to be used, and if I lay in bed, it only revved inside me, overheated me. We stayed at a luxurious hotel on the water, and Larry had breakfast brought up every morning, but I could not make him understand that I could not eat lying down and that I could not sleep late. I would roll out of bed early in the morning, sometimes before sunrise, and careful not to wake Larry, I would leave the room, walking the pink and gray carpeted halls of the hotel in my nightgown.

People left their room-service trays from the night before outside their doors, and I would scrutinize them. I've always found leftover things, old and used things, reminders of the past, somehow sad. I never say "the end" when I finish reading a story, because I don't like endings. Actually, I don't believe there is any such thing as an ending. There are no beginnings either, only moments when we realize what is happening. The day Jeffrey was born, his life began to me, but I am sure he was a force in the world before I held him in my arms, and he will be one after he is gone.

When I got lonely in the hallway, I would go back to my room and wait for Larry to stir. When he woke, he would ask me how long I had been up. I would always say, "I just now opened my eyes." A few mornings, we made love. I don't know if he believed my fake enthusiasm. I know it is terrible to admit it, but part of me is always with Jeffrey. He is the only thing in the world that completely needs me, and there will be a day when this need is gone. I expect Larry, Amelia, and Will will still be here, and I promise I will give them my undivided attention. I will initiate sex; I will buy lingerie. I will attend every play, concert, ball game, dance — there will be years and years and so much love to give them. I promise.

The week passed, and I would be lying if I said I enjoyed it. Ultimately, I was bored. Larry wanted to sit by the ocean reading crime novels, but I found it impossible to just lie there watching the waves roll toward me, crumble, recede, and roll toward me again. Anxious, I would get up to go for a walk. Most of the time, Larry let me go, but the first few times, he begged, "Why can't you just sit here with me?" I would concede, settle back in the lounge chair, but it took a great effort to lie there. If I brought up Jeffrey, he answered with the same five words every time. "I'm sure he is fine."

By Saturday, I was excited to get my son. It seemed like much longer than a week since I had seen him last, and I remember telling Larry, a little bit to his chagrin, that I did not want to send Jeffrey to camp again. "We're not going to have enough time with him as it is," I said. "When he dies, I'm going to wish I had this week back. When he dies, there will be plenty of time for trips to the beach."

It was raining, and the sand by the side of the road was the color of putty. I don't think it's good for us to avoid thinking about Jeffrey's death. Amelia and Will don't need to dwell on it, but Larry and I need to be prepared. "It's only a week," Larry said. "How much can change in a week?"

"The whole world can change in a week, a day even," I said. We were driving along a narrow causeway, and the rain was stirring up the sea in shades of gray and blue. The whitecaps twisted like long beards. "Yesterday we couldn't escape the sun. Today you can't even see it."

"Helen," Larry said. "I wish you could be happy when you are alone with me." He seemed to be concentrating very hard on the road. "We used to have fun together."

"I am happy when I am alone with you," I said. His hand was abandoned on the seat, and I picked it up and held it.

"I didn't get the feeling you were really with me this week." The headlights of oncoming cars emerged from the darkening sky.

"I was with you," I protested. "I had a wonderful week."

"Did you?" Larry asked.

"Yes."

He was quiet for a while. He switched the windshield wipers to a faster gait. The rain was getting stronger.

"I hope the cabins are warm and dry," I said.

Larry glanced in the rearview mirror and then over at me. "I'm sure they are," he said. Then he added, "I'll be glad to see Jeffrey."

"So will I," I said emphatically.

"I know." Larry shook his head. "I miss Amelia and Will too."

"Of course," I said. "But they don't miss us. They're so happy when they're at camp."

It was a two-hour drive to the camp, and as the rain continued to fall, I became increasingly convinced that something had happened to Jeffrey. I didn't share my anxiety with Larry. I was often worried for no reason, and I knew he would remind me of this fact and only dismiss my concern. Larry had the radio tuned to a classical station, but it was not loud enough for either of us to hear over the rain and the rhythm of the windshield wipers. Jeffrey had had a checkup about a week before camp, and the doctor said he was shockingly healthy, but it was still possible for him to die suddenly. His heart could stop beating; he could fall and hit his head or land in a shallow puddle and drown because he could not move. I have forced myself to imagine in great detail life without Jeffrey. I'll still have Amelia and Will. They will get married and have children; I'll have a rich and enviable life. I've told myself that I will find a way to be happy when he's gone. God would not want me to mourn forever. There is, however, a narrow window of time that I am not sure I will be able to endure: the actual day of his death and the few days or weeks after. If I can get through that, everything will be all right, but it is that specific time that I dread.

At the camp, we were ushered into the mess hall where other parents were waiting for their children. Open umbrellas rolled on their spokes, dripping water. One man shook his hands in disgust, as if the rain were contaminated. Around the mess hall were construction-paper collages, heaps of clay in unrecognizable forms, drizzles of paint on paper, the art projects of younger, less afflicted children. I watched the other parents greet their children as they were wheeled in. The counselors draped yellow ponchos over the wheelchairs, but the children still had streaks of water on their faces. Not everyone finds a disabled child a blessing, at least not at first. There were parents who strode forward, their faces set and their hands reaching in advance for the handles of the wheelchair. They saw the disease as a judgment. Those who covered their children with kisses and knelt at their feet were still blaming themselves and their own faulty genes. Those who had to be called twice and then walked wearily over felt themselves unjustly accused. So did the ones who smiled and talked too long to the counselors, pretending they didn't mind their burden. I could recognize it because I had felt all those things, and it was only recently that I had realized, or finally accepted, that Jeffrey's delivery to me was a compliment. It was no accident, and it was nobody's fault. These children must be born to parents who are capable of loving them, and as I watched these other men and women, wet and tired, like stray dogs, I wanted to tell them that it would all work out. They would learn to love their children, even to love the responsibility that those children entailed, because they were capable of it, and they would not have been given those children if they were not. In genetic terms, I am tempted to say that somewhere near the gene for muscular dystrophy that I carry is the gene for loving someone with muscular dystrophy.

Larry spotted Elizabeth with Jeffrey before I did. He took three giant steps over to them and blocked my view of my child for a moment. He squatted by the wheelchair, and I saw his hand reach up and cradle Jeffrey's face. Then I went cold all over, my body realizing before my mind that something was wrong. I followed Larry's arm to where his hand rested on Jeffrey's cheek, right underneath two purple and gold bruised eyes. By the time I was at Jeffrey's side, Larry was already quizzing Elizabeth. "How could he fall?" Larry demanded. "How could you let him fall?" I moved Larry to one side so I could see Jeffrey. The arch of his nose was red and swollen. The backs of his hands were bandaged. Jeffrey's skin is more tender than other children's. In sunlight, you can see a faint network of blue and red veins spidered across his cheeks. I am told this fine skin has nothing to do with his disease, but I don't see how it cannot be related. I began inspecting him from the top of his head down. Minor scratches can turn septic on him if left unattended. I pushed my fingers through his hair, checked behind his ears, the back of his neck. "Are you okay?" I asked him. "Does it hurt anywhere?"

"I fell," he said. Over my head, Larry continued to interrogate Elizabeth. "Weren't you aware of the responsibilities that this job entailed? Did you think this was just going to be fun? Something good to put on your college applications?" He didn't give her a chance to answer. "You thought it was going to be easy. Arts and crafts and singing songs."

I needed to concentrate on what I was doing and considered telling him to shut up and let me work. I pressed Jeffrey forward, balancing his head and arms against my stomach so I could examine his back. A slow rage was starting to boil in me, not at Elizabeth per se, or not at Elizabeth only, but at the entire camp, all the doctors and nurses who could allow something like this to happen. God gave Jeffrey muscular dystrophy, but it was the camp that allowed him to fall. There was a scrape from his wrist to his elbow, crusted and scabbed and left unbandaged. Because of God, Jeffrey will die young, but because of Elizabeth Gottlieb, he has had more pain added to his short life.

Larry kept right on talking to Elizabeth, but I was surprised at what he said next. "You don't realize what you've done," he groaned. "Now we can never go away again." I refused to look up or acknowledge what I had heard, though he was right. I was busy removing Jeffrey's shoes to make sure there were no broken toes. I have disliked Elizabeth Gottlieb ever since that day, not only because she allowed harm to come to my child—I am not insane, I recognize how hard it is to care for Jeffrey, how easy it is to let him fall—but because she stood there, in pink shorts and a tank top from Jacksonville Beach, and said, "I'm sorry. It was an accident," and cried not for Jeffrey but for herself.

I was not going to bring Jeffrey to this wedding, but he was with me the day I got the invitation. It was early spring, and I wheeled him to the end of the driveway to get some fresh air while I picked up the mail. He noticed the heavy white envelope right away and made me understand that he wanted me to open it and tell him what it was. I obeyed, and I informed him, "It's an invitation to a wedding. Someone is getting married."

"Who?"

"Elizabeth Gottlieb. Do you remember Elizabeth?" Jeffrey's eyes swept cockeyed in all directions.

"Am I invited?" It took me a while to realize what he had asked. I looked at the invitation. His name was included with Larry's and mine and Amelia's and Will's. It was funny to see them all listed there together, because I got used to thinking of Larry and Jeffrey and me as one family and Larry and Amelia and Will and me as another. Amelia and Will are so rarely home now. Amelia is in law school in Washington, D.C., living with her boyfriend who is, I think, too old for her, not a boy at all, but at least he is Jewish, unlike, from what I have heard, the man Elizabeth is marrying. Will is in college, only an hour away, but he rarely comes home. He is busy with his fraternity, and I can't keep track of the girls he dates.

"You are invited," I answered. "Do you want to go?"

His head was fallen over to the side, and one eye was angled right into the sun. He squinted up at me, and I thought he nodded. "You do?" I asked.

"Yes," he said.

I had to call Annette Gottlieb and make sure she truly intended to invite Jeffrey. He can be a shocking sight to some people. I tried to think of a way to phrase my question that would allow her to answer it honestly, but in the end, it's a battle with her own conscience, and I'm not sure there's a way to make that easier for people. I heard Annette hesitate before she responded, "We would love to have him. Is there anything special I should do? Anything you'll need?"

"No, I don't think so," I answered. I'm past letting those hesitations bother me. She made her decision. "We don't have to climb stairs, do we?"

"It's all in the front yard," Annette assured me. "I'll set the chairs up wide enough for his wheelchair. Josh's father is in a wheelchair too."

"Thank you," I said.

"Elizabeth will be thrilled to have him," Annette added. "Jeffrey is very special to her."

I don't think Elizabeth ever told her parents what happened at camp. She must have been ashamed of herself, and she did not want to share that with her parents. All children have pride. Of necessity, I've observed Jeffrey more closely than other parents observe their children, but I know there are still things he keeps from me. Someone who has not raised a handicapped child might wonder how Jeffrey, in his limited world, could possibly have secrets. All I can answer is that the world is big for those who can imagine.

It took forever to dress Jeffrey this morning. His arms and legs have a mind of their own, and sometimes I wish I could just sew the clothes on around his body. Amelia described dressing Jeffrey as such a struggle, like putting clothes on an oak tree. She was not wrong. His arms are like branches; you pull them into place and they snap away. Still, it was worth it to see him in a suit. We have not gotten Jeffrey dressed up since Amelia graduated from college, and I did not remember how handsome he could be, with his glassy blue eyes and his wet hair brushed back off his face. I kissed him impetuously, though I try not to do that too much. It isn't fair to him because he cannot pull away. I could kiss him a hundred

times a day, but I know he doesn't want me to. I allowed myself to think, just for a moment, of how handsome he would
have been without this disease. Nothing good can come of
thinking that way, but sometimes I just cannot help it. Larry
is stronger than I am in that regard. When Jeffrey was diagnosed and we were told that there was no cure, Larry gave up
hoping right away. It took me longer to accept, and I know I
caused him pain when I suggested that the doctors had been
wrong. Tests weren't perfect, I argued, and when Jeffrey managed to walk across a room or climb the stairs of his little
slide one day, I could convince myself that God had answered
my prayers and that this child had been delivered. God sent
Sarah a baby when she was ninety years old; he could lift the
curse from Jeffrey. God did not choose to answer my prayers.
I knew there had to be a reason, but it was years before I
discovered it. It is necessary that some people on this planet
have the capacity to love despite great hardship. It's not me
I'm talking about. It's Jeffrey.

As a baby, Jeffrey seldom fussed. He loved to be held, and
he would nuzzle his head between my neck and shoulder,
and gaze up beatifically. Even the babysitters loved him. He
had a little swing that you could place him in, with holes for
his chubby legs. The swing was on a spring, and he would
bounce up and down, laughing and delighted with himself. That swing kept him entertained for hours, but he was
equally amused by any of his toys: a colorful series of pop-ups
that a dog, a cat, and a clown leaped out of. He had a cobbler's
bench with square and round pegs and a dozen jars of Play-
Doh and the Fisher-Price barn, which he liked to fill and snap

open, watching the plastic cows and trees tumble out. He was fond of *Sesame Street,* and we had Ernie and Bert puppets, who went by the names Ennie and Bet, and there was a gigantic Big Bird emblazoned on his stroller. One day, while we were out walking, I told him that maybe Big Bird would flap his wings and take us flying. We ran a few feet and pretended to take off, and then I cried, "Look! We are flying! We're up in the clouds!" I asked him if he could see the clouds.

"Yes," he said. "And birds and airplanes." Buds and eplins.

"What color are the birds?" I asked.

"All different colors," he said. "Yellow and blue and red. And the airplanes are green." The next time I took him out in the stroller, to my amazement, he asked, "Are we going to fly again?" All mothers think their children are special, but Jeffrey was extraordinary. I knew he was going to surprise me.

He was in kindergarten the year he was diagnosed. His pediatrician, very astute, saw the signs before I could. Most children with muscular dystrophy are not diagnosed until they are around seven or eight, and I sometimes wish we had had those extra few years of ignorance, but I suppose it was important to find out. I was five months pregnant with Will at the time, and the doctor advised me there was a fifty-fifty chance that if I was carrying a boy he would also have MD. We had to go and have a dozen tests at the university hospital: sonogram, amniocentesis. I didn't want to have any tests done. I did not see the point. I was not going to abort the child. There was nothing I could do if he had the disease but bear him and raise him as best I could. We are compulsive gatherers of knowledge even though there is very little in this world that actually enlightens. I told the doctor the tests were useless, but he insisted that it was important to know, and Larry wanted to know. He really, really wanted to know. It puzzled and disturbed me. I remember asking him what difference it would make. "We won't abort," I told him. "You wouldn't want me to abort, would you?"

He never answered me. The tests came back negative. Will was born with dark hair that never fell out, and he plays tennis on the university team. His father says his serve is close to professional.

The whole time I was having the tests, I was worried about Jeffrey. I asked every doctor I met to explain muscular dystrophy to me. I was hoping one of them would say something different, but it was all the same: deterioration and death. "Isn't there anything anyone can do?" I asked. No. One nurse told me, "If I had a little boy with muscular dystrophy, I would pray to Jesus to take him quickly."

When I got home from the hospital, I would gather Jeffrey into my arms, lift him from the ground, and press him tightly. His legs swung behind him like rope. He laced his hands behind my neck and laughed. He thought we were playing. When I put him down, though, he often fell. He would seem a million miles from me then, as if I were gazing down at him from some high cliffs and he was on the rocks. I couldn't bear to watch him struggle to stand up even though the doctor said it was best to let him learn to cope. That way he would be independent for longer. Independent? He was five years old. I would bend down and gently help him stand up. His hand pressed into my shoulder, as small as a seashell. He would balance against me, and at first, until he was seven at least, I would let him go and he would usually stay standing. He held his hands out to the side as if he were walking on a tightrope.

That first year of knowing was a strange and sleepless time. Amelia was two and full of energy, crashing through doors and making constant demands. I had told her to be careful with her older brother and not knock him down, but she was two, and she did not listen to anything I said. She could not understand why Jeffrey was so slow. He had always played with her from the time she was a baby, wanting to hold the bottle for her and push her in the stroller and feed her. I did crazy things at night when I couldn't sleep. I calculated the number of seconds I had left with Jeffrey if he died at twenty. Countless nights, I sat up and watched him sleep. I saw omens — good and bad — everywhere. Jeffrey dropped a glass, but it did not break. That was a good sign. Amelia had inherited his Fisher-Price barn. She snapped it in two one day so it would never close again. That was a bad sign. Jeffrey's condition was stable, but I knew what to look for now, so I was constantly reminded of his death sentence when his knees buckled, when his hand reached for mine and missed, whenever he talked in his funny voice, which I once found so adorable, and I watched his tongue flounder in his mouth.

Larry was unpredictable. Sometimes he wept. I found him in our room one night staring at a picture of Jeffrey while the tears fell. Other times he was sarcastic. He lost his temper easily. We didn't fight. I am not a fighter, and when Larry tried to take out his frustration on me, I recognized it for what it was, and he stormed unopposed. Dinners landed on the floor. I still remember the way the blood of an undercooked steak looked against the white linoleum, and I know that jars of mustard shatter easily when thrown. Jeffrey and Amelia were unfamiliar with their father's rages. Larry had a temper at work, where he was a demanding boss, but he tried not to bring any of those frustrations home with him. Something in the desperation of knowing his child was dying made Larry, for a while, unable to control himself. Things settled down when Will was born. Larry doted on the new baby we knew was safe. He'd been dipped, like Achilles, in the waters.

When we arrived at the wedding this morning, Larry drove straight up to the house to drop us off. We have a van especially adapted to Jeffrey's needs, with a platform that rises and descends at the press of a button. That way, I can take Jeffrey with me if I have to go somewhere, and I don't have to worry about getting him in and out of his wheelchair. He is too heavy for me now, not because he has grown but because I have aged. I am not as strong as I used to be, and while I can handle bathing and dressing him, I don't have the strength and coordination to carry him up and down stairs or in and out of cars. Larry still carries him, and it always looks odd to me when he does, a sad caricature of romance, Jeffrey's frail body in Larry's arms. Larry started to lift Jeffrey out of the wheelchair when we got to the wedding. I reminded him that it was not necessary, and he hovered uselessly for a minute, and then said, "Oh, right. I forgot." I showed him where the button was, and I positioned Jeffrey's wheelchair on the ramp. Guests were arriving, pretending not to look at us, but the contraption makes a lot of noise, and I caught their sideways glances. Jeffrey's eyes immediately focused on the big bouquets of yellow and white tulips. He likes flowers, and in the spring, I take him to the botanical gardens, and we walk among the rows of azaleas and cherry trees. If there's no one else around — and there usually isn't on weekday mornings — I pick flowers and rub them one by one against his cheek. They feel different, each one. This is something that Jeffrey and I discovered when he was nine years old. Rose petals are sturdy, and azaleas are as thin as cobwebs, and tulips are cool and stiff, like glass. No one but Jeffrey has ever appreciated these things with me. Amelia is too tough for flowers, and Will's a boy, and Larry just thinks of them as something useful to prove he remembers our anniversary.

Larry asked me if I would be all right while he went to park the car. I assured him I'd be fine. I wanted to bring Jeffrey over closer to the tulips. I watched Larry back down the driveway. The van is cumbersome, but he maneuvers it well, better than I do. Someone called my name, and I turned to see Rita Lefkowitz, Marty's widow. She has all her children but not her husband. Who is worse off? I hadn't seen her since Marty's funeral, and I wondered if she'd be shocked by Jeffrey's decline. If she was, she hid it well. She didn't blink an eye when she declared, "How wonderful that you brought Jeffrey!" I was trying to remember the names of her sons, but I drew a blank. Her daughter came up behind her, looking uncomfortable in her flouncy dress. The dark purple birthmark still covered half her face, and I see medical science hasn't fixed that either. She was scowling as she approached, but then she smiled genuinely at me and Jeffrey, and said, "Hi,

Jeffrey." To her mother, she groaned, "I cannot bear to have another picture taken." Rita whispered something to her, and she stomped away.

"You look wonderful," Rita told me.

"So do you," I said. "How nice to see Carla here."

"She's a bridesmaid, but the boys couldn't make it. Eric is in Chicago, expecting his first baby, and Bill just got back from climbing Mount Kilimanjaro." She tried to stop herself before she finished the sentence. People always do that, as if I have forgotten all the things that my child cannot do and they are the first ones to remind me. Maybe they would feel better if they knew that I haven't forgotten. I haven't forgotten for a moment, but I am no more bitter that Jeffrey cannot walk than I am that I cannot fly. He can do what he can do, and if the list does not grow longer, it grows wider. He can't jump or run or climb, but he can think, he can blink, he can nod his head a dozen different ways.

"How is Larry?" she asked me, and I told her he was fine. "And the other children?" I told her they were fine and didn't go into details. She obviously didn't remember their names, and I only remembered Carla because of the birthmark. Extremes, both good and bad, imprint in memory. People always remember Jeffrey's name, from random people at the synagogue to the man behind the deli counter. I excused myself and took Jeffrey over to the flowers.

I know that people think I've given up a lot to care for Jeffrey. Annette Gottlieb is involved at the synagogue and plays tennis and golf. They travel with their children all over the world, some as far as China. Other friends of mine have had careers. They've gone back to school; one even became a doctor. They've had affairs; they've remodeled their houses more than once. With the money we have spent caring for Jeffrey, we could have circled the globe, bought a beach house, added another level to the house. Larry and I traveled before Jeffrey was born. We went to Italy and France once, Israel and Egypt, and Mexico. I've seen beaches and pyramids and temples and castles. They impressed me, I suppose, but they don't call to me, and I have trouble understanding what it is about travel that is so exciting to people. I don't need more reminders of what I do not know and cannot understand. The past—the kings who died and the wars fought for reasons we no longer know or comprehend—saddens me. I'm too superstitious, and my faith is precarious. It requires a special balance for me to feel that there is a purpose in life, and when I see all those empty castles, those dungeons where people suffered, unrelieved, and I arrive two hundred years too late, it upsets the balance, and I start to feel that things are futile after all, eternally repeated in pain and anguish. That is what I feel when I travel. I never feel that at home. I never feel that with Jeffrey.

I wish I could say that Larry feels the same way. My husband is fifty-nine years old. His hair is gray on the sides and thinning on top, and he has to wear reading glasses. He is still athletic. When we met in college, he was a swimmer, with a swimmer's broad shoulders that narrowed to his waist like an inverted triangle. In high school, he had been the star quarterback. He doesn't swim anymore, but he runs and he plays tennis and golf. When Will comes home, they might throw a football or even go to the batting cages, but Will doesn't come home very often. When we first moved into the house where we live, Larry asked if it was possible to build a swimming pool. He had a civil engineer assess the prospect, and we were told that the groundwater was too close to the surface for a pool. We almost didn't buy the house, but then Larry decided we'd buy it, live in it for a few years, and then move to a house with a pool, maybe even a tennis court. He was ambitious, and he had a right to be. He knew he would inherit his father's real estate business, but that was not enough. He was driven to succeed, got an MBA at night to add to his law degree, and he doubled the size of their holdings. He has done well. We sent Amelia and Will to private school, to Europe one summer each, and on trips to the Grand Canyon, but we were never able to move. Jeffrey's expenses are too high, and Larry is always worried about what will happen to him if anything happens to either of us. He doesn't want Amelia and Will to have to take care of him. We've never actually discussed this with them, but there are provisions in our wills, even a letter Larry wrote to them telling them to live their lives. I don't worry about this the way he does. I am certain Jeffrey will die before we do. In fact, I know he is going to die soon. There's very little left of him, and God won't make him suffer. Maybe then we'll move, spend all that money we've set aside for Jeffrey, and Larry can finally have a swimming pool. He's only fifty-nine; he'd have at least twenty more years to breaststroke.

What will I do when Jeffrey dies? I cannot remember if there were plans I once had. Jeffrey's been my job for twenty-four years. When he dies, I suppose I will just retire. I'll put on a pink warm-up suit and walk around the neighborhood

like the older women do. I'll bake cookies; I'll wait for grandchildren. My important work will be over.

Larry is sweating a little when he finally finds us in the courtyard. He had to park almost a mile away, down at the bottom
of a steep hill. Most of the guests have arrived, and I tell Larry
we should find a place to sit down since we will need an aisle
seat. People scatter for us when they see the wheelchair coming. We are among the first people in place. There's a row of
older people in the back, fanning themselves and trying to
stay awake. In the front row, I see an old man in a wheelchair;
his wife sits vacantly beside him. It must be Josh's father, who
I heard had a stroke a year ago. I tell myself it is worse for him
because he has suddenly lost a freedom he has known for decades. He knows what he is missing, but somehow it makes
my heart ache that my boy resembles that old man more than
he resembles the young ushers in their gray morning coats
and the nervous bridegroom whom I caught a glimpse of,
posing for pictures with his mother and father. I could not
love Jeffrey more, but I would be lying if I said I didn't wish
sometimes that he was just a normal child and could do the
things that normal children do. Roller-skate, sing, kiss a girl,
and get married. I feel sorry for Jeffrey sometimes, but I honestly believe that Jeffrey has never for a moment felt sorry for
himself.

    People fill in the seats around us. Sometimes I have to wipe
Jeffrey's mouth or position his hand in his lap. Larry greets
old business associates. He's busy shaking hands, and I smile
at familiar faces. Annette finds us and asks if everything is all

right. I tell her that we are fine, and I see that the next stop she makes is to the old man in the wheelchair. It is both hours and seconds while the seats fill up around us and the bridesmaids, young girls all, arms linked with young men, process past us. When the bridal music strikes, everyone stands up. I have to move Jeffrey's head so he can see Elizabeth coming down the aisle. "That's Elizabeth," I whisper to him. "Isn't she beautiful?" I wonder what Jeffrey thinks about all this life around him. He cannot tell me anymore. We communicate on faith. I think he thinks she is beautiful. I think he has forgiven her for dropping him. Actually, I think he was never angry. It was I who had to forgive. As she walks slowly, smiling and accepting all the love and admiration and good wishes that you can almost feel soaking her, warming her, scampering in front of her, and paving the way into a bright and painless future, I feel my anger toward her dissolve. Good for her. Lucky her. God chose this path for her and another for my son.

When we got Jeffrey home from muscular dystrophy camp, I had to tend to all the places he was hurt. In addition to the bruises on his eyes, his hands and arms were scraped. There were swollen red bumps on his legs from some kind of bug that had been allowed to feast on my child, a cut on his finger, a bruise on his back as if someone had hit him. I did everything I could to make him heal more quickly. I held warm washcloths to his face, and when that did not work, I switched to ice. I administered to his wounds with salves and soaps and bandages. Larry said it would get better in time, but meanwhile, neither of us could bear to look at him. It was too painful, those pale eyes framed by bruises. Jeffrey endured the attention. Once, a piece of ice fell from the washcloth, and I did not notice it until it was half melted in his lap. He didn't say anything. He didn't even point it out to me.

Larry allowed me to hover for a month, and then he decided that it was enough. He wanted to go out and see a movie. There was a nurse who would come and take care of Jeffrey. She was very good, and I trusted her. Larry called her, and he made the arrangements and presented the plan to me. My first impulse was to resist, but I saw that Larry was set on going, so I nodded and tried to smile. We were going to take Amelia and Will to see the new Star Wars movie. They were the only children in their school who had not yet seen it. I would have liked to have taken Jeffrey too. He was the one who loved space so much, but before I could suggest it, Larry let me know that it was out of the question. He said, "I'd like a simple evening. I'd like to not worry for an hour or so."

The nurse came. Jeffrey smiled when he saw her. Her name was Merry, not Mary, and he said he had missed her. He was happy to see her. I kissed Jeffrey goodbye, promised to be back soon. Everything went fine for a while. We went to dinner. Larry and Will discussed the baseball season. Amelia made a plea for a new wardrobe. She wanted sweaters from Benetton. Larry told her she could have one if she wouldn't throw it on the floor when she took it off at night. Then we went to the movie. I never have seen the end of that movie, but I assume that, as usual, the good guys won.

I sat there in the dark trying to concentrate, but I just felt so bad that we had left Jeffrey alone. I kept thinking that he would love the movie, how he could scan the sky with his telescope looking for the planet where Luke Skywalker lived.

Finally, I couldn't take it anymore. I got up. I didn't even notice that Larry followed me. I walked out in the harsh light of the lobby through the heavy popcorn smell over to the pay phone. When I reached for the receiver, a hand came and pressed it down, wouldn't let me lift it. I turned around to see Larry standing behind me.

"Come sit down," he said.

"I just want to call," I confessed.

"Come sit down," he repeated.

"Let me call."

"Helen, come sit down." Larry's face was steely. I saw his jaw tighten, then relax. "If you would just come sit down . . ."

"What?" I asked. I put my hand back on the receiver. I was holding a quarter, ready to drop it in. "Why?"

"Helen. Please. Amelia and Will asked where you went. They think something is wrong." I missed the slot when I went to put the quarter in. It dropped onto the carpet, and we both stared at it, this bright spot winking up at us. I went to pick it up, and he covered it with his shoe. I was squatting at his feet, looking at where my hand was about to reach. Larry bent down and slipped his hands under my arms and raised me up. "Come back," he said. "Everything is fine. Just come back and see the ending with me and Amelia and Will." He started to guide me back toward the theater. I followed him for a minute, but then I pictured the quarter behind me, embedded in the red carpet, and I said, "I'm sorry. They can tell me how it ends." I broke away from him. I walked over to the telephone, afraid to look back to see if he was watching me. I made the phone call, and it turned out that Jeffrey had thrown up, and the nurse was worried about him and hoping

I would call. I calmed her down and told her I would be right home, but I stopped myself from going into the theater and finding Larry.

I asked an usher how long until the movie ended. He told me five minutes. A line of people was already waiting for the next show. I sat on a red-velvet bench and waited. It wasn't long until Larry came out, holding Amelia's and Will's hands. They were excited and jabbering away about the movie, and I pretended to listen as they told me the ending. The ending of the second movie in a trilogy that is, in fact, not an ending at all. There will be other movies for Amelia and Will — I know it — and I hope one day they will understand why I had to give so much to Jeffrey. They will do the math and see I concentrated my love for Jeffrey into a very short span of time and stretched my love for them out over decades and generations. Maybe Larry will see it too. In his old age, I will care for him with the same skills I have learned caring for Jeffrey; I will bathe him, feed him, arrange his pillows, and smooth out the creases in his pajamas. He does not appear interested in the wedding; I can see him looking at his shoes, then up at the sky. Jeffrey has fallen asleep. I have one hand on Jeffrey's, and with the other, I reach for Larry. He smiles weakly at me, then glances past me at Jeffrey, takes in that he is asleep and looks away.

Elizabeth Gottlieb will soon be a married woman. Amazing. I knew her when she was in diapers. Jeffrey and I were at one of her birthday parties, seven or eight, when she got a bicycle with training wheels. I reach for a rose petal that has fallen into the grass. It's been crushed and creased, but it still has a scent. I place it on Jeffrey's lap, and his eyes flutter open. I can't stop myself from caressing his face with the back of my hand. We were sitting on the porch yesterday, and he got some sun, so there are two swirls of pink on his cheeks. It looks like he wants to say something, so I move my face closer to his. When I am closer to him, I feel I am in a better position to receive his thoughts. His head trembles slightly. I hold the rose petal up before his eyes, and I follow an imaginary line from the fragment of the flower to his face. Suddenly, I see something strange in his eyes, an expression I have never seen before, and it stops me for a minute. I try to decipher it. Is it sorrow? His eyes are rolled closer together, and his long lashes droop, and his mouth is opened to an oblong O. I hold the rose petal between two fingers and look more closely at him. Is it sorrow? No, no. It cannot be.

Come in

THERE WERE FOUR of us in a quad room our first year at the University of North Carolina at Chapel Hill. This was 1960, before there were any ideas about diversity and mixing it up and everyone getting to know one another and kumbaya. I must have been on a list of leftovers, stragglers who had to be plugged in here and there, because I was the fourth one in that quad of Jewish kids: Josh Gottlieb, Larry Wolf, Martin Lefkowitz, and me, Jack Chandler, a poor white kid from Troy, North Carolina. Before that day, I'd never met a Jew. Okay, I didn't think they had horns or anything, but there was an inkling that all the other things people said about them were true: they ran the world, they owned all the banks, they were cheap and show-offy and weaselly and small and stuck together in some secret cabal that worked to the detriment of the rest of humanity, especially Christians, a group that, at the time, I still considered myself a part of. I thought it was enough that I actually pried up a piece of the floorboard with my pocketknife and hid my cash there even though the minute I met those kids, some of those stereotypes started to go away. For one thing, Larry was over six feet tall and played high school football. He'd had some interest from recruiters, but that had all gone away when they found out he was Jewish. Marty sort of looked the part, but he was friendly with a great laugh that started quietly and rose in strength while it fell in pitch to a great guffaw. Josh was shy and quiet, but he has turned out to be the most generous guy I've ever known, and if anyone was cheap, if anyone was eyeing the other guys' wads of dough, if anyone wanted to show off what they knew, well, I guess that was me.

But man, forty-one years have passed. Marty's dead of lung cancer that hit him hard and had him carrying around an oxygen tank at our twenty-fifth reunion. Larry's got the best job title — *senior* vice president — which is funny since Marty and Josh were the A students, but that's what they say about C students — the A students work for them. They don't talk about D students, which explains why I had to find my own way. I should probably be the dead one, seeing as I was the one who kept going into the dragon's den, sometimes by choice (heroin) and sometimes not (Vietnam), but instead I'm at Josh's daughter's wedding, at Josh's big house in Atlanta, overdressed in a rented tux, all this for Elizabeth, who I held in my big paws seven days after she was born. I'm the one with the twee job teaching painting and photography to privileged kids who just missed the Ivies and spend the first two years at my institution convincing themselves that their lives have not been derailed and the next two years — if I have anything to do with it — changing their ambitions altogether and telling law school or B-school and Mom and Dad to kiss off and putting on a backpack and heading off to Myanmar.

Elizabeth, Elizabeth, come here a minute. Step away from

those other girls, none as beautiful as you. I see Marty's kid there, but I can't remember her name. She's still got that birthmark, makes her look like a Picasso with a divided face, half pale, half purple, I'd call it quinacridone violet to be exact. She has a face Oskar Kokoschka could love. Nevertheless, she looks pretty in her radiant yellow dress; all young girls look pretty in their dresses on a day like today, under a cloudless blue sky with a slight breeze and distant birdsong. Come here, Elizabeth. Uncle Jack has something to tell you. You look absolutely beautiful, perfect, that long neck so kissable, that tiny waist. Back in the day, if you hadn't been the daughter of the guy I guess I would say after all these years is my one true friend, I would have held you close and tried to feel your breasts against what was once my strong, fearless chest, but then if that was you back in the day, you would look, well, you would look like your mother now, attractive but not ravishing, doable but also forgettable. These are shitty things to say about a woman. Maybe it's just because I remember what she used to look like. She had a sweet, soft face with a little plump mouth, kissable lips. You wanted to trace them with your fingertip before you touched your mouth to hers. Her face is still relatively lineless — in fact, her forehead is as smooth as an egg — except for the crinkles around her eyes and the few brown splotches peeking through her makeup. The lips are thinner. The eyes not as fresh or liquid, like there's some kind of stale skin over them, the congealed oil that floats on top of a rain slick. She has spread out a little bit — Hey, who am I to talk? — but those legs are still tan and strong, golfer's legs swishing past me in her mother-of-the-bride pink chiffon number that probably set Josh back a grand or two. The first time I met Annette was on a golf course. She had on Bermuda shorts and a sleeveless top, and her breasts were perky in the way breasts were perky in 1960 — I miss those Playtex bras that lifted everything up so high and wide that breasts looked like two torpedoes heading off for different targets.

Okay, I'll stop thinking about breasts on your wedding day and what I used to dream about doing with your mother, Elizabeth. How about this? I am thinking that you are still the smallest and most beautiful thing I have ever held in my two clumsy hands, and the things that I have held in my hands are more glorious and more horrible than I hope you will ever know. Oh, yes, I have held things in these hands; I have held the heavy sun-soaked head of a woman I loved while it rested in my lap; and I have held the heavy blood-soaked head of a man who died in my arms. I have held and hoisted over my head a ten-foot canvas I have poured my soul onto; and I have held the last crinkled dollar that I fished from behind the stained brown sofa of one of a series of shitty apartments I have lived in. I have held a 1.2-carat crystal, a diamond attached to a ring that I hoped to put on someone's finger; and I have held the white crystals of opium and the burned shards of tinfoil and a dirty needle crusted with blood; and you, I held you when you were just born and during a few birthday parties when I happened to be in town; I held you when you were wearing a tutu and a costume that I think was supposed to be a lion because I remember the long tail that you used to tickle my face — you a child for a man with no children, who ran to me when I showed up, oblivious to whatever state I was in, and looked through my coat pockets for a present and masked your disappointment when they were empty.

You are getting married. I was married once and came close a few more times. I married Jenny Paxton at the ripe old age of twenty-two; that's what everyone did in North Carolina, married by twenty, three kids by twenty-five. She came from Troy too, though she went to the other high school, so I didn't know her when I was a kid, which is probably why she would even consider me. She didn't know that I was the one who slashed the principal's tires, the one who smoked behind the school instead of eating lunch so that I stood almost six feet and weighed 130 pounds my senior year. She didn't know that I stole and crashed the driver's ed car (and neither did anyone else, thank God, because that might have truly got me in trouble, and I didn't really want to get in trouble). Like all skinny teenagers with a brain, I just wanted to be someone else. I was smart and ashamed of being smart because it meant something somewhere had gone wrong — Mom must have screwed the mailman or they mixed up the kids in the hospital. Smart was nothing in that town of football-playing farmers, and if I didn't have the exact same crooked nose and close-set blue eyes of my father, he probably would have thought the same thing I thought — what the hell kind of alien life-form is this that reads poetry and wants to go to fucking Paris, France, with all the queers and cowards.

I married Jenny under false pretenses. We met in the spring of my senior year of college when I was starting to realize that I didn't know what I was going to do when I finished school. Gottlieb, Lefkowitz, and Wolf knew — saying that together sounds like a law firm — law school, med school, family business. That's not to say they didn't have dreams — Marty was hilarious, funnier than Lenny Bruce and Woody Allen — and who knows what he could have done if he hadn't loved his parents, but they all loved their parents — shit, *I* loved their parents, their mothers with their pots of soup and handwritten letters with ten-dollar bills inside and instructions to have a little fun; their fathers who had grandfathers who had all been poor, not the way we were poor in Troy, but poor like the roof's caving in and the ground is crumbling and the soldiers are closing in and people you love are going to die in horrible ways; their fathers who were so proud of them and wanted nothing more than to see them wear a black cap and gown, and take their rightful place on the golf course. I loved my mother, but she was dead, and my father and I didn't have anything to say to each other because everything I did was an insult to him — going to college, being skinny, smoking weed, leaving home, knowing Jews and blacks and thinking that other people in the world might be as worthy of God's love as the Christians of Troy, North Carolina.

I spotted Jenny in church, and in the last throes of thinking I could be happy being what everyone I grew up with was going to be, I kissed and screwed and married Jenny Paxton in that order. Jenny of the milky white skin and wide-set green eyes and strawberry blond hair, Jenny with acne scars on her back and Roman toes and a hip that jutted out in a way that I first thought meant she was challenging the world but later realized meant she was perpetually in fear of falling down. Thank God something was wrong with our parts — or maybe nothing was wrong with us individually, but the God that I don't believe in saw that we were mismatched. Through two years of marriage and plenty of sex — the only thing that both of us liked — Jenny never got pregnant. Her sisters got pregnant; all her friends got pregnant. Jenny did not. She blamed it on the books I read, she blamed it on the paint fumes I inhaled, she blamed it on the way I slept late and the fact that I drank too much and didn't talk to my dad or my brothers and didn't go to church enough. I knew then and still know that it was a gift, her barrenness, and if there had been a child wandering around this planet that I had created and been unable to love, I would feel really, really bad about that, and if I added it to the list of things I felt bad about, it might have been enough to make me want to die. And I am happy to say that at the age of sixty, I do not want to die. On this bright day I want to live, paint, dance, read, fall in love, and, yes, maybe even marry a woman I love while a string quartet plays classical music and someone arranges yellow flowers on tables with pressed tablecloths. I might, in fact, want to live the life that you, my dear Elizabeth, are heir to.

My wedding was nothing as elaborate as this, Elizabeth. We had a church wedding. Jenny wore a white dress but not a wedding dress. She bought it at Penney's, and her older sister sewed on some beading and extra lace and removed the black bow it came with since black isn't right at a wedding, although over there, being led out of your father's car by your brother, is a woman in a black dress and sensible shoes who is blinking in the bright sun of the beautiful day that Mother Earth has given us for your wedding, and she looks very much like she doesn't belong here, and I suspect that there are many people here thinking the same about me. This country boy married his country girl in the First Pentecostal Church on a sunny day too. Sunny days are among the few things that don't change with time, and maybe someday you will be attending the wedding of a child you love — your own, I would imagine — on a sunny day. I hope that child — and you, Elizabeth — are loved more than I loved Jenny Paxton. I didn't love Jenny Paxton. I liked her fine. She was a sweet girl, and she was deserving of love; she was deserving of someone who would make her breakfast in bed and watch her while she slept and have a ridiculous sloppy smile on his face when she did simple things like rising dripping wet from the bathtub or cleaning the muddy feet of a puppy, but I was not that man. Who are you marrying, Elizabeth? Your father told me his name and that he likes him, but he's not a Jew, apparently. Still, he thinks he will make you happy. He better, or he will have to answer to Uncle Jack, and I do not want to tell you, Elizabeth, the things that your uncle Jack can do when he goes to a dark place. With great shame, I will admit this silently to you now though I will never say it out loud: Jenny Paxton knows.

Your father and I did not move in the same social circles at UNC. The law firm of Gottlieb, Lefkowitz, and Wolf all pledged Alpha Epsilon Pi, and sophomore year they moved into the fraternity house full of Jews that, I am ashamed to admit, no good southern Christian boy or girl would ever enter. I didn't pledge a fraternity. I didn't have the money. I stayed in campus housing and lived in a shitty gray concrete building designed by some reject from the Soviet system of architecture with rooms built on a grid like a prison. I wish I was lying when I said there were visible diamonds of chicken wire built into the glass of the windows to make them shatterproof. The poor kids were cordoned off there in a far corner that the rich kids didn't know existed. Seriously, at our twenty-fifth I took your father to see the building, and he said that he didn't think that was even part of the campus. But I ran into Josh from time to time, in the dining hall or on his way to and from campus, and he always smiled big and stopped to talk. Your father is a generous man, and when I confessed I was flunking my math requirement, he tutored me. He got me through history, taught me how to write a paper. We used to sit by the fire — it snowed more in the sixties — and Josh would ask me, "What do you want to say in this paper?" My history requirement was American 101 and 102. George Washington to FDR. It stopped after World War II, before the country lost its way and started getting soft. Sorry, Elizabeth, the USA you live in now seems a land of plenty, but believe me, it is starting to live off its own fat, and I fear lean years lie ahead. My father thought the Commies would destroy America, but like most everyone, we'll destroy ourselves if you just leave us alone. Solitary confinement is the most dreaded punishment, hurts worse than bullets.

We would meet on Sunday mornings when the girls I wanted to date were in church and the Jews were studying — an activity that yields more immediate dividends than prayers do — and sometimes your mother would show up in her knee-length wool skirt and her oxford shirts, a strand of pearls around her perfect neck. Your father used to get flustered when she arrived. They were kids. I was actually the one to teach your father to shave. He didn't even own a razor freshman year. Annette was tiny; I could wrap my hands around her waist. She called me Jackeroo. When she leaned over to see what we were working on, she lifted up one foot, and your father grabbed it and kissed her ankle. Anyone would have loved her if she'd let them. She was the first girl I ever met who spoke a foreign language, French, and I used to tease her and say that in Troy we considered Birmingham, Alabama, a foreign city. She laughed when I called it that, and said, "Birmingham's not even a big city. New York is big." She and her mother went there twice a year to buy their wardrobes. Until I started teaching at my hoity-toity college, I never knew anyone who even had a wardrobe. Your mother was in the teachers' college, and she would pick up a pencil and correct my grammar, blaming all the mistakes on Josh though she must have known they were mine.

They had a regular Sunday afternoon date to go drive in the countryside. Josh would ask if I had had enough for one day, and I knew enough to say yes to that and no to their invitation to join them. The public schools of Troy, North Carolina, were not designed to generate scholars, but with our Sunday tutoring sessions, your father helped me eke out a degree. He told me I was smart, even tried to convince me to go to law school. He said the Jews had learned a few centuries ago that the only thing they can't take from you is your education. Your brains will find you a place in the world when your blood fails you. More than once, I wished I'd listened to him, but at the time I thought I knew my place in the world. First it was North Carolina, then it was New York City. Then the world had other plans for me, and like some twisted version of *The Wizard of Oz*, a tornado called the U.S. Army came barreling through, found me, and tossed me over to the other side of the world to a place called Vietnam.

I graduated with a degree in organizational behavior, the gut major that was chosen by the jocks and the losers, united at last — the skinny weed smokers and the thick-necked quarterbacks — in our academic failures. I moved back home, married Jenny, moved into a little rented house at the edge of town as far as I could get from my dad in tiny Troy, population 3,162. My degree got me a job at the hospital in Chapel Hill, an hour's drive each way, where supposedly I did something in management, but mostly I doodled, read novels, snuck out back, and smoked pot.

I discovered that my high school dream of being an artist hadn't died, and I started painting. There was nothing else to do at the end of the day after I came home from work, ate the dinner Jenny had cooked, and screwed her. I'd paint in the garage, awful things, trying to be Lucian Freud or Kandinsky. Jenny would come out, smoking a cigarette, and laugh at me, comparing what I'd made to the scribblings of her nieces and nephews. I'd tell her she wouldn't know art if it bit her in the ass, and she said, Maybe not, but I know what ain't art. She was right. I got embarrassed and frustrated. Is that a good reason to hit someone? I think you would say no, Elizabeth.

On our black-and-white television with the broken knob, I watched what was happening elsewhere, sit-ins, marches, love-ins, communes. But everything might have stayed the same if it hadn't been for that crazy kid in the hospital. He crashed his car somewhere off Highway 109, then took off running when he saw the cops, jumped into the Pee Dee River, and almost drowned before they got him out and brought him to UNC. I was told by one of the nurses that he seemed calm at first, so they took off the handcuffs and his wet clothes. He let them dress him in a hospital gown and a warming blanket to stave off hypothermia. The Pee Dee is fed by springs, so the water's usually around fifty degrees. Then, once he warmed up, he ignited, erupted, threw off the blanket, and ran out of the ER. First, he was screaming about the pigs, then the devil. He threw charts on the floor, crashed through the nurses' station, sent glass bottles of medicine flying, and shrieked for a full-on minute before he burst into song in a foreign language that for all we knew was an aria. It was so loud that I heard it from the back room where my friends, the orderlies John Caswell and Rick Sherman, and I used to hide and sneak whiskey. That kid didn't need technology to broadcast; his voice was high-pitched and urgent. John opened the door, and said, "What the fuck is that?"

I followed the sound over the blue-gray carpeting and the tiles out to the front of the hospital where several nurses were trying to talk the kid down off the admissions desk. The kid looked like Jesus — so many of them did — with long hair and a scraggly beard, but instead of an apostle's robe, he had a hospital gown. "It's all going to end soon." The perennial cry of the apostle. "And you all are gonna look back at your lives and say you never lived. You never loved. You never looked. You never saw anything, touched anything, felt anything. You're dying. Rotting. Blighted. Petrified. But it's okay." He reached out his arms the way a rock star reaches out to his adoring audience. "It's not too late. You can be saved." I stared at him from the far corner of the room. The doctors and the nurses surrounded him, white coats and blue scrubs, a soft pool of colors he could safely jump into. "You can be saved," he cried again. Salvation. Don't trust anyone, Elizabeth, who has never yearned for it. It is the fundament of all religion and philosophy, to be delivered and saved from fear, meaninglessness, the vulnerability of the body, the loss of loved ones, and our own inevitable deaths. Not nice thoughts on a wedding day, but death and our need for salvation are the two basic facts of human life, and everything else, our desires, our hobbies — my painting, your horseback riding, great books, golf games, and, above all else, love — are the necessary distractions that enable us to live. Pick your distractions well, Elizabeth, they will define your life.

It's ridiculous to have one's life changed by a college kid on an acid trip. I stood there in my khaki pants, my short-sleeved shirt from Penney's, and my loafers, and felt as unfree as the most chained-and-bound prisoner. Sorry for the hyperbole. It is a common criticism of my work — colors too bright, brushstrokes too broad — but this is something you see in white male artists of my generation, truly the last white men to be freed from bondage, the bondage of our own creation, the uniform of suits and ties, neat houses with green lawns, pretty wives, and sweet children. We burst free. We burst free.

The kid started throwing shit, staplers, pens and pencils, a coffee mug. He raised his feet and danced like some crazy Irishman. From the admissions desk, he climbed up onto a metal cabinet, the whole time shouting about how we were dying and he was living, we were darkness, he was light. You could see spit flying out of his mouth, his face flushed almost purple, until the head nurse, Mrs. Kilpatrick, got to him, jabbed a needle in his thigh, and let him tumble down into the waiting arms of the orderlies and nurses who, if there were any beauty in the world, would catch us all the way they caught that boy.

Alan Casterman, a guy who sat a cubicle away from me and made me look bad by actually working, said, "That was fucked-up." He went back to his cubicle.

It was almost four o'clock. I left for the day.

I went home to Jenny. She was in a sour mood, having spent the day with her younger sister and her sister's two daughters, ages three and thirteen months. She was the only childless one in the park, her two arms dangling uselessly. If motherhood is the apotheosis of femininity, what is its opposite? I was in a sour mood, thinking the whole drive home of how much I hated my life. In every car I passed, there was a man, by himself behind a wheel, and the road stretched on and on and led nowhere. We were all living the same lives. We were interchangeable. If I could have caught the eye of the guy in the green Dodge Dart, we could have swapped places. I would drive to his house, he to mine, and our griefs and frustrations would be the same. I was Vladimir and he was Estragon, or I was Estragon and he was Vladimir. I make the kids in my Intro to Modernism class read *Waiting for Godot*, but existentialism is old news to them. They don't care that their lives are meaningless; they check their email, they plan a hookup, they go on; duh, everyone goes on. In 1966, though, there were choices to be made.

I am making excuses for myself, Elizabeth. Inside some people there is a block of rage, a hidden organ that you cannot see with a CT scan or exploratory surgery, but it is there, solid, pulsating, bloody, and inoperable, and it has a life of its own. It is passed from generation to generation. At times, I have consoled myself with the idea that it is in everyone; and in some lives, it is fed by circumstances, crappy parents, lashes with belts and switches, hungry bellies, disappoint-ments in love, mush for brains, but I am not sure. If it is in you, Elizabeth, I am sure it is the tiniest nugget, vestigial like your appendix. It is in me, Elizabeth, and I wish the sight of a little girl I have loved, all grown-up, in a white gown, with the smoothest skin and a smile that forgives everything, could cure me. If anything could, you would think it would be that. It would be the fact that you once offered me a four-leaf clo-ver that you had found after the most painstaking and con-centrated search, gave it to me because you rightly sensed I needed the luck more than you did. I still have that clover, Elizabeth; they can last forever pressed into the pages of a book, dry and brittle but still green.

I left Jenny behind. She was bruised and bloody. I knocked out a tooth, and she looked up at me, gap-toothed, with the face of a five-year-old. Do not forgive me when I say I vom-ited in the driveway before I got in the car and left. It was the splattered drops of blood that made me sick, not her injured face. I did not call a doctor or an ambulance. I left a coward. I did not want to go to jail. I did not want to face Jenny's fa-ther or her sisters or her sisters' husbands who might do to me what I had done to her. I drove away from North Caro-lina in 1966, a place where there were so many opportunities for heroism, where the blacks were facing down fire hoses and the students were protesting the war and children were signing up to become orphans rather than continue the ways of their parents. I landed in New York where you could call yourself an artist if you shot dope in your veins and stood up once a month and recited poetry or put a dab of color on something white and blank or kicked a leg in the air and called it a dance. I fell in love about a thousand times between 1966 and 1969. I could tell you about those years, or you could just listen to Leonard Cohen. I think I was happy; I am honestly not sure even though I wasn't shooting as much dope then as I did when I came back from Vietnam. I loved the way heroin made me feel, but there were other things to do — walk down to the Battery and stare at the water, work a few shifts as an orderly at St. Vincent's so I could buy food, cook a pot of soup, feed myself and anyone nearby. Buy paint and canvas, paint on the canvas, try to sell it in Washington Square. Sketch tourists outside the Metropolitan and try to sell them the sketches. The days went by in a blur of fucking and cooking and eating and drawing. I make a mean Hungarian goulash, Elizabeth. I will cook it for you and your husband one day, in one of those gleaming new pots and pans that are wrapped in white and tied with golden bows and sitting on the table in the foyer next to the guest book that I signed with a big scrawl because years from now I want someone to know I was here.

Let me tell you something about the government of the United States of America. It is more powerful than God, omniscient, omnipotent. Letters notifying me that it was my turn to serve my country were mailed to every address I had ever lived at, three houses in Troy, five squats, two SROs, seven apartments. The envelopes went unopened. I knew what they were. Everyone who saw them or touched them or even sat in the same room with them knew what they were. They vibrated, they pulsed, they smelled, they emitted a signal that could be sensed by dogs, men under thirty, and their mothers. I ran away from them, all the way down to Atlanta, where your father was living in a ranch house on Lindbergh Drive near the Varsity Junior. He was married to your mom and starting his life. I missed the wedding. Unlike the draft letters, the invitation had not found me. Josh didn't blink an eye when I showed up, didn't ask how I had gotten there — dodging conductors on a series of trains because I couldn't afford a ticket, hitchhiking, then finally walking down Piedmont Road past Cheshire Bridge and the strip joints and the head shops — you would not recognize it now. Where have all the peep shows gone? Long time passing, gone to Whole Foods, everyone; when will they ever learn? It was dinnertime, and your mother was making spaghetti and meatballs. Your father welcomed me in and your mother came out; she had on denim hip-huggers and a white shirt knotted at the waist and a frilly white apron, and there was a dab of sauce on her cheek, and, forgive me, I confused the smell of tomato sauce and the warmth of the house and the relief of seeing your father, my best friend, with love, and I do not say this justifies what I did, but I was pretty sure I would not be returning from Vietnam. They said the stupid and the soft did not survive, and I counted myself among them. I heard someone say, "Mommy," and your brother toddled out in footy pajamas, hair freshly washed and brushed away from his face. Your mother picked him up, held him on her hip, and nuzzled his face, a spontaneous act of love the likes of which I had never seen or experienced. I honestly could not recall my mother ever kissing me, and I had a spasm of self-pity and envy, yes, envy of that two-year-old child.

Your father, your kind and forgiving father, thought he could get me out of the draft. Technically, I was still married.

If I enrolled in school and was married, I could seek a defer-ment. If that didn't work, he said Marty would do it. He was done with med school, was a first-year resident. Marty could come up with a reason not to go, astigmatism, bone spurs. Annette put dinner on the table. Since college, she had grown her hair long and straight, and filled out. Did you know that your mother was only sixteen when she went to college? We were babies; at sixteen now, the kids are still being driven to parties. When my students get to college — eighteen years old at a minimum, sometimes older because they have taken gap years in Europe or Thailand or Argentina — they don't even know how to do their laundry. With all their internet access and technology, they think they're so grown-up, but they stay children so much longer now that the Russkies aren't plant-ing spies among us or sneaking missiles into Cuba, now that there's no draft and the hookers and the homeless have been taken off the streets and sent to rehab, now that the crazy people are on the thirteenth floor of the public hospital, and now that it's clear that Eliot was right and it will end with a whimper, not a bang, so what's the point in carrying signs and protesting? Nothing changes, and a slow decline merits no tears. She looked so beautiful when she put the bowl of spaghetti on a table covered with a tablecloth in that house that she kept so clean, where I was sure no one had ever over-dosed or slept in a pool of vomit or sloshed bleach over a bloodstain.

The living room of the house on Lindbergh Drive had blue carpeting. I lay on the floor with my head on a pillow, and your father ran through the options. He was excited about the law as only people at the very beginning of their career can be. He warned me against fleeing to Canada or Mexico. Quoting legal precedent, he cited how I could be stripped of my citizenship, what this might mean for my career, for my Social Security earnings (paltry though they would be), or for my chances at graduate school. He judged that no one would be forgiving draft dodgers anytime soon, and though he and I and your mother all agreed that the war was unnecessary, we disagreed on the level of stupidity, the duplicity of our leaders, and the reason that it had started in the first place. They did not believe in conspiracy theories and had trouble conceiving of pure evil. Poor judgment was their tepid response to the slaughter of innocents, a response that can only come from the purely innocent.

Your parents said good night to me and went into their bedroom, to the bed they shared together, and this being 1969 and your parents being from good breeding, this was likely the only bed each of them had ever shared with another person. I wasn't tired. In New York, eleven o'clock was when everyone woke up. I had a couple of sheets of paper and a pencil, and I found their wedding picture. I thought I would make them a belated wedding present, a sketch from the photo. At the age of twenty-eight, I was absolutely certain of my inimitable talent. Now thirty-two years later, I am fully cognizant of my mediocrity. In fact, mediocrity is my aspiration, and I feel fairly certain that I often fall short of that. That is why we all miss our twenties, with its confusions and delusions. I started with your mother, in a long white dress and lace sleeves. I started with her hands, her arms, up to her face. I couldn't get her face quite right, so I worked on her face over and over again. I had to separate the face I had seen that night, the fuller face, the longer hair, from the one in the picture. I didn't know she was pregnant — she didn't know she was pregnant — but the part of my brain that is an artist knew, and I knew she was different from the girl in the picture or the girl on the golf course or the girl waiting in the lobby of our freshman dorm for your father since no girls were allowed upstairs. I crumpled the paper. I had a joint in my backpack and went outside to smoke it. It was November. November was colder in the sixties than it is now. All the trees were bare. There was a crescent moon. The stars spiked the sky. I knew I was too lazy not to go to war. I didn't love my life enough, and no one loved me enough to make it worth avoiding. In fact, no one had ever wanted me more than the U.S. Army wanted me at that moment. I went back inside, lay on the floor of the living room where I had left the pillow, and stared at the ceiling.

I fell asleep. I woke when your mother came out to cover me with a blanket. She was wearing a white nightgown, and for a minute, in my sleepy haze, I thought she was someone else. I swear I did when I grabbed her arm and pulled her toward me. She stared at me for a minute, then said, "I didn't want to wake you. I thought you might be cold. The house is old and drafty."

I said, "It's a palace compared to where I have been."

"I hope that isn't true."

I sat up. "It is." One of the straps of her nightgown had fallen down to show her bare shoulder, and she moved it up. In college, her hair had been bobbed and shellacked into place. Now it was loose and long as was the fashion. "I like your hair this way." I moved a strand aside as if that were necessary to see her better. "I'm sorry I missed the wedding." She was not sure what to do with the blanket now that I was sitting up. I took it from her and held it in my lap since the sight of her in a nightgown was doing things to my body that were better kept to myself.

"It was a wedding," she said.

She sat down on the couch behind me. I could have kissed her bare legs, her clean feet.

"What time is it?"

"Probably about three. The baby used to always wake up hungry at three, so I got used to it. He sleeps through the night now, but I haven't been able to readjust." She shrugged. "I guess this is how it will be from now on."

It is a weakness of mine that I respond to loneliness in a physical way. It gets me in trouble a lot, and it is one of the reasons I don't have tenure. I touched your mother's leg. I think she shivered. She shivered, but then she had just told me the house was cold. I left my hand on her leg.

"I wish you didn't have to go to war," she said.

"I'm not too keen on it myself." I moved my hand up her leg, and I felt something change in her, something invited me farther in.

"Why don't you want me to go?" I asked.

"I don't want anyone to go." She touched my hair. "It will change you."

"Everything changes you."

"Jack, Jackeroo," she said. "Why were you drawing pictures of me?"

If I were honest, I would have told her that once the image starts to form on the paper it isn't her anymore. It's partly me and partly a dream and partly a story, but it isn't ever the physically and morally flawed person who breathes in oxygen and breathes out carbon dioxide, because that person, who-ever she is, even the woman whose ever-perfect form was the basis for the Venus de Milo, is a mix of the divine and the disgusting. She sings, and she shits. The image, the art, has to be more than that. It has to be beautiful in a way you be-lieve human beings can be beautiful but in a way they never are. It isn't real, those pictures we draw, not the yellow and green scribbles you drew that I pinned to my bulletin board for inspiration, not the butterflies, not the landscapes and the horses you drew and sent to me, Uncle Jack, the artist, until one day, around fifteen, you realized you weren't any good at it. You weren't bad — everyone recognized your butterfly as a butterfly, your golden sun as a sun, but not more than that, and it is the more than that that makes an artist. That makes someone think, when you have drawn a picture of her — un-less you do some Lucian Freud version of their face — that it means you love her. Picasso chopped his lovers' images up like the worst serial killer, but when he reassembled them, he put in the more than that, and they spread their legs and sac-rificed their youth for him knowing it would never last.

"I wanted to give you a wedding present," I said. I sat next to her on the couch, and she leaned her head against me. Then we kissed, a real kiss, parted mouth, tongue, and with-out thinking, automatically as if she were any girl, I felt for her breast with one hand and pushed her nightgown up her thigh with the other. Neither of us planned it, and as soon as we realized what we were doing, we stopped. She stopped first and pushed my hand away, and with that movement, she came into focus and was Annette again, my best friend's wife, not just the body of a young woman. She removed my hands from her body. And I remember this distinctly: she wiped the back of her hand across her mouth the way you did once, around age five, and truth be told, it stung as much when you did it as when she did.

"I'm sorry," I said.

She nodded, mumbled something, went back to her room. In the dim light, I could see the outlines of her body, ghostly, almost translucent, carried away from me. I found the picture I had been drawing uncrumpled, pressed flat, and sitting on the kitchen table. I went back outside for a minute and stood in the empty street under the crescent moon and burned it so your father would never find it.

The next day I went to the draft office on Peachtree Street and registered for basic training.

War, Elizabeth. What can I tell you of the filth of war, the heat, the sweat, the exhaustion, the rot, the corpses, the lost souls, the screaming babies, the inside out, the upside down? What can I tell the girls swarming around, carrying yellow and white flowers and smiling for the picture, girls who seem to me at this moment made not of flesh but of some kind of soft marble? If I could sink a hot knife into them, their thighs would be white and smooth and cold all the way through. No blood would spurt, no muscle spasm. People who have been to war are different from everyone else. Yes, we know more about life and humanity, the boundaries of goodness and evil, but it's like the bite of the proverbial apple. Whatever is left of Eden in your heart is lost when you obtain that knowledge.

I can't be sorry for kissing your mother because she wrote

me letters after that, and aside from a rare note from your father, they were the only letters I received. She loved your father. I don't think it is a lack of fidelity to want your soul to
be known by another. These days everyone smears the soul
across the digital universe — the things your generation tells
one another on the internet — but if the mother bird drops
the worm into the mouth of the wrong baby, she feels no joy.
You have to know the recipient, and your mother thought
she knew me. She didn't. She doesn't. Those letters were sent
some thirty years ago, so there are some truths I knew once
about her, but I don't know if they matter at all to the well-
preserved woman who is directing today's greatest show on
earth, an American girl's wedding.

The first news was that she had given birth to a baby girl.
I read that letter on leave in Saigon while a whore massaged
my feet. She said she had been certain it would be a boy, and
she remembered Daisy's line in *The Great Gatsby* where she
hoped that her daughter would be a fool, and she thought
that if we were going to send our men off to kill one another it
seemed obvious to her that the men were the foolish ones and
it would be better if the boys they sent to die were also fools.
War was nothing more than a wrestling match with blood,
and she wondered if we couldn't just resolve our differences
in the boxing ring or on the tennis court. Russia and the U.S.
squared off everywhere, at the Olympics, in the United Na-
tions. Vietnam was their new wrestling arena. She implored
me to be safe, but then in the same sentence, she wrote, "I
imagine in war most often there are no choices. On those few
occasions where there are choices, please choose your own
life, for those who love you if not for yourself." She never said

she loved me, and I was fairly certain that she didn't. I wrote my letters to your father or both of them. I never wrote to her directly. I told myself that this was honorable. I told myself I did not want to share this war with her. I wanted her to remain innocent. In truth, Elizabeth, in love, as in war, I have always been passive, and your mother wasn't worth it. It wasn't worth losing your father's friendship, hurting him, hurting her. Don't take this personally. Although there have been women I have loved, women I have wanted to grow old with, there has never been a woman I would fight for. Maybe I came to love too late. Like war, love's battles are best and most fiercely fought among boys.

They made me a medic. I exaggerated my hospital experience to get that job because I thought it would be safer. It was not. If anything, it was more dangerous because bandages, morphine, and tourniquets took up space in my pack where ammunition or food could have been. The medic gets put in the spotlight. While everyone fires his gun — and no one has the time to see who is advancing and who is huddling behind a tree, who is spraying bullets blindly and who is squeezing them off at targets — they all notice the man down, the man bleeding and screaming for help and waiting for the medic to come and pull him to safety and either save him or finish him off. Did you know that when a man's leg is blown off, you have less than five seconds before the femoral artery retracts into the muscle? You have to grab that artery, slippery and spewing blood like a garden hose, and tie it off, or he will bleed to death; the blood will swell his thigh as if it were a water balloon; he will die before it bursts. We tried not to leave him there, but depending on the day and our weariness and the number of bullets and grenades and our fear, we made different choices. I plunged the morphine in as much to silence his screams as relieve him, and sometimes we shouldered him up until we could call for a helicopter; sometimes we tipped him into a shallow grave; sometimes we walked away and left him there for the rats. Sometimes I chose. There were men I favored and some I didn't like. I would like to say it was logical, that I could judge the men who were kinder or had more to give the world, but it wasn't. I could have tried harder for a father of twin boys, and perhaps that guy from Pensacola wasn't worth the risk. When blood dries on your hands, it cracks the same way paint does. I am sure blood was the first medium used to make the first image on a cave or in the sand, the blood of a man or the blood of a beast.

Your parents and your brother and sister moved to this house where we are standing now, and they could not afford new furniture, so your grandfather had a living-room set delivered, and your mother hated it. Your sister did not sleep well, and your mother wrote letters to me one-handed, holding her with the other. A baby's cry is weak, she said, compared to the scream of a man, but she was certain she would hear her child cry for her even if she was on the other side of the world and it made her think of the mothers of all the other soldiers. She didn't know me well enough to know my mother was long dead. Your mother liked the world at 3 a.m., the quiet and the absence of human activity and striving. The branches of a pear tree she planted in the courtyard — that pear tree right there — rubbed up against one another. The night sounds of insects and owls went unappreciated. The world did not exist for human beings; it just was. If we disappeared, the owls and fireflies wouldn't care. She doubted they would even notice. She wondered what animals slunk through the jungles of Vietnam and how they made sense of the explosions. She told me to be careful. Full of care. I dissected that word and decided it was the one thing someone in war should not be, but if you were lucky enough to return, it would be a noble aspiration. A really good idea, like western civilization.

Those few letters survive, Elizabeth. They have moved with me from apartment to house, from California to Nebraska to Minnesota, and right now they are in a box in the basement of an old Victorian in Massachusetts that I share with three people because, unlike your father, I have never owned a house, and the poor salary they give me as an adjunct professor at the semiprestigious school where I teach does not give me the luxury of both meeting my deductible and living alone. Truth is, I don't mind it. I have never been good at intimacy, but I rather like the presence of other human beings as long as they are not trying to kill me.

In one letter, your mother said, "I am sure you have seen a man die by now. Death and birth, the only things shared by every human being on the planet, yet only women really know birth." I think your father was busy setting up his law practice, providing for his growing family, and she was alone with the babies and the maid and no one to talk to. She never got to be a teacher, so she taught me, her anonymous student, who studied her letters more assiduously than I had studied anything in college. If you want to make a scholar, send him to the jungle and put a loud stopwatch in his ear counting down the seconds of his life. Still, I never acknowledged her thoughts, and I don't think she cared. A true artist creates without a need for recognition. Your mother was a real Emily Dickinson, writing letters while she rocked a cradle, with a baby at her breast, waiting for the dinner to be done, in between setting the table and changing a diaper. She sent them off to me in Vietnam, but I was pretty sure she could as easily have put them in a bottle and sent them bobbing over the Atlantic. She wanted to be known by someone, anyone. We never talked about it when I got back. It helped that we didn't see each other for several years.

I got through the war with nothing more than a few scars. At the beginning of it all, I wrote down the names of the boys I watched die, but that list mysteriously disappeared, and I could not re-create it, so I gave up. I think I would be a better person if I could give you an exact number — more than fifty but less than five hundred — but one of the things about war is that you learn how little your life — or anyone's life — matters. Even Saul Logan, whom I grew to love, who started with me on day one and lasted 123 days by my side, whose loss briefly shattered me until I discovered that I could forget about him with opium in my veins, even Saul, whose black eyes and skinny body I swore I would commit to memory — and shouldn't an artist above all else remember the shape and form, the angles and the shadows, of a body? — I have lost. Saul was a poet interrupted. The day he got his draft letter, Saul started to memorize the poems of his fellow black Irishman William Yeats. I had never heard of William Butler Yeats. English 101 skipped from Shakespeare to Dickens to Hemingway, a greatest hits of literature, even though everyone knows the songs on the B sides of albums are more real and raw. Saul's father had fought in a war, as had his grand-father and his great-grandfather and almost certainly the one before him. He said in his family you weren't grown-up until you'd watched someone die. You couldn't be a father until you made room in the world for your child. He would say some-thing beautiful like that, and then follow with "Logan sperm don't start swimming 'til the life of another be dimming." He didn't have an Irish brogue, though he could put one on. It sounded real to me, but what did a boy from North Caro-lina know? He was four or five generations removed from the Emerald Isle, and his natural accent was pure Brooklyn, the sound of the English language after it has churned through the mouths of a thousand immigrants. Like all of them, he had a girl back home he thought he loved, but he actually looked at a picture of his little brother more than he looked at hers, and he wanted the war over before his brother, Pete, aged sixteen, would be called to take his place.

"I dreamed that one had died in a strange place / Near no accustomed hand / And they had nailed the boards above her face / The peasants of that land." That was one of the poems he recited as we lay down to sleep whenever we found a place where the jungle parted and left us a bare patch of earth. Af-ter he died, after a bullet pierced his eye and came out the other side in a way I thought might be a relief for someone whose head was so full of thoughts, I started reading the po-ems of the mad Irishman. If you don't write or paint, you leave nothing behind. Fortunately for the vast majority of the world, either this thought has not occurred to them or they don't care. Actually, on second thought, we leave children behind. I won't—too old for that, though I suppose by the grace of my gender I still could—but your father and mother will, and you will probably give them another baby or two to hold before they die, and though babies are no doubt more beautiful than paintings, my students still have to pause and think when I ask them about the flood and which one they would rescue, the Rembrandt or the baby—so in some cases, we can give them a run for their money. There are, after all, more babies than masterpieces, and though the depth of feeling that is the love of one human being for another has never been approached by even the greatest works of art, I might venture to say that the impact of the masterpiece is wider and more enduring.

You are getting married, Elizabeth! I have been advised by a friend, a poet herself, to use exclamation points sparingly, just as I have been advised to use caution with the colors red and orange, but as I age, I find my paintbrush heading more for the reds and my pen wants more exclamation points. That man, who better be good and kind, has kissed your lips! You have taken his hand, and you are gazing into his eyes with an unmatched ardor! Yes, ardor, while he gazes back at you with exactly as much joy as anyone who has ever loved you could pray for. I have a stupid, sloppy smile on my face, and I see that most people have the same smile, even through tears, though the old man in the wheelchair has fallen asleep and is drooling. And Marty's kid, Carla! Ha! I remembered her name and that she's actually kind of clever, poor thing, with that terrible birthmark—in real life, Picasso's women would never get laid—trying to make up for her looks with her intellect. Carla looks fatally bored, and the man in the row behind me is scowling. Don't worry, Elizabeth. There is always a scowling man. We take turns being him. We take turns being the one who will console him. We take turns falling down and lifting up.

After the war, I went back to New York. I could use Saul, the Vietnamese children, Jenny, my unrequited whatever with your mother, my father who beat me and my mother and my brothers, mortality, or poverty — any of them might make acceptable excuses for the choices I made, to slouch from squat to sublet, to steal when I needed money for heroin, to screw with abandon. I suppose, since it is your wedding day and you are no longer a child and the relationship I have had with you is changed forever, I suppose I should be honest. I came to Atlanta and told your father I needed help, but I didn't really want help. I thought about who I knew who still had money, who I knew that would let me into the house, give me a place to sleep, and who I could rob blind when his back was turned. It was similar to the journey I took before the war although in the course of four years your brother had reached the ripe old age of six, your sister was three and a half, and you, my sweet baby girl, had just been born and were one week old. Your parents had moved from the house on Lindbergh to this house, more uptown, farther from the bus line so it took longer for me to trudge past a series of manicured lawns and mailboxes with their numbers discreetly displayed since if you had to ask, you shouldn't be visiting. I carried a rucksack, and I had a long beard and was in need of a hot shower, and I am probably re-creating this in memory, but fathers cut off their lawn mowers and white-haired women walking poodles stopped to stare at me; children paused midleap through the sprinkler and bicycle bells went silent. This is a fancy way of saying I didn't belong there, where there were National Guard deferments and maids in uniforms and everything was lemon scented and artificially flavored.

Your mother answered the door. She was cradling you, and I could tell by her loose blouse and the gloss of milk on your lips that she had just been nursing you. She had cut her hair short, and her face was still full from the pregnancy, and for a minute, I didn't recognize her, and it occurred to me that my friend Josh Gottlieb might have had the good sense to move and abandon me, but she recognized me. Her jaw unhinged, and her eyes moistened, and she said, "Jesus Christ," which is a funny thing for a Jew to say. She balanced you one-handed and reached the other out to me, and said, "Come in. Jack, come in." I stepped inside of the house, this house that is always clean. Your sister was running up and down the halls dragging a doll by its hair. She stopped to stare at me. She cried. She ran to her mother's leg and clung to it, sobbing and terrified. Without thinking, your mother said, "Here, Jack," and handed me the baby. You were wrapped in a white blanket. With your full belly, and already knowing your place in the world, a world that wanted you and welcomed you, that set a place at the banquet for you the minute you arrived, you looked up at me and I swear you smiled. I couldn't believe your mother trusted me to hold something so precious. My arms felt weak and fuzzy, not up for the job, and I stood perfectly still, terrified of dropping you, stunned. Your mother picked up Katie, whose sobs switched to wails, and they disappeared for a minute. Your face has never changed, the shape of your doe eyes, the tiny upward tilt of your nose. You looked at me so intently and frankly. I would like to say that those few minutes I spent holding you were enough, that the kindness your parents showed me was enough, that your father's embrace or the roast chicken dinner we all ate together that night was enough. The most I can offer is that I believed it may have been the start of something.

We had to pick your brother up from the bus stop. It was springtime — you know that since your birthday is in April, the month of diamonds. We walked up the street. Annette pushed a pram, and you lay swaddled in your blanket watching the blue sky, the clouds, the azaleas in bloom, the daffodils. The world is beautiful. Atlanta in the spring, the jungles of Vietnam, the play of sunlight on the Hudson River, the blue mountains of North Carolina where I grew up. This is an observation that has been made by the joyful and the troubled alike. I daresay it may be the last thought of many a suicide. Those four simple words often floated in my brain before I drifted off to oblivion. The beauty of the world is not enough to sustain a human being. In fact, it can be your undoing, the knowledge that it exists, existed before you and after you, your own inconsequence. We waited with a few other young mothers, a spattering of toddlers. Annette said hello to them and introduced me. "This is Josh's college friend, Jack." A yellow school bus groaned to a stop, and like something magical, it released a set of children, girls in white shirts, boys in blue shorts. Benji jumped down, skipping the last step. He was carrying a spelling book wrapped in brown paper and a lunch box. He peered into your pram and waved. I pushed the pram back so that your mother could hold Benji's hand while we walked. The politicians told us that this was what we were defending. That the plague of Communism would spread from Asia to Europe to America, and all the mothers pushing prams would be turned into slaves, their pink blouses and white pants ripped from their bodies, replaced with gray woolen shifts. The green lawns would be plowed under, and the houses torn down and replaced with cement blocks. But we lost the war, and here it all was, as perfect as ever.

Back at the house, I took a long hot shower and used your father's razor to shave off my beard. Annette gave me a pair of his pants and a clean T-shirt. She must have called him, because Josh came home from work early, and without asking how I felt about it, he drove me to Marty's office, where I got a physical exam. Marty saw the track marks on my arms. When he parted the gown to listen to my heart, he saw the curvature of my empty belly, the ribs, the scars. He told me he could put me in the hospital to help me over the withdrawal. I said I just needed money. Marty had lost a lot of hair. He was left with just a rim of dark curls around his skull, so he looked like a monk. A Jewish monk. He told me that when he was in training — at Bellevue in New York, it turned out, only blocks from where I lived — he had seen many heroin overdoses, many deaths. Then he asked me a question that no one, I think, had ever asked me before. He said, "Jack, what do you want to do with your life?"

I didn't have an answer for him at the time, but I thought about it when I put my clothes back on. He came back with a prescription for Percodan and said to use that to ease my cravings. I said, "You know, Marty, I've always wanted to be a painter."

He shrugged his shoulders. "If you want to be a painter, shouldn't you be painting?"

I got off the drugs. Not right away. If I were a better man, I would buy your mother a pair of diamond earrings to replace the ones that I stole, the ones I hope she never noticed were missing or just wondered where they were or at least blamed me for their disappearance, not the maid. I was in and out of their lives for a few years after that, and I fail to believe they didn't notice how things went missing after my visits, but somehow, miraculously, the door was never closed to me, and eventually I got my shit together. I started teaching. I sold some paintings. I sold some more. There is one hanging in the living room of this house. After all I took from him, your father tried to pay me for it. At least I can say I didn't let him. After all they gave me, I gave them one of my best, a giant slash at the sky, stabbed through with stars and pools of tears. Most of my paintings are untitled, but that one is named *Come In*. Those two words, with their double entendre, were what your mother spoke to me before she handed me a baby to hold: Come in, yes. Come in. We aren't all equally blessed in this world. You have had and will have so much more than most others, growing up in this house with those parents, loved and safe and beautiful. They will raise champagne glasses to you and your new husband. It is a sunny day, and you know what I say about sunny days. They are timeless and free, shared by the rich and poor at the same time on the same patch of earth, and therefore, like you, and love, and newborn babies, miraculous. Come in.

The fucked-up nipple

ELIZABETH GOTTLIEB HAS ONE NIPPLE that dimples inward. I know this because my sophomore year of college I got to second base with her. I think I may have been the first one to get that far even though she was already a junior in high school and I would have thought someone would have at least fingered her by then, if not more. She was pretty hot, so this must have been because of her saying no instead of a lack of interest from your average high school boy who is, in general, not super picky. Don't ask me why I'm at this wedding. I've barely seen Elizabeth since that night when I got her drunk (also maybe a first for her), and that was more than ten years ago. My mom said I had to come today because my sister Debbie is a bridesmaid and Mrs. Gottlieb was my mom's sorority sister a million years ago, so they are tight. I feel ridiculous in this suit; I can barely breathe; it's way too small for me. I'm just hoping I don't see anyone I know because they'll probably freak out at the sight of me. The meds make me fat and pimply, and if Elizabeth Gottlieb remembers me at all, she probably remembers a pretty good-looking guy, popular, on top of his game.

So here's how I met Elizabeth. I was talking to my cousin

in front of the frat house, and he mentioned something about Debbie, and one of my brothers overheard and asked who Debbie was, and when I said she was my little sister, he said, How little? And I said, Sixteen, and he said, That's the good kind of little sister. He told me I should have her come up for the party that weekend and tell her to bring friends. I said I didn't want him touching my little sister, and he said, Duh, that's where the friends part comes in. Then he asked if she was hot, and I said, How should I know, she's my little sister. He said, C'mon, you know. I looked at him like he was crazy, and then he said she must be a dog, so I said she was pretty. He asked if I had a picture of her, and I said no, which was true; what nineteen-year-old has a picture of his little sister in his dorm room? Debbie had been begging for an invite since my freshman year, so we lied to Mom and Dad, and said she was coming to go to the Georgia-Florida game — which is huge, and I am just lucky that my dad was on call that weekend or he would have wanted to come too — and then she was going to look around the campus because it was time for her to start thinking about colleges.

The truth was we didn't have tickets to the game — it was huge, like I said, and had been sold out for months, mostly to rich alums and season-ticket holders. I thought Debbie would share that fact with her friends, but she assumed they didn't care, and then when they got there and found out we weren't going to the game, they were all okay with it except for Elizabeth because it turned out her dad was going to be there, and he wanted her to come find him. I told her nobody could find anyone in the stadium anyway because it was so huge, but she was really nervous like she was going to get in trouble, so I found a guy who said he'd look for her dad and tell him Elizabeth wasn't feeling well and had gone to this girl in Kappa Delta's room to lie down. The girl was a friend of her family's, so she thought that would be okay with her dad. But even after we worked all that out, she still didn't look so happy. It turned out she actually wanted to see the game, and it was the promise of the game rather than a party with college guys that had made her sign up for this trip in the first place. Debbie and the two other girls, Jennifer Abrams — who I see is also a bridesmaid and as fuckable as ever — and a girl whose name I can't remember, had come for the party, and before I knew it, they were downstairs (where we were watching the game on TV), drinking beers and cozying up with some brothers. I pulled Debbie aside and told her not to get too cozy, but she shrugged me off, and I got pretty drunk later and I'm not entirely sure what she did that night except she promised me she didn't fuck anyone.

Of course, I got stuck with Elizabeth, who was sipping her beer as if it were a fine wine, and the beer got warm in her hand and looked like piss before she was even a third of the way done. She was trying to watch the game, but people kept getting in front of the TV. She told me she wanted to go home, and I said Debbie's too drunk to drive, and she said, Why don't you take me? And I said I was too drunk too. I said her beer was warm and got her a fresh one, and she drank it down. She got giggly, and said, I don't even know why I care about this stupid game. I want to go to Yale, so I should be rooting for the Yale Bulldogs. I told her she must be pretty smart if she was going to Yale, and she shrugged. I said, Don't be fake and modest, you just said you're going to Yale, so obviously you're smart. She said, I didn't say I'm going to Yale, just that I want to. That's not the same thing. I said, It's not fair to be smart and pretty, usually girls are just one or the other. She said, Why just girls? And I said that was just how it was in my observation, and she said that there's lots of pretty girls at Yale and Harvard; she knew because she visited Harvard once. Then she looked at me sideways and said the guys were cute too.

I got her another beer. She asked me what my major was, and I told her premed, and she was drunk by then so she said that was lame, that premed was a job, not a major, and she suggested I study literature or history because I would spend the rest of my life being a doctor. I said that was fine with me as long as being a doctor put a good chunk of change in my pocket. She said I wasn't very idealistic, and I told her I guess I was just mature for my age. She laughed so hard she spat beer all over me, and that was how we ended up in my room, and I wrote a note to my roommate on the memo board outside our door: FGA, which meant Fucking, Go Away, but, in fact, there had been very little fucking in the room, a few make-out sessions, some what my school sex-ed teacher called "heavy petting," but the only girl I fucked that year was Margie Herman, and she was a dog who'd already been humped by half the frat house.

I didn't fuck Elizabeth Gottlieb; though my cock was willing, my conscience was not. We kissed; I unbuttoned her shirt and saw that weird nipple — which, having not seen that many tits in person, I thought might be common — felt her tits, tried to undo her pants, had my hand swatted away, and felt her actually pass out in my arms, so I laid her down on my filthy comforter with her shirt unbuttoned so I could take my time examining her chest, her pretty breasts, her small belly button, the soft hair on her belly, and the peek of some pink lacy panties, even a few dark hairs springing free. It's horrible to admit, but I jacked off while I was looking at her — part of me wanted to come all over that pure white chest, but I wouldn't know how to explain that to my sister's friend, so I used Kleenex, cleaned myself up, and left her there to sleep it off. I have never told anyone this, not even Dr. Gruber — who I have been seeing twice a week now for four and a half years with my parents footing the bill — and certainly not Debbie, who pities me now when she used to admire me, and least of all Elizabeth, but I am pretty sure her pretty white tits were seen — and perhaps even fondled — by several of the brothers that night after I left her there and went back to the party because I came up later to find the door open, her shirt wide open, the pants looser, and my roommate typing on his computer as if there weren't anything more interesting than a half-eaten sandwich on the bed. I pulled up her pants and buttoned her up and covered her and told him to get the fuck out of there, and when she woke up, I was working through a chemistry problem set, and she thought I was some kind of fucking hero or gentleman, and she used to ask Debbie to bring her up to see me, but I couldn't face her again, so I told Debbie that Elizabeth had gotten too sloppy drunk and that she wasn't invited to any parties anymore.

My mom is all excited about this wedding, since my sister is engaged now to a nice Jewish attorney — hah, one better than Elizabeth's Lutheran or Protestant or whatever — and she is on some kind of anthropological mission to attend as many weddings as possible and synthesize their customs so Debbie's wedding can be a life-changing experience for everyone who attends. Maybe she's hoping it will be life changing for me too, will accomplish what Dr. Gruber, olanzapine, electroshocks, Zoloft, Wellbutrin, and lithium have not — get me over this persistent sorrow, this certainty that happiness is not for me, not for anyone, really. Even people who think they are happy are just in some kind of altered state, a fugue, a fog, a dream, from which they will all eventually wake up and either see the truth or take a drug that, if they are lucky, works for them or decide to just sleepwalk through life. I have to admit that a lot of people are doing a good job looking happy here. Elizabeth's mother gave my mom a big hug, and she had these tiny tears in the corners of her eyes. (Hasn't anyone besides me ever wondered why people cry when they are supposedly their happiest? It seems so obvious that the incredible effort expended in forcing their fake joy beyond its natural boundaries makes them sort of, well, leak.)

She said it was the happiest day of her life, seeing her daughter married, though, of course, that is a relative term. The day a refugee from the Sudanese civil war lands at the shitty Atlanta airport and tastes his first Wendy's hamburger and settles into a crappy apartment with stained wall-to-wall carpeting in some distant suburb of this polluted city is the happiest day of that guy's life. The day the Russians rolled into Auschwitz and the living skeletons that were the survivors (one of whom, legend has it, is a distant relative on my mother's side) hobbled out to meet them, smiling so hard that what was left of their teeth fell out, was the happiest day of their lives. You get it. It seems weird to me that this could be the happiest day of a mother's life, because all it means is that tonight her daughter, her little baby — who, based on this collage of photos someone has assembled next to the guest book we are supposed to sign, used to have a poochy belly that showed through a lemon-yellow bathing suit she wore to the beach when she was about five years old — this girl in Mickey Mouse ears standing in front of Cinderella's castle, this girl in a pink leotard and ballet slippers, is going to have the shit fucked out of her tonight by the guy who is smiling stiffly for the cameras right now. She is going to be turned every which way so he can find novel ways of sticking his cock in her hole and is probably going to have to put that lovely mouth with its perfect teeth around said cock and suck. Is that really a mother's dream? Well, at least there's some old guy drooling in a wheelchair who has been left directly in the sunlight and totally forgotten, and who is about to have heat-stroke in addition to the stroke he has clearly already had, who seems to be as miserable as I am.

I am thirty-one years old. In two months, I will turn thirty-two. I should have been married, living in a big house with two kids, and been on the board of the synagogue by now. That has been the fate of most of my Alpha Epsilon Pi brothers, whose holiday cards and wedding invitations and birth announcements I continue to receive. My mother opens them and insists on sharing the news with me, to which I reply with a vacant uh-huh, refusing to either cry or pretend to be happy for them. Then I tell Dr. Gruber that Joel Rosenthal had a baby girl last week, and she asks me how that makes me feel, and I tell her it doesn't make me feel anything, and I am not lying. Joel Rosenthal had terrible acne in college and used to beat off to pictures of tied-up girls and kept a pair of someone's dirty panties in his desk drawer. Now he is Dr. Joel Rosenthal, completing his ophthalmology residency at Columbia, married to a girl he met in med school, who, according to my mother, is gorgeous and, apparently, fertile. I wonder if he ties her up. Dr. Gruber says it is important to let things go, but I find that these meaningless facts are branded in my memory. While I cannot remember the elements of the periodic table, which I once had memorized, or the twelve cranial nerves or stoichiometry, I know that Joel Rosenthal has a big mole behind his ear, because he showed it to me once and asked if I thought he should have it removed. Dr. Gruber wants to know why I think this happened to me. I don't know. Is it because my father put so much pressure on me and had a temper and had affairs? Or because my mother starved herself close to anorexia so that she could wear a bikini well into her fifties, by which time, although she looked good from a distance, she was actually a crinkled, deflated mess of a body, a blow-up doll with the air let out of it that sagged in all the wrong places? I have explored all these things with Dr. Gruber. She says it is biochemical.

I graduated from the University of Georgia with honors and was accepted to seven of the ten medical schools I applied to. I was going to be a heart surgeon. My dad's just an internist, and he always said that if he had it to do all over again he would be a surgeon. They make a shitload more money, and everyone thinks they're amazing, and no one asks them to do heart surgery on them in the middle of a bar mitzvah party, unlike the poor internist, who has to dole out advice on hypertension and impotence over the bagels and lox. That summer, I went home to relax. Med school was going to be hard, and my parents let me do whatever I wanted to do, which was nothing. I was like that guy in the movie *The Graduate*, lolling around the country club pool, ogling the teenage lifeguards who had the good sense or the innocence to be unimpressed with my imminent attendance at the Emory University School of Medicine.

My sister had an internship with our congressman in Washington, D.C. Debbie is a lawyer now, though the JD is the new MRS degree, and once she's married, she'll stop pretending she gives a shit about corporate law and take her place at the country club and the gym, which is her destiny, and she, wisely, and to preserve her sanity, is embracing it with no opposition. I went to D.C. to visit her that summer, and I think now the first sign that something was wrong was that I found that all I wanted to do was ride the Metro from one end of the city to the other. It was cool on the Metro, even in the blistering summer heat of our nation's capital, which we all know was built on a swamp, and I loved the feeling of being carried down those long escalators into its subterranean world, where soft lights throbbed on the ground to indicate the arrival of the next train quietly whooshing into the station. There was almost always a seat on the Metro, since I rarely took it during rush hour, and I would lean my head back and ride it all the way to the last point in Virginia, then Maryland, feeling a huge amount of accomplishment at having visited two states and the District of Columbia without even standing up. The train made a comforting thump-thump sound over the rails, jostling me gently as if I were a baby in a crib, and sometimes I slept and woke up to a person looking at me curiously, an older woman with kind eyes or a homeless guy or someone in a suit sneering at me, aware before I was of my uselessness. When Debbie was done with her day, we would go out to dinner at nice cafés in Dupont Circle (I paid; I had Mom and Dad's credit card), and I would lie about my day, which I found stunningly easy to do, particularly because my sister is not that smart and I think she still believes what I told her about there being two *Mona Lisas*, one of which is in a secret room of the Smithsonian.

I stayed there a week, and then I went home, and Mom and Dad bought me a condo since they thought that would be a good investment, and I started med school. The first course was embryology. They thought they'd ease us into the process with something easy; what idiot thinks that embryology is easy? Granted, the professor was a nice guy who graded on a curve, and if you went up to him after class with questions, he would basically tell you what was going to be on the test, but still it's horrifying, seeing how the morula turns into a blastocyst and then into this little shrimp thing with a giant fish eye and a tail. To tell you the truth, it's disgusting, but I put my head down and got through it and got my A because cardiothoracic surgeons don't have to know any of that shit, but we do have to get As so we can get into a good surgical residency program and then into one of the coveted CT surgery fellowships. I met Serena in embryology, so I guess you could say that the beginning of life, of all human life, was also the end of mine, because I fell in love with Serena: the would-be heart surgeon took out his bloody red heart and handed it to the beautiful dark-haired girl from California, and she looked at it curiously for a moment, and then squeezed, really hard, so that it oozed and spurted through her fingers, and then she ground her foot on what was left of it as the blood soaked into the ground. I used that image on Dr. Gruber once, and she said she thought that really captured what I felt at the time, but did I really think Serena did that on purpose? Did I really think Serena was a monster? Fuck yeah, she was (is) a monster, a monster who lives and breathes hot breath out of every pore of her body, in Los Angeles, California, where she, of all things, delivers babies.

Serena Goldstein, half Jew, half Mexican. Her dad is a Jewish tax attorney in Beverly Hills, and her mom is a Mexican American princess, a MAP, daughter of a drug lord or a corrupt government thug or both, because who else gets filthy rich in Mexico? Maybe I should have listened to my parents. She wasn't a real Jew since her mom never converted, and though I think my parents would have been cool with her as long as she didn't have a Christmas tree or celebrate Easter or stage a pogrom, the Orthodox rabbis in Israel would have spat on our kids. Given what she put me through, maybe those rabbis are onto something.

Serena was raised Catholic, but had a Bev Hills bat mitzvah, with Cyndi Lauper singing "Girls Just Want to Have Fun" and the average gift a check in four digits minimum or something from Tiffany's with a diamond in it. When I met her, she said she was thoroughly confused and thinking about being a Buddhist or something, some religion as different from Catholicism and Judaism as you can get, with a God who doesn't give a shit if you have cheese on your hamburger or if you've said "I do" before you get laid or what you do with the unwanted pregnancy she tearfully confessed to me she had sucked out of her uterus her senior year of college when the condom on the giant cock of her last boyfriend broke and he spilled his seed into her. Because of the abortion, she had developed some kind of fuckaphobia, so I didn't screw the girl for a whole year, though we did everything but.

At first, I was amazed by Serena. I think I spent three months just staring at her, slack-jawed, probably drooling. She had thought about so many things. I know I sound like I'm making fun of her theological angst, but she actually had reasoned through it, studied the Judeo-Christian traditions, Buddhism, Hinduism, Confucianism; she was a religious studies major and a classics minor who threw in her science courses on the side while, it sounded to me, she managed to break the hearts of half the guys at Stanford before getting a full scholarship to Emory, where she honored us with her presence not because of the money (her parents had mucho dinero — I about died when I saw their house in Beverly Hills) but because she was curious about the South, with its history not only of racism but also of heroes and genius, Martin Luther King, William Faulkner, Jackie Robinson, B. B. King, Elvis. I hadn't thought about any of that crap, and I think she was pretty disappointed in Atlanta because it doesn't feel southern at all. Half the kids at Emory are from New York, rejects from the Ivies who spend their four undergrad years telling themselves they chose this place. She dragged me to the Martin Luther King museum (I didn't even know there was one and had never been there in my twenty-three years living in Atlanta), and it was pretty pitiful, especially compared to the flashing lights and glass escalators of the Coca-Cola museum, where a magical machine spat out different soda flavors from around the world into small paper cups that we lapped up like puppies being drugged.

When she came back to start our second year of medical school, she said she had missed me over the summer while she was stuck in the cultural wasteland of Beverly Hills and then cloistered like a princess in her grandparents' mansion outside Mexico City, where she was guarded by two big and lustful thugs who were needed to prevent kidnapping but who, she said, undressed her with their eyes and stared at her ass when she swam laps in the pool. She finally spread her legs for me, though I had the sense, based on some kind of warmth and softness, that her pussy was broken in and that she had spread these legs for someone else over the summer, so she felt that I, her loyal servant who had accompanied her to museums and on a weekend pilgrimage to Milledgeville, a small city famous for its horrible insane asylum and the fact that this weird writer named Flannery O'Connor had lived there a long time ago; I, who had attempted to read books by that writer, and by William Faulkner, both of whom clearly needed some serious psychiatric help but who, I think, lived before the development of Thorazine or maybe, for all I know, tried it, like me, and found it to be no help at all; I deserved a fuck at last. It was good, and I was hooked.

Jennifer Abrams is walking toward me and smiling. All the girls are wearing these floaty yellow dresses, and I can see her legs almost all the way up. She's still gorgeous, and Debbie reminded me this morning that she's not married. I told Debbie I was sure I was just what Jennifer Abrams was looking for, a fat, unemployed, internet-porn-addicted thirty-one-year-old who lives with his parents. Debbie made a face, and said, You don't have to be that. You did finish medical school. As far as Jennifer knows, you just took some time off. Maybe you wanted to give your professional golfing career a shot. Tell her you've been in Australia for the last four years. It would be peachy to think that Jennifer Abrams doesn't know what happened to me, but the whole goddamned Jewish community of Atlanta, and probably Savannah and Charleston too, knows what happened to me. She's talking to that dog Carla Lefkowitz with the fucked-up face, er, port-wine stain; she has some syndrome where the leg's too big and something's wrong with the brain or the optic nerve or the auditory nerve, I can't remember the name. That stuff used to roll off my tongue. Jennifer and Carla appraised me and softened their eyes like they're looking at a three-legged dog.

I ran into Carla at the grocery store, like, two years ago. In high school, Carla was a total loser. How could she not be with her limp and her purple face and her straight As? I was supposed to be nice to her because her dad and my dad were partners, but I never claimed to be Mother Teresa, and she was disgusting. My parents let me throw this huge high school graduation party, even gave me enough cash for a few kegs, and conveniently took off for our beach house right after the ceremony. I invited everyone from tenth grade on up except for Carla Lefkowitz and about ten other losers. She knew about it too. How could she not? Everyone was talking about it. Her mom called my mom up and complained to her. She said, How could you raise someone so heartless? My mom asked me if it was true, and I told her that, yeah, Carla was gross and that I didn't care whose daughter she was and that I didn't want her anywhere near my house, wouldn't even want her to touch our mailbox, and my mom just said, Oh, and walked away, didn't tell me it was okay or that I should make my own decisions or tell me I was a shithead. (Dr. Gruber, I'm sure, thinks I am a shithead; Serena would have hated me for it, but I'll bet there were girls like Carla even at Beverly Hills High, and I am sure she didn't give them the time of day either.)

Anyway, there I am pushing a grocery cart full of all the shit I like to eat now that I don't care what I look like anymore and because the meds make me constantly hungry, like there is a pocket in my stomach that if I could just find and fill it would make everything okay, and here comes Carla, skinny and wearing a suit but still ugly. I'm sure some plastic surgeon should be able to fix her face — or she could put on some makeup. She's not even trying. She says, Steven? Steven Shapiro? And I say, Yeah. I am not going to let on that I recognize her. Carla was a nobody. I shouldn't remember her. She looks me up and down, and says, How the mighty have fallen, and then just pushes right on past me. I think she wants to run over my foot with her cart because she angles it a funny way, but she misses me. Bitch. She turns back to look at me, and I think she is trying to decide what to say, whether to pity me or enjoy the spectacle. Finally, she says, There is a God. I watch her walk away. She has a run in her stockings, and she is trying to look all grown-up and important in some high heels, but they are too big, and her feet keep slipping out of them, so she makes a lot of noise with those shoes slapping the ground, and I actually feel kind of sorry for her. (Progress, Dr. Gruber would say. Empathy helps us survive even our greatest sorrows. She says feeling the pain of others thins out our own, like when you spread out a thin layer of paint so it dries quickly. I said, Well, but once it dries, there's no changing or erasing it. All you can do is paint over it. Hmm, she said. I hate it when she says hmm. It means she wants me to think about it some more, but thinking makes my head hurt. It makes me want to climb up to the top of a snowy mountain and sit there until every bit of me is frozen solid.)

Jennifer says, Hi, Steven. The wedding is starting. You want me to help you find a seat? God, she is gorgeous. I'll bet her nipples are perfect. Kevin Holderman, the high school quarterback, supposedly went all the way with her, but I think that was just a rumor. She was too good for him. She's a grown woman, so no doubt someone's tapped that by now. Lucky shit. Carla's just squinting at me, and I know she's laughing at me, but she won't do it out loud.

I say, No, that's okay. I can find a seat.

We both look at the pictures of Elizabeth when she was a little girl. I realize now I have been standing by them for a long time, so she probably thinks I'm a pervert or something. Wasn't she cute? Jennifer says. This is not something guys do, look at baby pictures and comment, so I just shrug. Jennifer points to the rows of chairs on the right. That's the bride's side, she says. She looks at me. Unless you know the groom. Do you know Hank? I tell her that I do not know Hank. I see my parents sitting at the end of a row. There is a seat in between them, but I don't know if it's for me or Debbie. I can't remember how the bridesmaid thing works. Do they do their thing with the dress and the bouquet and sit down, or do they have to stand up there or what? My mom is looking around. When she sees me, she smiles and pats the chair between her and Dad. I feel such a sudden rush of gratitude for her that I almost start to cry. I have failed her so many times, have called her names, wrecked her car, drunk her booze — even some crazy expensive champagne they bought to celebrate their thirty-fifth wedding anniversary — and still she saved me a seat. I sit down next to her. There's such a thick cloud of perfume around her, I'm surprised she's not covered in bees. My dad is sitting with his thick hands on his thick thighs. He has some kind of program thing rolled up like he is going to swat a dog. He doesn't look at me. He says to no one in particular, Debbie's wedding is going to be indoors. It's hot as hell out here.

The chairs are wedged in tight. My mom is talking to the lady in front of us, and a few rows up are some pretty girls, but mostly I'm surrounded by middle-aged and old people. The lady sitting behind me is murmuring to herself in a foreign language. German or Polish or Russian or something. Time was when I'd think she was a spy or an assassin, but I've made some progress, and while I am still pretty sure she's talking about me, I don't think she wants to kill me. Just to be sure, I turn around and look at her hard for a minute, so she knows I'm onto her. She isn't even looking at me. She is staring at her lap and kneading her hands together like there's some tiny bug trapped in her palms that she urgently needs to destroy.

The music starts. Everyone turns to look. First there's a little girl throwing flowers and some little boy in a suit and a clip-on tie that's coming off, then the bridesmaids, most of them gorgeous, and somehow, with the music and the sunshine, even Carla Lefkowitz doesn't look bad. I rub my eyes to make sure I'm seeing right. She kind of has a nice smile, and I think maybe I could do her after all. She catches sight of me and narrows her eyes. I am pretty sure I can hear her hiss, and I start to hiss back at her until my dad slaps my knee. Debbie comes along and does a little low wave at me and my parents. When Elizabeth comes down the aisle in her long white dress, she looks so beautiful and perfect it's ridiculous, and I feel an urge to shout out, That girl's got some fucked-up tits, but at the same time, I feel a wave of shame, who am I and half of AEPi to have seen the tits of that beautiful girl, someone's daughter, someone's wife, maybe soon someone's mother. Probably all these girls have crazy tits. I start to see them all, green tits, tits with eyes where the nipples should be, tits with mouths, talking tits. Elizabeth gets to the front, and I hear the rabbi say something in Hebrew that I know means the devil is coming; he'll be here any minute. He's going to make this whole place go up in flames. Everyone smiles and murmurs amen.

I have to get up. I have to get up. I stand up fast and edge past my mother, stepping on her feet. My chair falls backward into the lap of the old lady who says something in her foreign language — probably calls me a shithead — and she drops her hands and lets whatever she was holding fall to the ground. She stares down into the grass, scanning for whatever I just caused her to lose. I bolt out of there, going as fast as I can until I find myself in the shade of the woods behind the garage, where the florist has discarded the wilted flowers and unwanted stems of the bouquets and centerpieces. In the garage, the caterers are setting out glasses of champagne. There's water in the vases and a big punch bowl we could use to put out a fire if it started. It seems safer here. I don't remember any of the Hebrew from my bar mitzvah. I don't know the Hebrew word for the devil. I lean up against a tree to catch my breath.

I was on my way to having it all. I was top of my med school class, some of the attendings may not have liked me all that much, but they had to admit I was good. Our third year of med school, we finally got unleashed on patients. On my surgical rotation, the first surgery I scrubbed on was a basic appendectomy with the head of the surgery residency, Dr. Bill Jenkins. Lucky for me, there was a guy from AEPi in the class ahead of me, and he gave me these notes. He said that if you scrub with Dr. Jenkins he's going to quiz you on all this shit, but they're always the same questions. I wasn't too worried. I had it down. Anatomy made sense to me in a way that biochem and microbiology didn't. Once we got past embryology, it was like I had built the body myself; I knew where everything went, what connected to this and that, what was vital and what could be destroyed. There are blood vessels and nerves that basically go nowhere, so you can cut them out and no one's the worse for it, but then, for some reason that only God knows, each finger only gets one nerve. Cut it and you're fucked. You'd think He'd give us a spare, especially for the thumb. We're not much better than dumb animals without a thumb, but one nerve, one big blood vessel, that's it. Cut them, and at best, you've got a useless thumb; at worst, the whole damn thing turns rotten and you have to chop it off. The surgeon, Dr. Jenkins, kept quizzing me — how long is the small bowel, where besides the right upper quadrant can you find an appendix? (Certain people who look otherwise normal are freaks on the inside, the appendix wedged next to the rectum, the heart on the right side, only one kidney, and you may not know it until you open them up. It's called *situs inversus.* There's a metaphor for you, Dr. Gruber.)

So there I am, in the fierce lights of the OR, as bright as an interrogation room in some third-world police station, and Dr. Jenkins and the resident are using laparoscopic cameras to mush through this lady's belly. We're all staring at her juicy insides, and Dr. Jenkins says, Mr. Shapiro, what happens if you cut the vagus nerve? (It can't secrete gastric acid and you freeze motility from the stomach.) What's the most common malignant gastrointestinal tumor? (Colon cancer.) Second-most common? (Stomach.) Another name for stomach cancer? (Signet ring cell carcinoma.) What's a carcinoid tumor? (A neuroendocrine malignancy most commonly found in the ileum that secretes excess levels of serotonin leading to the carcinoid syndrome.) How do you test for it? (Serotonin metabolites in the urine.) Nailed it, nailed it, nailed it. Dr. Jenkins was impressed. After the surgery, he invited me into the doctors' lounge where *no* med students ever get to go, and he put his feet up on the table, told me to help myself to coffee while he ate a package of graham crackers, breakfast of champions, he said, and he asked me what I wanted to do with my life. I said I wanted to be a CT surgeon, and he said, You'll make a fine one, and offered me any help I needed getting into a surgical residency. I told Serena I loved her that night. I was so fucking happy. I was going to be a CT surgeon, and I had the most beautiful girlfriend in the world.

The rest of the month was awesome. I scrubbed in on a

liver transplant, a thoracotomy, and this amazing procedure for esophageal cancer where you take the esophagus out and replace it with a piece of the small intestine — metaphor again, the poor guy has to eat through his crapper for the rest of his life — but the body's smart, it turns it into an esophagus, and voilà, he's chewing and swallowing and getting on with life, seeing his kids grow up, walking his daughter down the aisle — the whole life shebang — when otherwise it would be certain death. I saw a Whipple procedure, a nine-hour surgery to save another dude with pancreatic cancer, watched some surgeon take out these black lymph nodes filled with melanoma — that guy was fucked, no saving him — tacked up some bladders, tossed a few more appendices and gallbladders. It rocked.

The next month I was back on medicine wards — yawn. But I still had to suck up, had to get those A's for the surgery residency. Then pediatrics, you could have shot me, sick, snotty kids. Only one of them needed surgery; at least they let me go see that. The peds attending, Dr. Waltzer, said, Shapiro, I'm going to reward you for always being here on time and knowing what you need to know. I can see you are not a great lover of children and you have done due diligence despite that, so I am excusing you to go see them fix this baby's complex transposition of the great vessels, with the requirement that you will follow him during his ICU stay and through the remainder of your rotation. That baby was named Ethan Madsen, and he was the bravest little guy in the world. He had a heart the size of a walnut, with the arteries turned backward and a hole so small you couldn't fit a pinky through it that was killing him. He died, but I was okay with that because we tried, and if we hadn't tried, he would have died for sure, so there wasn't anything to lose by trying. It would have been awesome if he'd survived, and I felt really bad for his mom and dad; they cried and cried and cried. Dr. Gruber wants to think that my depression started when Ethan died, but she's wrong. I was really okay with it. I know it should have made me sad, but it just seemed like part of being a doctor. It didn't make me not want to be a surgeon or anything, though for a second during Ethan's operation, I had thought it might be cool to do pediatric CT surgery, and maybe Ethan's death, along with the fact that adult CT surgeons make way more money and there are only, like, ten peds CT surgery fellowships in the country, made me dismiss that thought before it was fully formed.

Serena was probably more upset about Ethan's dying than I was. She had watched his delivery on her ob-gyn rotation, and when she found out I was taking care of him, she came to the ICU one day after rounds to check on him. She walked in wearing her green scrubs and a little camisole — that was, like, my favorite outfit of hers; for one thing, it's incredibly easy to take off a pair of scrub pants — and she gave me a little wave. I was rounding with the ICU team, so I couldn't take time to talk to her, and I was actually a little nervous since she wasn't supposed to be there because, in a way, I had violated patient confidentiality by telling her the name of the little boy with the fucked-up heart, and they were nuts about patient confidentiality at Emory.

We had to go to these stupid ethics conferences, where some prissy attending would remind us not to talk about the size of some patient's dick or how fat some other patient was while we were in the elevator. The ethics conferences were the biggest waste of time. I tried to sit in the back and study note cards because the class suck-ups would always come up with some supposed ethical conflict that really just involved some attending or resident being an asshole and were in no way ethically ambiguous. One girl, Jane Martin, always sat in the front of the class and asked questions even if what the professor had just said was patently obvious. (Two plus two is four. Ooh, Professor, is that true if the patient is in renal failure? Yes, Jane, you idiot, two plus two is four regardless of the function of your kidneys or your uterus or your cerebellum.) Jane always had observed someone doing something terrible who she was in a big hurry to rat out, like a resident saying a patient was nothing but a drug addict or a whore or a piece of shit from the county jail (which they said all the time, but only when it was true), and then the attending teaching ethics would say, Is that an appropriate thing for a health care professional to do? And everyone who was awake or paying attention (usually Jane and the Jane clones) would say, Oh, no. One day, for some unexplained reason, Dr. Greene, the chief of neurosurgery, was leading the ethics seminar — I am sure he had better things to do — and when Jane brought up whatever scenario she had saved for the day, Dr. Greene said, Well, Jane, that is really not an ethical conundrum, is it? It was beautiful.

But I was pretty sure Dr. Greene would not have wanted me telling my girlfriend the name of the little baby whose life was leaking away in the cardiac PICU no matter how hot said girlfriend was. I calculated what I would do if I got in trouble. I would say, Well, it was just really emotionally draining, and

I had to share it with someone. They would love that. I was still a med student, and I was allowed to let my emotions get the better of me. Not just allowed, encouraged.

Serena came out from Ethan's room and put her face in her hands and cried really loudly. The rounding team could hear her. She locked eyes with me, but I couldn't leave rounds. One of the nurses comforted her. After work, I met her at a bar where a bunch of us were hanging out, and she said she understood why I couldn't come over to her, but she didn't understand why I hadn't told her how bad off he was. She said, I wasn't prepared, and I let Roberta down. Roberta was Ethan's mom. I said, Roberta doesn't know who you are. She said she recognized me. I said, Roberta does not count on you in any way. She said, I went in there all smiley with a little present, and she looked at me like I was an idiot. I said, You didn't let Roberta down, you're just embarrassed. She called me an asshole and left the bar and didn't return any of my calls. When she saw me in the cafeteria a few days later, she said I was immature and spoiled and that I would need to grow up if we were going to have a future together. I said, It's not like I've asked you to marry me. I tried to pretend she was being a crazy girl, you know, the kind who starts sketching her wedding dress after the first date, but she knew I was full of shit, because once, in a state of postcoital delirium, I said, I think we should have three kids, two boys and a girl.

Serena and I stayed together, but then we had to decide where to do our residencies. She was doing ob-gyn, but in true Serena fashion, she wanted to go to the best program possible even though it's not a superhard residency to get. I had to go to an awesome program, because it's really hard to get into a CT surgery fellowship, and they're not going to take losers from some crappy program. Here's how the residency thing works. You have to apply to these programs and go on interviews. If you are doing something that's really competitive, like you want to be a cardiothoracic surgeon, you apply to all the top programs, and then you try to do some away rotations at those places. I went to Mass General, Vanderbilt, and UCLA. (Though I went to that one only because Serena was from California, and she said she might want to train near home since a lot of people end up practicing in the city where they train. I should have known she wasn't going to do the couples match, because when I told her I was going out there, she just shrugged her shoulders and didn't tell me to call her mom and dad or anything, even though the med school put me in these crappy dorms with graduate students, where I managed to be surrounded by the only ugly people in California, and I really could have used a home-cooked meal, courtesy of Maria, their Mexican housekeeper, and a dip in the heated pool or a couple of rounds with Señor Goldstein on the golf course at the Bel-Air Country Club.)

After you apply, they tell you if they want to interview you. You have to pay for all of this yourself, so the poor kids are kind of screwed, but, hell, that's only one of the many ways they are screwed in life, so I'm not going to cry for them. Then you fly all over the country kissing various people's asses. Finally, you make a list of where you want to go, and all the programs make a list of who they want to have come train there, and then some computer matches it up, and one day in March you find out where you are going to spend the next three to ten years of your life. Some poor fuck always ends up in Peoria or Omaha, but you work so hard in residency that you might as well be in Siberia, so it doesn't really matter.

Serena didn't say anything about whether we were going to do a couples match so we could be together after med school until I finally had to ask her. She showed me her match list. It was nothing like mine. I said, I don't want to go to UC San Diego, their surgery program sucks. Well, she said, I don't want to go to Northwestern. It's too cold. She said, My career is really important to me, and yours is to you, so let's just do our own thing, and if we make it, then we make it. I said that we could be apart for nine years. She shrugged; she was one cold bitch.

I said, Are we breaking up? And she shrugged, and said, Why not? That's how she ended three years of love. Why not? There would always be a guy willing to grovel at her feet like I did, willing to lick her pussy and rub her back and make her a bubble bath. All the shit I did for her, a million other guys would do it too. All she had to do was ask. She went to the senior banquet with this loser gastroenterology fellow and wouldn't even look me in the eye. Fuck her. I matched at Mass Gen, my number one choice, and she ended up in Dallas, which was like her sixth choice. Fuck her.

I can tell by the music and the general shuffle that the wedding has ended. I don't want anyone to see me here leaning on this tree. The old foreign lady is wandering in this direction, talking to herself and shaking her hands at the sky. At first, I thought she was looking for me because I am the reason she dropped whatever she'd been holding on to so tightly, but she is walking in no particular direction. In fact, she looks like she is lost, like she was not invited to the wedding but instead just came out of the woods after being asleep for a hundred years. She looks into the woods, past where I am, and I can see she is crying. For some reason, she takes off her shoes and sits in the grass, still looking at the woods. She lies on her back, and if I were still a doctor, even a doctor in training, I would run over to her, take her pulse, see if she is having a heart attack or a stroke or a syncopal episode. I would start CPR; I would save her life. I don't remember how to do any of that, but I walk over to her anyway. She looks up at me, and says, "My sister, Eva, never had a wedding. She was in love with a boy named Elias Auerbach."

I say, "Okay."

"He kissed her in the woods."

Behind her, people are streaming into the tent. The ceremony is over, and it's time to get this party started. The waiters have sprung to life and are carrying around trays of champagne. Some guy is laughing really loudly, a fake loud laugh. Maybe he was in love with Elizabeth, and now he knows he's screwed; she's married someone else. Or maybe he's telling someone about Elizabeth's crazy weird tits. The lady says, "I can't see. You." I move aside, and she stares up at the sky. I look up too, thinking maybe there's something there, though I am not sure what would be in the sky that is interesting — a hot-air balloon, maybe a plane trailing a banner that says, CONGRATULATIONS ELIZABETH AND HANK. There is nothing there, not even a cloud. This lady is crazy, I think, and then I start to laugh, because so am I, and neither of us belongs here with all the people who are managing to live normal lives. I shuffle behind a few other trees, crush a pinecone,

and then find myself at the edge of the Gottliebs' steep driveway. I am not going back to the wedding. I walk down the
driveway into the road, then past the rows and rows of parked
cars, past all the big houses.

Every once in a while, maybe just once a year, you'll see a
guy walking on the highway. I mentioned this to Dr. Gruber
once, and she said she had never seen anyone walking on the
highway, but I said, You must not be looking. It's not often,
but everyone has seen it at least once, someone just walking on I-85 or I-285, not hitchhiking, not carrying a gas can,
just walking. The cars whoosh past the guy (or girl, once I
saw a girl); their clothes are whipped by the hot breeze and
the car exhaust, and they disappear in the shadows of giant
semis and then reappear. I walk to the end of the Gottliebs'
street and then onto a busier street. There is no sidewalk, and
I have to jump onto the scraggly grass of no-man's-land. A
dog barks at me from behind a tall gate.

I had a great apartment in Copley Square in Boston. My mom
and dad and Debbie and I spent a week on Cape Cod drinking
craft beer and complaining about the rocky beaches the week
before I started residency. Then they deposited me in my
apartment and took a cab to the airport. I could see this huge
flashing sign outside my window. My mom had stocked my
refrigerator because she said there wouldn't be time for me to
do anything. I had milk and eggs and frozen dinners and ten
different kinds of cereal. She had bought like a hundred pairs
of underwear and socks so I wouldn't have to worry about
laundry. The last thing they did before they left was take a
picture of me in my white coat with my name embroidered

on it, STEVEN SHAPIRO, MD. My dad said he was proud of me. My mom had tears in her eyes. She said I was so handsome. Debbie told me to find a cute doctor for her to marry.

The next day was orientation, and something was not right from the very beginning. For one thing, the chief surgical resident was this fat bald guy who talked like Elmer Fudd and had some indeterminate stains on his coat pocket. He said, We follow the ACGME standards, and you will have an eighty-hour week. When I was a resident we sometimes had to work over a hundred hours a week. This does not mean you will work less, so you will have to work smarter. Be organized. He said the first-year residents mostly just change catheters and place central lines, so don't get any illusions that you're going to be some great surgeon at the end of the year. He told us to be respectful to our attendings, to one another, and, above all, to our patients. He sounded like Jane Martin, another prissy suck-up. I looked around, and most of the other residents were taking notes. *Be organized,* the guy next to me had written down. Seriously.

We got our assignments. I was starting out at Dana-Farber, the cancer hospital. Tumor call. I reviewed my anatomy textbooks that night, set my clock radio, set my watch alarm, set my cell phone alarm, and then slept right through every fucking one of them. It was light when I woke up, which meant I was screwed, since I was due at the hospital at 5 a.m. I saw my pager blinking; I had missed, like, a hundred pages. I jumped into my scrubs and ran to the T stop, thought better of it, got a cab, which was a mistake since it was rush hour in Boston; and I didn't get to the hospital until 8:45. I paged my resident, and a nurse answered and said he was scrubbed in surgery. I heard the resident shout, Tell that dumb fuck to wait outside OR 8. I didn't know where OR 8 was. We'd had orientation on all the hospitals, but all the different maps had blurred in my head, and I had to ask, like, five nurses how to find the operating rooms, then got scolded for entering the OR area without shoe covers and a hat, and this nurse slapped one of those bouffant things on me that fry cooks wear since I had forgotten my cool surgeon's scrub hat, and then she finally let me through the swinging doors, and I found OR 8 and looked through the window in the door just in time to see blood spurting straight in the air.

It was quiet. No one said shit or what the fuck. I heard the suction machines and the cautery buzzing and the ping of the heart monitor. I wasn't sure if I was supposed to go in or not. A team came up to the sinks outside OR 7 next door and started scrubbing. They looked me up and down, and dismissed me. The smell of the surgical soap made me queasy. I had not had time for breakfast. I had no idea how long I was going to have to stand there. The light was crazy bright. It was cold. Orderlies walked by with stretchers, and I was suddenly certain that everyone on the stretchers was dead. Or if they weren't dead yet, we were going to kill them; that was what we were there for, not to save lives but to end them, first by gas, and then by cutting open these stunned bodies and removing whatever essential organs we could find. I had a flash of thought that we would cut open some old man, and inside we would find not heart, lungs, and kidneys but a carburetor, a bicycle wheel, a broken doll, a wedding ring. Serena told me once about how they had to induce labor in this lady who had been carrying twins, and they had died when she was twenty-nine weeks pregnant. She said, We could have put her to sleep and done a C-section, but then if she got pregnant again, she'd probably have to have another C-section, so she decided to be awake, and she had to push, and out plopped these two warm blue babies, warm but dead, with their eyes closed and their mouths open. They were boys. She asked if she could hold them, so the doctor wrapped them up in blankets and gave them to her.

I left the hospital. I walked out with the blue paper shoe covers on my feet, in my bouffant cap, down the halls where all the people were dying, into an elevator full of people who were innocent and ignorant of our purpose there, out into the bright sunlight of Boston in July. It was crowded in the street, lots of people in suits and doctors in white coats and nurses carrying cups of coffee, smiling and laughing and talking on cell phones. It was brutally hot outside, especially compared to the cold freeze of the hospital, and as I walked, I got hotter and hotter. I took off the hat and threw it in the street, but I was still hot. I took off my shirt. I fully expected the Charles River to be in a full rolling boil when I got to its banks, but it wasn't. It looked cool and dirty. A beer can floated by. I took off my shoes and my scrub pants, and I jumped in.

A car is honking at me. A giant metal thing on wheels with big glowing eyes. It has been following me for some time, but I am going to ignore it. I am almost to the highway. I want to be one of those mysterious and brave people who walk along the highway, who say, Fuck you, cars and trucks, I have two legs and I can walk all the way to fucking Canada if I want to. The car pulls up next to me. I can feel its hot breath, but I won't look at it. I hear the door open, and someone calls my name. It is my mother. She reaches over and opens the door for me. She says, Steven, get in. Please. I look away from her.

A car honks at her, then realizing she has stopped, goes around. She crawls over the center of the car and gets out on the passenger side. She says, Steven, come back to the party. Or I will take you home if you are ready to go. If you have had enough, I will take you home. I tell her I have somewhere I have to be. She says, Where? Where do you have to be? I say, Somewhere. I cannot tell her. I know it and I don't know it. I am certain that I will know it when I get there. I tell her I can walk home. It isn't far. She says, It's five miles. I say, I can walk five miles. I smile and tell her that it will be good for me. She says, I will walk with you. Suit yourself, I say. I start walking, and she is tottering next to me in her high heels. She can't keep up. I can hear the highway. She says, Steven, I can't walk five miles in these shoes. Please get in the car. Where are all those people going? I wonder. The world is so cruel and wonderful, with all its millions and millions of places that one can disappear into. My mother calls my name loudly. My whole name. Steven Joseph Shapiro, like she used to say when I was little and in trouble. I turn to look at her. She is old. I think she wants to help me. I think she loves me, but she's so old. No one that old and frail can help me, not without magic powers. I need a superhero. Someone who can fly and turn back time. Someone who knows the secrets of the universe and can forgive me for the terrible things I have done. A car drives by and honks, and she jumps, teeters, catches herself. Even from where I am standing, I can see the veins throbbing in her neck, and I have the sudden, certain thought that she won't live much longer. She holds an arm out to me. I wave to her, the same wave I gave when they got in the rental car to go to the Boston airport. I know that I need to get away from her. I turn into the woods, away from the honks and screeches of the highway.

It's a hot day, and the pine straw feels like lava under my feet. There is nothing that can hurt you in these woods, just chipmunks, squirrels, blue jays, crows, and copperheads whose bites will wound but not deal a mortal blow. The bears and wolves and rattlesnakes have been chased from Atlanta. It would be better for us if they were still here, so we could know who the enemy is. The vilest thing here is the sun, and it chases me from tree to tree. I know it's following me, the sun, other things too. There's a squirrel with half a tail, wounded I guess by another animal or hit by a car, and it keeps disappearing under ferns and behind trees, and popping up again in front of me. Part of me knows that squirrel isn't following me, but then again, how many half-tailed squirrels can there be? Animals do not like me. Serena had a cat that peed in my shoes and hissed at me whenever I came over. She said he was jealous. I told her that was stupid — unless she fucked the cat too. As I walk, the blue jays squawk louder. Asshole blue jays that take whatever nest they want and push out the eggs of the other birds. They eat their young. That was something people used to say about senior residents at Mass Gen, watch out for them, they eat their young. The crows are loud with their ugly caws; black and shining, they are following me too, spreading their wings and watching me as if they know where I am going. I have gone in the wrong direction. Again. I have lost the sound of cars, the smell of asphalt. But that's okay. Somewhere in these woods is a creek that flows to a river. I'll follow that instead of the highway, see where it takes me, maybe all the way to the Mississippi River or the Gulf of Mexico.

Someone is walking toward me. Something. Frail and unbending as if it were made of sticks. It makes a sound, a squeak, a groan. I try to remember what we learned in Boy Scouts—stay still or run? That was for bears and mountain lions, not the supernatural. For the supernatural, it probably doesn't make a difference what you do. Right? They'll find you, like God. I think I am pretty well hidden behind a bush, but the next thing I know, it's looking up at me. There are hands on my arms, and it's at least part human. It looks up at me with an ancient face, wrinkled, almost reptilian except for the gray hair in a bun, and it smiles joyously. "We looked for you for years. We thought you were lost. But you were here all along."

I say, "Where is here?"

And she answers, "Here."

Mushrooms

THE WOODS BEHIND OUR HOUSE in Hesse, in Germany, were darker than any I have seen since. The dirt was black and soft, like crumbled velvet, and the tops of the trees were knit together so tightly that even in the middle of the day, after just a few steps, I could hardly see anything at all. The spruce trees were fat, with thick dark green needles, and among them grew elms and ash, with heavy leaves that would tear free, one at a time, and fall silently to the ground. It seemed to me, as a child, that there must have been some rule in the forest. Things happened singly, all alone. That is how I remember it. The ominous caw of a crow. Then silence. Then the rapid terrified scuttle of a small animal, a rodent of some kind. Silence. An owl hoots. A wolf howls. Silence. The rat-a-tat of a woodpecker.

My sister, Eva, took me to the woods. The last time we went there, we were searching for mushrooms. I was six and she was seventeen. She held my hand tightly. I was afraid of the woods, and she knew it. I think she was also a little afraid. I could feel the blood pulsing in her wrist. She breathed rapidly. We stepped into the darkness. She was carrying a basket. It was springtime, and it had been raining, and the forest smelled wet and ancient, the smell I always associated with mushrooms; the air was warm, but the ground was still cold when I dug my hand under the wet leaves. Eva read fairy tales to me at night, usually the Brothers Grimm, but when we walked into the forest, she always reminded me that they were nothing but stories. She told me no father would ever leave his children in that darkness, no silent princesses sat alone weeping in the trees. There was an abandoned castle in the forest — years later, when I went back at the invitation of the mayor of Lauterbach, I saw that it was less a castle than a small estate crumbling with only a remote air of aristocracy — but at the time it seemed like a castle, and I always chose to believe that an exiled princess had once lived there, that her father had found his way to her through a magical ball of yarn, that a prince, cursed to be a baby deer, was rescued by that princess and eventually saved her from her exile, so one day her sad father followed his ball of yarn to an empty castle and never saw her again. It would be nice to believe that the people who are taken from us have run off to different kingdoms to marry princes. It would be a much nicer ending than what happened. To my mother and father and two of my three brothers. And to Eva.

Before we had even started digging for mushrooms, someone stepped out of the darkness of the woods, and my heart stopped. Eva and I stood perfectly still, and the sounds of the forest, one by one, ticked off, howl, chirp, snapping twig. I could see by the outline that it was a man, tall and young; his feet pounded the forest floor and interrupted the order of sounds. He was running in our direction, but I was not sure if he was running toward us or away from something else. He came close enough for us to see his black eyes, and then my sister froze. She said, "You scared me."

The man stopped in front of her. I squeezed her hand because for a moment I thought I might have become invisible. He said, "You're late. I've been here for hours."

"Not hours," she said. "Rachel needed to finish some schoolwork first." When I heard my name, I was relieved. She had not forgotten me.

He said, "You should have come alone."

"I wouldn't be allowed to come alone. There can be strangers in the woods."

He touched her waist. "Am I a stranger?" he said. A shaft of light broke through a tree and lit his face. He had a light beard and mustache, and I thought he was very handsome. His hand was big, and her back seemed small. It seemed so big that it looked like it had crashed into her back and flattened there, and like it would be there forever now, so I was relieved when she reached back and peeled it away.

She bent down so that we were face-to-face. "Rachel," my sister said. "I am going to show you a good spot to look for mushrooms, and I want you to stay there and look and promise me you will not leave. I am going to be very nearby, also looking for mushrooms."

"I want you to look with me," I said.

She said, "We need to find a lot of mushrooms, and it will be better if we look in two places." She brought me to a spot we had been to a few times in the last year. We had pulled two fallen logs together to make a place to sit and eat the snacks we packed, just an apple and bread. The logs were still there. There was a small creek nearby, and sometimes deer came there to drink. If I was quiet enough, I could hear their tongues lapping and then the swallowing as the cold water rolled down their throats. She left me there, and I found a basketful of mushrooms in no time, and then sat on the log, scratching two bites on my ankle until they bled. I looked up at the ceiling of trees. In that spot, there were a few breaks, and the sunlight came down in cones and highlighted a tree stump covered in dark green moss, a stone in the river that created an eddy of seething water, a small white flower. When my sister finally came back, her hair was messy, and the collar of her shirt was crooked. She was alone. She examined my basket of mushrooms and told me I had done a marvelous job. Eva always chose superlatives. She would not say *good* when she could say *marvelous*. She would not say *love* when she could say *adore*. She would not say *scary* when she could say *terrifying*.

Eva was going to marry that boy. I met his sister two decades later in a small café in Washington Heights. She said that she doubted I could be related to the girl her brother had loved, but she had lost everyone and was looking for any kind of connection. When I told her that Eva was my older sister and that I remembered her brother, she trembled all over. Although the war had been over for more than ten years, she was still terribly thin, and her hair grew only in clumps, leaving patches of pale skin. It was a faint red color; she had tried to tame it into a bun. I could see scars on her scalp, but most people had scars, and I did not try to imagine where they had come from, because imagining was never worse than reality. When she stopped shaking, she asked me if my sister had survived. I told her that Eva was dead, and she started trembling again. She then asked me if I looked at all like my sister. I told her my sister looked like my father — tall and thin, with light hair and blue eyes — and I looked like my mother. She could see for herself what I looked like — slanted black eyes, small pointed nose, jet-black hair, and not much bigger than a coffee table, though some of that was due to malnutrition. In my first year in the displaced persons camp, I grew six inches; I could almost feel my bones stretching, painful and exhilarating at the same time.

Her name was Miriam Solarz. She lived in Sweden. She gave me the address of her house and told me to call her if I was ever in Sweden. Before she left, she showed me a picture of my sister with the boy from the woods. His name was Elias Auerbach.

My sister never got to have a wedding. I didn't want one. I married my husband, Julius, also a survivor, in front of a rabbi and two strangers while we were still living in the DP camp. We had two sons, David and Simon. Simon died of a cerebral hemorrhage when he was twenty-six years old. David married a girl from Miami in an elaborate wedding in a synagogue that looked more like a church, with a choir and a gold-plated bimah and gigantic flowers. He lives in Miami in a house with a pool, and he has two children who call me Grandma and are too busy to say much more than that.

When Julius died, I stayed in New York for several years, but after I had a mini stroke, David insisted I had to move to Miami. I did not want to go to a place where I knew no one, but then friends started to move, to Florida, to California, to places where their children lived, or worse — they died — and when I realized I knew more of the dead than the living, I agreed to move, but not to Miami. I knew what life would be like in Miami. They would put me in the most expensive nursing home and leave me there. My niece Annette was always sweet to me, and she told David I would like it in Atlanta. She invited me to come here. At first, I lived with her, but I saw I was a nuisance, so I moved to the Jewish tower, where I could have friends. It's like when the boys were little and I sent them to preschool so they could make friends their own age. Now I live where all the other old Jews live. Officially, it is called Zaban Tower, but my friend Agnes calls it Zombie Tower for all the old men clomping along with their walkers, the clomps admittedly softened by tennis balls on the legs so it is more of a thump. Thump, shuffle, thump, shuffle. I am glad Julius died before he was reduced to such a state. Annette is a good girl, but she is busy, so I've learned how to fill the days. We play mah-jongg and bridge, and talk about the grandchildren we never see and the husbands who have died. The husbands— they have become more wonderful with each year since they left the earth. To hear Agnes tell it, her husband could fly. I am not complaining. Annette could just as easily do nothing, like the children of many of my friends. We have Shabbat dinner together almost every week, though sometimes it is just Chinese food arranged on plates, and sometimes it's just the two of us, sometimes the children are in town. I know it isn't easy. Annette has to pick me up, driving through terrible traffic since they live on the other side of town and I now limit my driving to a three-mile area, which includes my synagogue, the drugstore, the grocer, and the YMCA swimming pool where I do water aerobics.

Julius died twenty-one years ago, when he was seventy-two. He was twenty-three years older than I was. He lost his wife and two children in the war, and then he lost another son. But he never complained. He had been a pediatrician in Poland, and he became a pediatrician in New York. At first, all his patients were Jews and Italians, but later there were more blacks and Mexicans. He still loved it. A baby is a baby, he said. Julius loved all forms of celebration: a bris, a birthday party, a bar mitzvah, a wedding, even that thing the Mexicans do when the girl turns fifteen. He never turned down an invitation. I would say, What are we going to say to these people?

He would say, Put on something pretty, Rachel. What are we going to say? What everyone else says, Congratulations. Then we eat some cake, maybe we dance. What could be wrong with that?

Once we went to one of the blacks' weddings. I was used to black people by then, but when I was in the DP camp and I saw black American soldiers, I had never seen a black person before. I tried to look up their sleeves to see if they were black all the way up. I changed colors in the summer so why shouldn't they? The wedding was in Harlem. I thought we would be killed, but Julius said he had known the boy since he was born. The boy had had something wrong with him — a kidney problem, I think — and Julius said weddings are not just a celebration of love, they also mean a boy has become a man, and for this boy in particular, that alone was reason for a big celebration. Julius drove. I wanted to take a cab, but Julius said it would be a waste of money. There were burned-out buildings and bums everywhere, huddled under newspapers and wrapped in plastic bags. Loud music came out of the buildings, and girls, almost naked, danced on the street corners, a scared and defiant dance I recognized as desperation. They were prostitutes, I knew, like the ones I used to see after the war trying to get the American soldiers to give them something. I said, Why is this happening in America? And Julius said, There have always been people left behind. There were whores in Germany too, even before the war, and drunks and crazy people.

I thought our car would be stolen, but there was a parking lot behind the church and two men in tuxedos were helping people out of their cars and up the sidewalk. One of them, a giant of a man, recognized my husband. He said, What's up, Doc Rosenblatt? Julius looked at him strangely, and then smiled. Ah, Deshawn, I told your mother you would be more than six feet. You had the biggest feet of any six-year-old boy I have ever seen.

The boy, Deshawn, walked us into the church and sat us in the second row in an area marked RESERVED. He said the Andersons would be so glad we came. He shook my hand and told me that my husband was the coolest guy in all of the Bronx. It was such a lovely day. The mother and father of the boy getting married—I can't remember his name; it was a regular name like John or Joe—came to see us and make sure we were comfortable. The mother wore a hat with a lace veil on it, and she smelled like roses. Then the grandparents, the cousins, the uncles, the boy himself. Julius shook hands with everyone, and when they thanked him for saving the boy's life, he said the boy had saved himself.

I think that was my favorite wedding of all, including my own son's. A lady in a light blue dress sang a beautiful song, and everyone was crying. The groom was so handsome, and the bride was a tiny thing in a poufy white dress with a long train. I told Julius she looked like an African princess. He whispered, Just tell her she looks beautiful. I knew that! There were things I told him that I wouldn't say to other people. Like when a Mexican man came one time to fix our pipes, and when he couldn't understand me, I figured he did not speak English. I got the superintendent, and when he started speaking in Spanish, the man said, I speak English. I just can't understand her. I wanted to die. When people hear my accent, they ask me where I am from. Washington Heights, I tell them, though I know what they mean. What am I going to say? If I say I am from Germany, they will think I am German. I am not German. I am a Jew. I never belonged to that country. I don't belong to this one either. They tried to make a Jewish state in Israel, but the land the Jews should inhabit doesn't exist anymore. Milk and honey, a land of sweetness and soft green hills, and enough rain and piercing sunlight. I think it is on the other side of the clouds. Not heaven. The promised land.

Julius did not like it when I talked that way. His family were Zionists. He was very proud of the state of Israel. We both went to Palestine after the war. Julius never told anyone else, not even his sons, that when we arrived in Palestine his family, who had left before the war, refused at first to accept him into their home. They were ashamed of him, ashamed of all survivors. We had let ourselves be led like lambs to the slaughter, they said. We didn't fight like they fought against the English and the Arabs. Julius had let his wife and children be murdered — where were his scars, where were his bullet wounds? He should have died defending them. Believe me, this is something Julius thought himself, so when he stood there in the sandy street outside his uncle's house, a house with glass windows and olive trees in the yard, and was told there was no room for us, he understood and walked away. It was only when the Jewish police went back with us and ordered his family to take us in — the shelters and hospitals were stretched thin, so if you had a relative, they put you there no matter what condition you were in — that they opened the gate and embraced him. Me, they said nothing to. Julius introduced me as his wife, and then the man — an uncle of an uncle, I think — looked me up and down, and said, Pretty enough. Julius was not angry with his uncle. He understood that they could never understand. He felt the same way about the guard who smashed his baby's head against a wall. He was an animal, he said. We heard once of a child who fell into the tiger cage at a zoo and was, of course, destroyed. He said the guard was like that. They did not shoot the tiger. It was being a tiger. If he could find the guard, he would put him in a cage, but he would not kill him.

I am not like Julius. I can remember the face of the German soldier who dragged my mother down the stairs in 1938 on the night of the November pogrom that is called Kristallnacht in the history books. He had been in my brother David's class at school; his father worked in the lightbulb factory, and his mother had skinny legs with dark hair, and she used to wait until a Jewish child walked by their house to sweep the dust and crumbs out their front door into the child's face. Kurt Boller. He dragged my mother by her beautiful black hair, and then they harnessed her to an oxcart and made her pull the cart, along with my friend's mother, tossing shit at them, emptying chamber pots on their heads. I can remember the face of the soldier who shot my brother Levi because he was deaf and did not turn around when the boys who were rounded up for deportation were told to turn around. My mother and I saw it from where we were standing, and she gasped but said nothing. Although I was a hundred feet away, I can remember his icy eyes, and the way he laughed, with a crooked front tooth, his hands red and inflamed with the cold, and wrapped around the butt of his rifle. He poked my brother's body, and then shot him again. This man would now be eighty-eight if he is alive. I would know him if I saw him, and I would kill him. I would kill him in a terrible, slow way.

Annette insisted that I come to Elizabeth's wedding even though I told her I am tired of weddings and funerals alike. No more celebrations or mourning for me. The time has come for me to pull up a chair and just watch. Annette sent Benjamin to get me. I haven't seen him in two years, since he moved to Minneapolis. While I was waiting for him, I mentioned this to William the doorman. William asked me what Benjamin did in Minneapolis, and for the life of me, I couldn't remember, and then I said, Who knows? Does it matter? I waited in the lobby for a long time. He was late. When the boy walked in, he looked around, as if there were a hundred little old Jewish ladies waiting for him, and then, having determined that I was the only one, he crossed over, and said, "Aunt Rachel?" I looked up at him. "Are you ready to go?"

Was I ready to go? I was sitting there in a dress with my

purse watching them set up for lunch. Maybe he thinks this is what I do every day. "Of course," I said. He walked quickly to the door, pushed it open, and then realized I was a dozen steps behind him. He held the door open, letting all the hot air in, and I waited for William the doorman to say something, but William was reading the newspaper and couldn't be bothered.

The car was parked out front, a Mercedes. All the Jews drive German cars now. Benjamin did not open the door for me, and it took me a minute to work the handle and then figure out the seat belt. He said, "For the record, this is my father's car. I would never drive a car like this." He lurched out into the street. "Gas guzzler."

We drove in silence. His mother must have told him that I hated the highway because he took the long way over the surface streets, past the gigantic houses that have sprouted up all over the city. My friend Mila Goldstein's house was torn down, and now the Taj Mahal stands in its place. Mila's house was lovely, and now, like Mila, it is no more. The obliteration of the past is a human hobby. Sometimes we try to re-create it in our own memory, but what's gone is gone. If you cut down an apple tree and then plant another in its place, it is not the same tree. I was contacted by authorities in Hesse twenty-five years ago. They had received funding—probably from a Jew—for a new project. They were going to make bronze life-size statues of children to stand in front of the houses those children had been taken from. They would put their names on the statues—Yakov Spivak, age eight, murdered in the Holocaust—and when people walked past, they would think of the little boy. This was their idea. I said, Why are you doing this? Those who care already care, and those who do not never will. Give the money to hungry children in Africa. They said, But we must remember, and I said, Someone will put a baseball cap or paint a mustache on the face of the boy. It is such an easy mark. The best intentions always are.

The Germans and the Poles have made a great industry of the desire of Jews (particularly those with no personal connection to the Holocaust) to visit the places where their great-great-grandparents came from. It is a regular Jewish Disney World there now, with Shabbat services in the synagogue, Jewish restaurants, and klezmer music, but the funny thing is: there are no Jews. It is like the Museum of Natural History only we are the dinosaurs on display behind the glass. The truth is, this is a feeling I have everywhere. Someone from Annette's synagogue asked me to come speak with the children on Yom HaShoah. One of the little boys asked to see my tattoo. When I told him that only people who had been in concentration camps had tattoos, he looked confused. Their idea of the Holocaust is shaped by movies and television, so seeing a survivor in person has the same excitement as seeing an elephant in the wild; something that is only rumored to exist suddenly becomes real. But then it does not fit their preconceived notion of what it should look like — too big, too small, not sad enough, not scarred enough, too sad, too scarred. When people ask me where I am from, I say Washington Heights. I know what they mean, but I say Washington Heights. When they ask me when I came to America, I say 1952, and when they ask me where I came from, I say somewhere else.

When we got to the wedding, Benjamin honked his horn

and drove up the driveway. There was a large van in front of us unloading an elderly gentleman in a wheelchair. The boy said, "There's Bubbie and Zayde." An elegant woman in high heels was attempting to maneuver the wheelchair over the grass away from the van. I thought Benjamin should get out to help, but it was not my place to say anything. I also thought he should open my door, but he sat there with the engine idling, and he finally said, "You can get out if you want to. I have to help drive people up the driveway."

A man I recognized took the wheelchair from the older lady. It was Annette's brother-in-law. I have met him only once or twice, so I forgave myself for not remembering his name, just Annette's complaints about him. He was not a man of great accomplishments, but look, my David is accomplished but not so nice, and here was this man caring for his father. I wished I had not come. They would be eating lunch soon at the tower. Agnes and I always took the first shift. Eleven-thirty, then we try to walk a little. If Julius were here, he would tease me. What's the rush? But now, when I have all the time in the world and nothing to do, I wake at dawn. I watch the smoggy sunrise and think of all the people who have died. I can't even watch television. Nothing makes sense. When I complained to Annette, she got worried. She took me to the doctor to see if I was maybe getting demented, but I am fine. I am completely sane. My memory is perfect. I remember what happened sixty years ago, and I remember what they served for dinner last night. In the end, the doctor agreed with me: nothing on television makes sense.

Everyone was walking in one direction, so I followed, and

then found a row and a seat. It was an unusually hot day for April, but the sun was shining, and a nice waiter offered me a glass of water. Most of the other chairs were empty, and I realized I had arrived very early, probably because Benjamin had other things to do. Annette has a pretty house, big but at least it was not a monstrosity. It was in a modern style, with large windows. The wedding was being held in the courtyard that opened to the back where there were woods mostly full of scraggly pine trees, a few oaks, nothing like the woods in Germany. Julius once went to a meeting in San Francisco, and a colleague there took him to see the giant redwoods. He said that was the closest he ever came to feeling the darkness of the European forests. The giant trees, he said, looked like a fairy tale come to life, which was believable in Eastern Europe, where the wonderful and the horrible mixed so easily.

Annette must be busy. Usually, she would come and find me and make sure I was comfortable. She feels responsible for me, like the daughter I never had, even though we are distantly related by American standards. Her mother's sister married my brother Michael. Annette's mother used to bring her to New York to go shopping. They would come to Washington Heights for a visit. Julius nicknamed Annette the *meshuga hun,* the crazy chicken. She had so much energy, showing us the clothes she bought, telling us about the shows she saw, the Statue of Liberty — as if we had never seen it. She always wanted David and Simon to come with them, be tourists. Sometimes Simon would go if it was a museum. Shows and shopping he didn't like. Simon was quiet and studious, like the little heder child he was, with his nose in books all the time, though they were books of fantasy with elves and witches. I would have liked for him to read something useful once in a while, history or science, but Julius told me that everyone grows up on his own schedule. The boys who got tallest early end up the smallest. Don't rush him, Rachel, he would say. After all, the world is small and there really are not so many places to go. Walking through the noisy streets of the city, jostled by strangers, with cars honking and mysterious things falling from the sky — paper, drops of water, once even an egg fell and smashed right in front of me — I would wonder how he could say such a thing. To me, I had gone as far away from Lauterbach as another planet. I am one of the few people who can say she has lived in two entirely different worlds, the Earth and somewhere that has yet to be named.

David was the practical one. He didn't care about where he was from, only where he was going. If I tried to talk to him about my brother, his namesake, he would shift from foot to foot for a moment before saying he had to go, he had baseball practice or a big exam or a date. He studied business in college, and then more business, and now he does something with money, I don't know what, but he must do well, because the house is big, the swimming pool is big, the children each have a car, and they ski and take trips to Mexico and all have healthy tans. I am happy for him, but I do not know him. If I had not carried him in my body, I would wonder if he was my son. He idolizes his father; there are pictures of Julius all over the house, but I do not see Julius in this man.

People ask me if I think the Holocaust could ever happen in America. I usually say no, because that is what they want to hear, but I think human beings are capable of doing the most horrible things to one another at any time and any place. Nowhere is safe. This makes life rather bitter, I am aware, but anyone who has been tormented as a child by otherwise seemingly normal adults must know its truth. I used to play dolls with a little girl named Trudel. Trudel and I were the best jump-ropers in our grade at school, and every day at recess we counted higher and higher, trading off the title of champion with ease. Her house was not as nice as my house, but she had an excellent collection of dolls by dint of being the youngest of five girls. Her mother worked as a domestic in a big house, and her father was a truck driver, so they were seldom home. Her older sisters managed the house and cooked the meals. One day her mother arrived home early. She was an ugly woman. If you wanted to draw a witch, you might choose some of her features. She had a large mouth with a loose lower lip that drooped low almost to her chin. Large eyes, almost all white, with small dots of gray in the center, surrounded by chapped raw skin that she worsened by constantly rubbing. She stood in the doorway; I felt her presence for some time before she said anything, and I carried on playing, nervous for Trudel, because the presence of a silent adult usually meant someone had done something wrong. We had concocted a tea party, and Trudel's doll asked my doll if she would like some more. Hep! Hep! Trudel's mother cried from the door. At first, I thought she was coughing, but then she blocked out the light, her large shadow swooped over me, and she shouted, Hep! Hep! and clapped into my ear. Then she laughed. Hep, hep! She pushed me over. I scooted away from her, and she flapped her hands as if she were shooing chickens. Trudel stared blankly at me. Her mother clapped and flapped at me until I had no choice but to gather my schoolbooks and run away.

My mother was in the kitchen when I arrived panting and crying. I told her what had happened, and she forbade me to ever go to that house again. Hep, hep is a herder's cry. It is used on cattle, sheep, chickens, and Jews.

Annette finally finds me at the wedding. She is in a rush, like always, *meshuga hun,* and fanning herself with the program. She sees that I am seated. There is some kind of problem with the caterer or the dress or the music, and she can't stay. She asks me if I am hot, but when I say yes, she doesn't offer to do anything about it. She rushes off. A man and a woman sit in front of me, and the woman puts her purse down to save a seat for someone. The man is large and broad shouldered, and I realize I will not be able to see over him, but I don't care enough to move.

Other people's children have never mattered much to me. Julius was different, but then Julius was a pediatrician. Other people's children were his whole life. The boy who died was named Joshua. The girl was Judith. He refused to give these names to any of our children. He could not bear to speak them, and when he treated a child named Josh or Judy, he made up a nickname. He called the boys little bear, little sheep, and the girls little kitten. The parents thought he did this to all the children, but they were wrong, only those named Josh or Judy.

Sometimes, when I was sadder than usual, Julius brought me to the office. He said he needed help, but what did he need with my two left hands? He had good nurses to help, and I only made things more difficult. I couldn't type or write prescriptions. He said people liked meeting his wife. He was proud of me. He would tell the young mothers to ask me how to soothe a crying child, how to make a baby go to sleep, how to break a fever. He said, Rachel, show them how you rub the baby's back. The mothers handed over their babies with so much trust. I felt them, warm and hazy, in my arms. They nuzzled into my neck. Who hurts a baby? I would wonder. Their necks were damp and soft; there is a spot between a baby's shoulder blades that you can press ever so firmly with your thumb, and it works like pressing a button. They get quiet and relax, and just like that, they sleep, suddenly slack against your shoulder, formless in your arms. Once it was a Joshua he wanted me to hold. He said, This little bear is making life hard for his mother. He doesn't want to sleep. When the mother, a tiny little thing who still looked like a child to me, with her liquid black eyes and soft mouth, handed the baby to me, and said, Help me with my Joshua, I glanced over at Julius. He met my eyes and looked away. I knew what he was thinking. Somewhere in the human heart is the ability to take this small thing by its pink crinkled feet and smash it. Julius and I had to learn to live with that knowledge.

After Kristallnacht and the murder of Levi, my father moved us to Frankfurt. Trudel's family moved into our house. I know this because in 1976 the survivors from our town were invited to return. There were twelve survivors, but only I and one other man elected to return. Julius did not want me to go. He knew of my anger, and he warned me that I would not be able to obtain the justice that I sought. Justice in this world was not something Julius believed in. He was miraculous in that way: he was comfortable with giving and not receiving; with the fact, even, that he gave willingly and others grabbed and yanked and stole from him. I don't know what I was thinking. I went alone. A man named Moses Frankel also went. He knew my brother David. He asked me if I knew what had happened to David, and I said I had heard that David was killed at Buchenwald, and he said that this was true. Trudel had grown up to look just like her mother, fat and pink. When she saw me, her eyes grew wide, and before I could say a word, she said, We bought the house legally. The Germans sold it to us. I said, I don't want the house back.

Her daughter hid behind her mother's bloated calves, blinked at me with the same eyes that Trudel had blinked at me the day her mother interrupted our tea party. I said, I live in New York now. I have two sons. If you are wondering why I am tan, it is because I have just come back from a cruise. Then I wondered why I was explaining myself to this woman. Trudel's little girl stuck her finger in her nose. We own the house, Trudel said. I can show you the deed. I closed my eyes. I don't want the house, I told her. I asked her if she knew where the Bollers lived. She told me Kurt and his two brothers died in the war. His mother was still alive, in the same house where they had always lived. I wondered if Julius would let that count as justice.

Everyone was trying to get to America before the war, but you needed someone to say that you would not be a burden to the nation. My mother's aunt and my father's cousin were there, but they helped their own families first. Then my father managed to secure passage for my brother Michael and Eva.

Eva and Michael went to the train station. I do not know what happened after that. They got to Hamburg, and something was wrong with Eva's papers. She was not allowed on the boat. She eventually came back to Frankfurt, but I was gone by then. My mother found a way to send me to France where I would live in a convent as a Catholic orphan. She took me to the train station. We had to walk in the street. My mother had washed my dress the night before. I complained because it was itchy, and she said that she was sorry, but she had to use cheap soap; it was all that she could find. The ends of the sleeves had not gotten all the way clean. There were rims of gray sweat around the cuffs, and I pulled my coat down to hide them. I was ashamed. I looked at my mother. Ever since the night she was pulled down the stairs, she walked with a limp, and she hobbled quickly, afraid we would miss the train. She looked old and tired. We passed a German mother pushing a pram and holding the hand of her daughter. The girl was about my age, but she was a city girl, with a black velvet coat and a white rabbit-fur muff. I could see the girl's perfectly white collar — no stains — and the white satin ribbon that tied back her hair. It seemed to me at that moment that the girl had never been and never would be dirty or soiled in her entire life. She met my eyes and looked away. Her mother did not look at us. She stared straight ahead. I do not know if it was because we were not worth her gaze or if she was saddened by the fact that we were forced to walk in the street. She had on black patent-leather shoes; even the wheels of the baby carriage were bright and shiny. There was a very slight squeak as it passed us. My mother was wearing torn white stockings, and I could see the flesh of her legs through the

rips. She looked so human and pitiful that I remember wanting to cry and hug her and never leave her and also wanting
to run away and pretend that I did not know her. She held my
hand. Her hand was damp and soft. I snuck my head close
to it and smelled its salty, soapy scent. To this day, this is the
smell of my mother and everything too good for this world.

The train station was very crowded. We had to shoulder
our way through the crowds. It was obvious when we got to
the part of the train that would be taking the Jewish children
because it smelled of boiled chicken and bread and onions,
the food our mothers had packed for the journey. In my rec-
ollection, none of the children spoke, though I am sure this is
not true. What I remember is that over the hum of the usual
train station noise, the announcements of arrivals and depar-
tures, the greetings and the goodbyes, there was a condensed
cloud of collective anguish, of mothers all at once pushing
their children out into the world, a feeling I have never experienced since that day because, like the sounds of the woods
where I went with Eva, things in nature happen one by one.
Each baby bird is nudged from the nest. Each leaf falls. It was
the most unnatural thing to have all these children heaved
overboard all at once into the great unknown. My mother
pressed me into her body; her coat was coarse and thick. She
held my head with ungloved hands, then knelt down to look
into my eyes. In my memory, her whole face is glazed and
shining, as if she were encased in a coat of thin glass. In my
memory, I poke at her cheek to see what she feels like. Of
course, I know she was crying. I know that when she put her
hands on either side of my face and held me still she was mem-
orizing the look of me; she was trying to imagine the whole of

my life in that moment. When my son Simon died, I caught sight of my tear-streaked face in the mirror of the hospital and saw my mother's face that day. Even if we had grown old together, we couldn't have loved each other more or known each other better. We would have just had more time, more days to brush up against each other and either smile or apologize, and then get on with living. Life is meant to be lived in the general orbit of those who love us, though we cannot protect each other, not from heartbreak or injustice or murder. Love is the weakest shield, but here is the truth. It is the only shield. My mother put me on the train, and then I lost her face in the sea of the glassed-in and fogged-over faces of women in coarse wool coats watching their children leave.

The man in front of me at the wedding complains about the heat. He says, "We're having Debbie's wedding indoors. It's hot as hell out here." The air is very still, and I am sure that if everything got quiet all of a sudden we could hear birds singing and maybe the slight rustle of whatever lives in those woods, but it is not quiet. Someone is tuning a violin; glasses are clinking. The seats are filling up, and there are human sounds all around me, a cough, a cleared throat, someone calling someone else's name and waving. I have a feeling that everyone belongs here but me, but that feeling makes me belong to myself, since I have it all the time, at dinner in the dining room of Zombie Tower, at the grocery store in front of all the cereal boxes, by David's pool. Sometimes I think I would prefer to be in totally foreign places, like that Negro wedding, so it would make sense feeling this way. The seats all around me are full. A clumsy young man sits in front of me, scooting his chair back so that it is practically touching my knees. There are tender red pimples on his neck, and he is sweating. He belongs to the angry man and his wife. The woman puts her hand on the boy's knee, but the man looks at him and looks away. The music changes to a Bach cello suite. Julius loved Bach. He said not everything the Germans did was bad. There had to be a Germany so there could be a Bach and a Mozart. I said that I would trade Bach for my mother. He said, No one offered that deal. It is fair to say he lost more than I did since he lost his children, but I lost my childhood. The world has never been safe for me. You might as well have condemned me to live my life at the edge of a hot and smoking volcano. I have spent my whole life waiting to be destroyed. Everything that had been added to my life, my wonderful husband, my children, my grandchildren, only makes me a bigger target.

The bride walks down the aisle, and then the music stops and everything is quiet. I don't hear well, so I can barely make out the sound of the rabbi.

Trudel said that her mother had died thirty years ago, though she survived the war. Things were hard for them after the war, Trudel said. They were very hungry, and she lost an uncle and two cousins, one of whom she had hoped to marry. Then she told me where Kurt Boller's mother lived. I thought I remembered the house, but I wanted to be sure. I went there by myself. It was at the end of a small street that backed up to a field. The town had not changed very much, though the field was gone, and now there was a cement factory in its place. I knocked on the door. At first, it seemed no one was home. I waited a long time. I looked at the other houses. The doors were shut, and the curtains were drawn. I am sure people knew the Jews were in town. There was supposed to be a ceremony asking for forgiveness the next day. They were going to erect a plaque for all the citizens of Lauterbach who had died in the war, the Germans and the Jews alike, all listed together. I do not know if Moses Frankel attended the ceremony. I did not. I knocked again. I was about to leave when I heard the locks clicking. It sounded like there were a dozen of them, click, click, click, and then the doorknob turned and a tiny old woman with a shrunken face looked up at me through the smallest of cracks.

She had clapped for her son when he pulled my mother out of the house by her hair.

The woman's eyes were whited over with cataracts. I have a cataract myself now, so now I know I must have looked like little more than a miasma to her. I spoke in German when I asked if she was Mrs. Boller. I do not know why I asked. I knew the answer. She asked why I wanted to know. I pushed the door open; it was easy, and I walked into the house. The house was dusty and smelled of bleach and mildew. I told her my name. I asked her if she remembered my mother. She shrugged and said that she wasn't sure. She said she had trouble remembering things. I walked over to a table covered in a yellowed lace tablecloth. There were pictures of her sons when they were young, posed in a photographer's studio, and from later when they were in uniform. I asked her which one was Kurt. She pointed to a round-faced boy with small eyes. I asked if she was sure, and she pointed to another photograph. I picked it up. It was him. I asked her if she had loved her sons. She said, Of course. I took the picture and smashed it on the table. The glass shattered. I shook the frame so the shards of glass fell to the floor, then I wrenched out the photograph and tore it up in front of her face. I told her that her son was a monster and that I hoped he had died a slow and painful death. Then she spat on my shoe, and before I had time to think, I kicked her. She fell down, and I kicked her again. She started to scream.

I am lying. None of this happened. I put the picture down with nothing more than a thumbprint on the dusty glass where Kurt Boller's face gleamed out at me. I wanted to punch her. I wanted to kick her and pull her hair and shove her down the stairs, and then, while she was screaming and begging for mercy and reminding me of all the kind things she had ever done, I wanted to shove her face in a heap of cow manure and laugh when she looked up at me, filthy and hideous, more animal than human, so that the only natural next stop was to harness her to a yoke and whip her while she pulled the cart. If there was any justice in this world, I would have done at least half of that, but I was scared. I was scared of that tiny brittle woman, who could bring the whole town down on me with one scream, so I told her, I am a rich woman now, and I live in a big apartment in America. My husband is a doctor. I have two sons. She looked at me curiously. Her lips were dry and parted. She said, "Who are you?"

Then she turned and shuffled back into the dusty darkness of her house. I heard her plunk down in a chair. She started singing to herself. I let myself out. I went back to the small hotel where I was staying in a room on the second floor. There were giant roses on the wallpaper. I took my red lipstick and

I wrote MURDERERS across the roses. Then I checked out, walked up the street — it was almost empty because it was dinnertime, and the windows of the houses were lit yellow, and the whole town smelled of my childhood, boiled potatoes and fried onions. A baby cried behind one window covered in lace curtains, and music seeped out of another. I closed my eyes to it all. I should never have returned. All the people who had refused the invitation had known what I knew now — that returning would only breathe life into something that was dead. It would be better if not just my childhood but the memories of it were erased, so that as far as anyone is concerned, I did not begin living until June 6, 1952, when I arrived in New York and saw my brother Michael again, who had become a stranger to me during the thirteen years we were apart. I was twenty-one years old, married to Julius and pregnant. We arrived on an airplane if you can believe it. We flew through the air.

Everyone is clapping. I assume the ceremony is now over. I cannot hear very well anymore, but I hate the hearing aids David bought for me. They make all the wrong things loud, so when someone clears their throat, it is like a clap of thunder in my ear, and yet I still cannot hear the conversation going on across the table. People are standing. At some point, the pimple-necked boy in front of me got up and ran away, and his mother ran after him. People can be so emotional over nothing. Annette told me that Elizabeth was marrying a non-Jewish boy as if it were some terrible crime and I had to forgive her. She was actually crying. My father would not have allowed me to marry a German because German boys wanted to kill us. And we were the chosen people, keeping the 613 commandments so God would protect the Earth, though we learned the hard way that this didn't necessarily include the Jews on the Earth. This boy is American, whatever that means. What does anyone in America have to cry about? Maybe the pimply boy was in love with the bride, but there are, of course, lots of other girls out there, even for a *mieskeit* like him, and what has history taught us if not that human beings come and go as quickly as mosquitoes. There was a girl I saw earlier with a birthmark, a purple face; a girl in Hesse had one too, but they married her off to a farmer. The two of them could make a go of it maybe. The sooner you learn how to replace one person in your heart with another, the better you will survive. Julius would disagree. He would say you make room for another, but the ones you have loved never leave. I said, Isn't there a disease where the heart gets so big it doesn't work anymore? Yes, Julius said, cardiomyopathy; it leads to heart failure, but human beings are so much more than the workings of the body. There is a soul, Rachel.

I said, What good is a soul? Can you touch it? Does it keep you warm at night? Tell you stories? Protect you?

It makes us who we are, Rachel. Good and bad.

The world is too crowded with souls. I look at the father of the pimpled boy. He has a thick neck with dark stubble on it, numerous scratches, as if he is angry when he shaves, uses the razor like a scythe across his skin. He grimaces at nothing, glances at me and out across the sea of strangers. I stand up, intending to follow everyone to the tents. That is where they are going, even the angry man heads in that direction, but instead I see the woods, the disappointing American woods. It seems quiet over there, and I want to gather my thoughts for a minute. I am, of course, regretting coming to this meaningless event, but then Annette was right, what else did I have to do? Sit in the airy, overly lit dining room of Zombie Tower unable to hear Agnes and Anna's conversation about the children and grandchildren they never see, listening to the clomp and shuffle of walkers that are as regular as the ticking of a clock, clomping and shuffling us closer to our last day, to the death that I, at least, have been expecting to arrive at any moment since 1938. The only thing that has kept it from arriving, I understand now, is my expectation of it. Death likes to make a grand entrance; nothing would disappoint it more than for me to open the door before it has rung the bell and quietly fall into step with wherever it is going.

These are thin and pitiful woods. I can see other houses through the spindly trees, but at least there is some familiarity in the scent of decaying leaves and animal fur. How ridiculous. I am crying. Eva never had a wedding. She was in love with a boy named Elias Auerbach, who I realized many years later must have kissed her in the woods while I looked for mushrooms, and the sound that I took for screams was really laughter, and the silences were their lips touched together. Elias was murdered. Eva was murdered. My mother was murdered. My father. Levi, right before my eyes. He crumpled to the ground, and all those around him scooted away while his dirty clothes soaked up the warm blood that spilled from his body. I am so tired. I cannot move another inch, in this world, in this life. I take off my shoes and sit down, then I lie down and look up at the white clouds drifting across the hot blue sky. The angry man was right about how hot it is, and these thin woods do nothing to shelter us from the heat. I am ready to die now. I would be happy if I never got up, but as I have said, death will not do me the favor of coming when I expect him, so I will have to go look for him. I step into the woods and start walking.

A slice of leftover cake (with raspberry filling)

WELL, THAT'S DONE. Thirty thousand dollars, done. A large chunk of my husband's yearly earnings, done. Check to band, done. Ten thousand to caterers, done. Five thousand for flowers, done. I don't know how much for wine and champagne and cocktails, for the valet service, invitations, hairdresser, for the bags of Jordan almonds and the colored lanterns Elizabeth wanted and the wedding dress, done. The service is over, but there will be more bills to pay. The photographer, maybe we went over on the catering, Elizabeth asked the band to play an extra set. We will be paying for these four hours for a few more months, I am sure.

The stiff white wedding dress, a magnificent chrysalis, hangs from my bedroom door. Elizabeth wanted to change before she left for the hotel. For the last time in my life, I undid the buttons down her back, slid my hands over her hips, felt her balance on my shoulder while she lifted one leg, then the other, and stepped free. Twenty-five years ago, I would have reached for a pair of soft pajamas and slipped them on in place of the dress she had just abandoned, but she left the dress, a ball gown with a frothy skirt, on the floor (three thousand dollars) and put herself into a pair of blue jeans and a

T-shirt, then reached behind her head to pull her long hair into a loose ponytail. It's ridiculous to think that she won't need me anymore. A mother's work is never done, but the part that ropes you in, the part where you enthusiastically surrender your worldly ambitions, the part where you give your love, body and soul, to ensuring the joy and existence of another human being, that part is done. The lifting from the bath and cradling, the smell of her damp hair, the knowing every fold of her body more intimately than you know your own, the ear tuned to the slightest cry, the anticipation of her needs and the ability to fulfill those needs because they are simple, food, love, protection, that is gone. The sweet breath is gone, the velvety warmth of her skin, the poochy belly, the explosion of her smile, the rushing to you in the morning, and the clinging to your leg, gone.

Was it perfect? No. Steven Shapiro left in the middle of the ceremony — and not quietly. He knocked over all the chairs in his row, and he made his mother cry. Eddie's little boy stuck a finger in the cake before it was cut and messed up the whole bottom layer of icing. Would it have killed Carla Lefkowitz to wear a little makeup and smile a little more for the photographer? Ida should have made sure Albert was in the shade instead of, as usual, insisting on being in the front row and grandmother-of-the-briding all over the place. Josh had to rescue his father right after the kiss before he had heatstroke. I have honestly never seen a face that red. I would have preferred it if Jack Chandler had danced a little less with Debbie Shapiro. The thirty-two-year age difference had people talking, not that Jack cares. But that's Jack, who claims to be Elizabeth's godfather even though I have told him that Jews don't do the godfather thing. If he wants to think he's her godfather, let him think it; what harm can it do? Then again, what good? If I needed a godfather for my children, I wouldn't choose Jack Chandler, who probably still can't balance a checkbook and who still owes me a pair of diamond earrings. I know it was he, not Eulah, who took them. While showing off his disco moves, Brad Perry threw his wife into Bunny Walton, the wife of Josh's senior partner, and made her spill red wine on her St. John dress.

But those are the bad things. The food was good, I am told, not that I had time to eat anything. I watched Josh and Elizabeth in their father-daughter dance, Josh so stiff and Elizabeth so perfect after years of ballet lessons; there was not a dry eye in the house when he bent to kiss her cheek. She has chosen a good man. Hank loves her, I think, and his family seems sane and stable and kind. Although what does anyone really know of someone else's family? Still, happy families must exist. It's just that no one gossips about them. What is there to say?

I would have preferred a Jew. Marriage is hard enough without having to debate whether or not the Messiah has come. But the days of disowning your child for marrying outside of the faith are gone. Did the Jews really marry one another to keep the chosen people pure, because the God of Moses said the world would crash down if we didn't obey all those commandments, or was it because the goyim wouldn't have us? It's always best not to want the things you can't have. That's a talent my youngest daughter seems to have perfected. Anyway, we cooked the calf in its mother's milk, and by that, I mean we had a buttercream cake and beef tenderloin, and look: the tent is still standing. The milk of the cow with its baby. When you think about it, it is cruel. In the small villages that rule emerged from, you can see the peasants guiltily wiping the blood from their plates under the giant-eyed gaze of their life-sustaining cow. Now that cow is far away, and the meat is packaged in plastic and Styrofoam. There is no blood on my hands, no blood on the hands of the caterer who prepared the meal. Everything gets diluted, the milk, the meat, the religion, and the relatives; everything spread into a thin film, almost invisible and powerless.

Out my window, I can see the caterers cleaning. They are gathering glasses still half full of champagne, plates smeared with icing, untouched slices of cake, vases tipped over, flowers crushed into the dirt. I sent people home with centerpieces, with lanterns, with extra dessert, with open bottles of wine that could not be returned; and still there is a colossal waste out there, the extra money to have white linens around the chairs, the stained tablecloths, the silverware that has landed in odd places, behind a bush, the front seat of Josh's car, the bathroom. They are folding it up and taking it all away. The tent will stay standing until tomorrow, but the band has packed up their microphones, and the colored lights are gone. If — when — Ben gets married, tradition states this job will fall to someone else. Who knows if Katie will get married. In older societies, this marriage would not have been allowed. The youngest would have had to wait for her older siblings to make their choices. Maybe we could have convinced Hank to take Katie too, like Leah and Rachel. Poor Leah, poor Katie, cursed with a prettier, more graceful, and desired younger sister. Katie left before the party ended to go see some kind of concert downtown. I gave her permission. When Josh asked where she was,

I told him that she had gone to join friends, and I watched him decide whether to be annoyed, but I stopped him. "She put on the dress and walked down the aisle," I said. "It was enough. Be happy she has friends."

I know these three creatures better than I know anyone else in the world, certainly better than I know their father. That is not to say that I know everything about them. I'm thankful that I don't know exactly what Elizabeth and Hank are doing right now in the hotel that her father and I paid for since the flight to Italy leaves in the morning. The things that only grown-ups do, sex and cheating on taxes, these might remain dark to me, but I know the fundamentals of who they are, those you know in the first five years of life. That Ben was a dreamer, but one who preferred to hitch his star to the dreams of others, I knew that early on. He is a follower, but at least the ones he chooses to follow have lofty aspirations. There is nothing wrong with being an assistant. We all know the names of Gandhi, Martin Luther King, Abraham Lincoln, but someone read their speeches and offered comments; someone booked their train tickets. As a mother, I am not sad that he has chosen to stand next to greatness, not pursue it. That person is not the one who receives the bullet.

I also knew that happiness would not be easy for Katie. She was hard to comfort. When I held her close to me, she wanted to look out; when I faced her away, she clawed back to me. She was either born too early or too late. This is not the right age for her, and her spot in the world will be difficult to find. She will have to scrape and drag it into place, but lately she has stopped complaining and started seeking. She reproaches Josh and me. We should not have sent her to

Mansfield High, a place of terrible conformity. We should not have given her piano and dance lessons. We should have seen that her fingers slapped the keys and her legs were too strong for an arabesque. She has taken to climbing mountains. She thinks it is our fault we did not know to make her a bed outside under the stars, but I did know. I knew she went to the creek with Emerson, the Labrador retriever we bought for her. For *her*, when she was nine years old. Ben was busy with the drums, and Elizabeth is not an animal lover, but Katie, Josh and I both knew, needed a dog. She is the one who loves the most, will be hurt the most, will care for us in our old age. Ben will drift away, as boys do. Elizabeth will write checks, bake banana bread, drive us places, but the dirty work, which I hate to think about but know will come, the doctors' visits, the loss of teeth, the failing eyesight, the bruised skin, and worse indignities, the management of that will fall to Katie, who will do it dutifully if not cheerfully.

As for Elizabeth, she was an easy baby, a beauty from the minute she entered the world, the last one and the only caesarean section. Josh and I have said she chose the C-section because she didn't want to mess up her hair. All my children were pretty, but Elizabeth was exceptional. She had big unblinking brown eyes, as sweet and gentle as a calf, and a face that seemed wise but was really just placid, accepting. Wherever I went, the synagogue, the grocery store, Ben and Katie's preschool, people stopped to admire her. She gazed up at them with a serene smile, and no matter who held her — my mother, a complete stranger, the nurse at the doctor's office — they all said, "Oh, she likes me." That was Elizabeth's gift; she didn't have to nurture it. She was born with it, and I think it will probably take her further than genius or strength or courage, that ability to make someone feel loved and lucky, admired and safe.

My friend Rita once said that your children come to you perfect, and the best you can hope for is not to allow too much damage, from yourself first and foremost, and then from the world. I am not a powerful person; other than my children, I have almost no influence anywhere; but over them — when they were small, not anymore — I had a terrifying dominion. The harsh words I spoke, impatience, preferring one to the other, and the slightest inattention wounded them in ways that can take a lifetime to heal. All parents started as children, and it takes a combination of arrogance and amnesia to join this endless march of generations, to create offspring who will be totally and utterly dependent on us, on what kindness we can muster, on fleeting scraps of knowledge that have to pass for wisdom. All of us carry the imperfectly healed wounds of our childhood injuries; why then would we choose to try to care for others when we ourselves are still so in need of caring? Why is it that I can conjure up moments of regret so vividly that even twenty years later my stomach turns and I speak the dreaded words out loud or carry on a monologue of undoing, but I can't recall joy through anything but a thick haze? Ben broke a Waterford Crystal vase at Bunny Walton's house, and I pulled him into the backyard and called him an idiot. His face shriveled like burning tissue paper, and tears spurted from the corners of his eyes. Bunny Walton was an idiot for leaving a crystal vase on the coffee table when children were invited over, but I was so stupidly scared of her, of her husband, of her beautiful house with white furniture,

223

and of her two sons who were aiming for golf scholarships that I took my shame out on my own child. That moment comes to me at odd times. It wakes me at night or rains down on me from the showerhead, gets served to me in a plastic cup on an airplane flight, my son's disappearing face, Bunny trying to piece the glass back together instead of waving the whole thing off, the sudden realization of what I had done and the suffocating hug I gave Ben immediately after as if I could squeeze the memory out of him. My mother did the same thing to me, different house, different broken objet d'art (mud, Oriental rug, the Porters' living room, the sharp knife of the sun through a sliding glass door, and my piercing realization that I could lose my mother's love). The difference is: my mother never gave it a second thought. Her job was to provide food and shelter, teach manners and respect, give me a little encouragement on the way toward the right husband and a replication of her own life but with a little more luxury, a little more insulation from disaster. My safety was important to her; my happiness, not a big consideration, and if happiness was something I desired, like a beach house or a fur coat, it was my responsibility to obtain it.

From her perspective, I did well. I married a Jewish lawyer, and my education degree was the MRS degree she expected it to be. She herself never went to college, but you didn't need college to help in the shoe store, and my father prospered, expanding to eight stores in small towns across Alabama. He moved us to Birmingham, the big city compared to Adamsville, the town of a thousand residents where they were the only Jews, the town he dragged my mother to, away from New York and her family. She grew up poor, but being from

New York, she always considered herself more sophisticated, more cultured, more knowledgeable than the Alabamans, even in Birmingham where there were old families of German Jews whose children attended the Ivy Leagues and ran banks and became neurosurgeons. She insisted on taking me to New York to buy my clothes at Bonwit Teller and Gimbels — failing that, to Atlanta where Rich's and Davison's at least had the good sense to copy the inventory of the New York stores. She said we had to set the tone for fashion in poor backward Birmingham, and before shoes became the craze they are now, before Imelda Marcos and Manolo Blahnik, she had a closet full of pumps and sparkling sandals, arranged on the floor under the matching dress by color from white to black with brown, beige, baby blue, pink, red, navy, and even lilac in between.

I do not think my parents loved each other, though I never heard them fight. My oldest sister, Jeanine, told me that my father stayed in France for a full year after World War II ended, and when he came home, he was different. She was seven when he left, and she remembered a man who liked to carry her on his shoulders, who took her out on the lake and rowed the boat with strong arms and practically caught the trout bare-handed. Jeanine told us that in the Adamsville store she was a princess and was allowed to clomp around in any pair of shoes she chose, with the salesmen calling her Miss Jeanine and joking with our father about fish stories and baseball games. He got richer after the war, in money, in children, but with each new possession came a loss of hope, of joy, of friendship, like some fairy-tale bargain struck in which the greedy man always gets the raw deal. It was a well-known family secret that he had had a lover in France, that he would have abandoned his family if my uncle Marvin, my mother's oldest brother, rumored to have ties to the petty Jewish mafia — not Meyer Lansky but Lansky's seventh cousin twice removed — didn't finally go over to France and make him come home. From that entrapment grew a successful business. I guess my father figured he had nothing else to do. He stayed late at the store. He never hired an accountant, did the books and inventory himself. If one pair of Mary Janes went missing, he knew about it. Eventually, he had two kinds of stores in Birmingham, your basic family store and a fancy one for women only, which was next to his friend Henry Cohen's furriery. He and Henry would fly to France to look at shoes and the latest fashions, and do who knows what else. Only as an adult did it occur to me that he could be seeing a lover or maybe something worse, prostitutes. My mother didn't seem to care. Those were the weeks she took us to the city, and we stayed at the Plaza and visited her sisters and spent my father's money.

They're both gone now, now that I have so many questions for them. Did they have other dreams beyond the big house with two maids and the five well-married daughters or was providing for the next generation all they ever allowed themselves to hope for? Who were their parents and grandparents? The past moves away from us, a small boat on a swift river, and my children will forget their grandparents, and their children will not even know them, and my grandparents and great-grandparents might as well never have existed, at least as far as concerns this world where a wedding just took place and an empty tent is standing, devoid of chairs and tables, lights and guests, one loose panel flapping in the soft wind, sheltering only a few flower petals and an empty wine bottle.

My life is supposed to start now. As the old joke goes, the kids have moved away and the dog is dead. Nothing really changes for Josh. He goes to the office, golfs on weekends; the small hours he would have spent engaged with the children can be turned over to other things, mystery novels, bike riding, documentaries on PBS. For me, my life's work is over. What did the pharaoh do when the pyramids were done? Build a new temple? Women's lives are ruled by biology. I will not start on another round of children now. I suppose that biology makes sense; we can't keep having children when we may not be around to care for them. If the pharaoh didn't finish his temple, the next pharaoh could take over, finish the job, and carve his name into the stone. Temples are infinitely more fungible than children; kings will gladly take possession of someone else's castle but not his offspring. I look around to see what my other friends are doing — throwing themselves into tennis and golf, shopping, volunteering at the synagogue and the hospital, shopping. These things don't interest me, but I don't think I'm smart or passionate enough to do anything deeper with my time. Growing up, I liked to write poetry, but I was an education major in college and thought I would be a teacher at least for a few years before marriage and children.

I never had a career. I got pregnant quickly with Ben, and though now I think that I could have worked, back then everyone with children stayed home. We had help, Eulah when we lived in the old house and then Betty when we moved to this one, but none of us had jobs. And yet we were so busy!

We woke, and we dressed the children and walked them to the bus stop. We put away the milk, shook the crumbs from the toaster, sat down and drank coffee, read the newspaper. Betty came and did the laundry, washed and folded, swept and tidied; but I did the grocery shopping, walked the dog, maybe played tennis or went to the hairdresser. Before you knew it, school was out. We waited at the bus stop and walked home with the children, started dinner while they worked on homework. Betty set the table. When they were too small to be left alone, the children piled into my station wagon, and we drove Betty to the bus stop, then I bathed them. Josh came home. We ate dinner. They went to bed. Josh and I might have watched television or read for a while. That was the day. Looking back on it, I feel so spoiled and lazy. How many more things I could have done in those hours — learned French, studied for another degree, grown my own vegetables, even started teaching when the children were in school. Those hours are gone. I am not going to mourn them; they felt full at the time, and even if I look back now and see all the gaps and holes, what does that matter? I must look forward.

I am only fifty-seven years old. I know I am invisible to everyone under thirty. Everyone says ma'am to me now, not just the polite southern-bred valet at the club but the tall coltish girls with foreign accents who seat us at the fancy restaurants we venture to for anniversaries and to celebrate promotions of Josh's junior partners. There are sundresses that I will never wear, mountains I will never climb. I am not going to sit at a bar and be picked up by a stranger or dance until dawn, arms in the air and laughing the way Elizabeth's friends did at the wedding, kicking off their shoes, no partners needed, dancing for sheer joy. We missed that, my generation, married before Woodstock, and if we got divorced, as many of us did in the seventies, we looked ridiculous trying to disco dance and snort cocaine when we had been young at a time of A-line skirts and sock hops, gin and tonics, and strict curfews. In New York there were young men and women listening to jazz music and destroying themselves with drugs, but that didn't reach Alabama for ten years — my mother was right, it took ten years for styles to find their way south, at least in those days when flying on an airplane was still a privilege — among my friends, I was one of the only ones who had ever had such an adventure. We had to marry to have sex, and although we never talked about sex when we were younger and wanted it so badly, some years later my roommates and I, tipsy at our twentieth college reunion, admitted our wonder that anyone got married anymore now that premarital sex was no longer forbidden. It didn't seem like a good idea to us then, at least not for women. We still subscribed to the old why-buy-the-cow-if-the-milk-is-free theory — and yet, here I am, significantly poorer after my daughter has donned a white dress — white dresses still de rigueur though virginity less so — and promised herself to one man for eternity, and he to her. Maybe love is purer now that sexual gratification is only one part of it. Or maybe no one really knows what love is; we think we have it, then it's gone, and then it's back again. It's shy and slippery, and doesn't like to stay in one place very long and doesn't hold up well under a direct gaze.

Other than doctors, Josh is the only man who has ever seen me naked as an adult. When I was young and lithe, with what I see now in photos were beautiful breasts, a narrow waist, a desirable neck, I was scared of wanting men. I had a boyfriend in high school, Jacob Steinberg, the name sounds like an old man now, but Jake was tall, and he would have had wonderful curly hair but he cut it short, the crew cuts of 1959. He had the slight hint of a mustache, but his cheeks were still soft and untouched by a razor. His arms were strong for the reasons a boy's arms should be strong, throwing balls and raking leaves and pushing a lawn mower, daily life, not weight lifting or personal training. There were no gyms, only gymnasiums where basketball games were played, cheerleaders cheered, and girls tumbled in acrobatics. Jake and I kissed and kissed. We made out in his car, in the woods behind school, in the storeroom of the drugstore his father owned. We touched each other through our clothes. Any further and I pushed his hand away because I thought he wouldn't respect me. We were taught that boys, even boys who insisted they loved us, would change when they won the battle and got from us the secrets of our body. I pictured a Roman soldier, his golden cape over his shoulders, surveying in disgust the ruined landscape of a battle, his pathetic vanquished foes. I had been taught that sex would hurt; that it was a responsibility of a married woman; that although a girl could love being kissed, that although kissing could bring up a whole confusion of feelings, it was a trick of nature; and beyond kissing, the contact of human bodies brought nothing but shame and pain for women. By the time I realized my mistake, I was married and had sworn off all other intimacies.

My children would die to hear me say that their father is a kind and gentle lover. Our wedding night, he undressed me as carefully as I undressed our newborn babies, undid the buttons one by one, slowly eased my dress off my shoulders. He folded it over a chair before he turned back to look at me. He told me I was beautiful. He still tells me I am beautiful. When I become flustered over flat tires or tangled jewelry, he always says, "It's okay, beautiful. It can be fixed."

I think it is true that tyrants give birth to poets. At least it has held so far in Josh's case. When we first started dating, Helen Berman told me that Josh was a catch. So many of the Jewish girls in Atlanta wanted him. Handsome, smart, kind, and rich. His father had built an empire, and he was sure to inherit it. But, she warned me, his father was a horror. Albert Gottlieb ruled over the synagogue in his front-row seats bought with annual donations that were double any of his rivals except for the Schiffs and the Riches, and they brought their money with them from New York. Josh's father started with nothing. He was a man devoid of pity. He famously was once asked to donate to Holocaust refugees, and he refused, saying, "I only give to people who bear no responsibility for their misfortunes." Albert Gottlieb's father had died of colon cancer, so he gave money to the cancer society. That and the synagogue, and he grumbled about the synagogue and called the rabbi a shyster to his face. I used to fear that one day my kind husband would become his father, but despite frustrations with his career and a brother always begging for money and worries about the kids, he has remained calm and affectionate, and I have never doubted his love for me or the children. He didn't blink an eye at the cost of this wedding, although I did find him late at night with the checkbooks out on his desk, copies of bank statements, and a calculator. When I massaged his shoulders, he touched my hand. I said, "We don't have to spend all this money."

He smiled. "Don't worry, beautiful," he said. "This is the reason I worked so hard and saved."

Josh is not the type to share his worries with me. He tells me about bad things once they have been resolved. A few years ago, a young man appeared at Josh's law firm and claimed to be Eddie's son from some unknown dalliance. It was ridiculous; Josh shook his head as he told me. He got copies of the boy's birth certificate, and the problem went away. He has helped his ne'er-do-well brother through two divorces. His father's stroke destroyed the family business, but Josh has handled untangling the finances, paying the creditors. People think we inherited a fortune, but although my father-in-law built a very profitable business and lived like a rich man, Josh now tells me that once his father's care is paid for and his mother's uncompromising needs are met (my mother-in-law will not give up the weekly hairdresser, lunches at the Neiman Marcus café, trips to Canyon Ranch, lessons with the tennis pro at the country club) there won't be much of an inheritance, and what there is will need to go to Eddie, since he's as poor as a church mouse, and now he has a child to provide for. But never mind, Josh says, he has worked hard and saved, and we have no need of handouts. His brother has no such compunctions.

The whole wedding went by so fast, I barely ate and didn't even get to taste the wedding cake. It is wrapped up now, the top layer in the freezer for a year, and all the rest, at least what I couldn't convince people to take home with them, is in my refrigerator. I am going to get a piece to share with my husband at last.

The kitchen is spotless. I must remember to thank Rita for suggesting an extra cleaning crew for the house. I open the refrigerator and find slices of cake already cut and sealed in Saran Wrap. I find a smallish one, pour a glass of milk, and put it on a tray. Josh still likes to drink a glass of milk before bed, one of the more endearing things about him. In the den, Josh is in his tuxedo pants, but the shirt and tie are gone, and he is wearing a Carolina sweatshirt. His face glows in the reflection of the television. "Are they winning?" I ask. I don't know who "they" are in this case. For me, it's just another sporting event, the modern-day battle of titans that draws men of all ages, with their loose and useless testosterone, not really so vital in the modern-day world where there are no chariots and the clash of armies is far away on unseen soil.

"Yes, but they don't deserve to."

I set the tray down on the coffee table. Josh clicks the TV to mute.

"It was a perfect wedding," he tells me. "Except for the fact that the mother of the bride looked so gorgeous that she almost upstaged the bride."

I roll my eyes. "No one upstages Elizabeth."

"Not if she can help it." He takes a bite of cake, says *mmmm.* "Are there raspberries in this?"

"The filling."

"So good." I lean my head on his shoulder and he kisses my hair. "You must be exhausted."

"I am hollowed out," I say.

233

"Let me draw you a bath."

When he is grateful to me, Josh fills the bathtub that serves only me. He lights a candle, draws up a chair, and sits next to me while I soak.

"Did you see Theresa and Brad Perry dancing?" he asks.

"Unfortunately," I say. I close my eyes.

"They looked like John Travolta and what's-her-name, disco dancing, dipping; and then Brad threw Theresa into Bunny Walton. You'd think Bunny had been set on fire. She actually shrieked."

"Bunny Walton," I murmur. "She'll tell everyone the wedding was awful."

"Let her," he says. "She's probably going to go to bed dreaming of being thrown around the dance floor by Brad Perry." He turns the hot water on to keep the bath warm. "Did I tell you I have a new client? La Maison bakery. Apparently, a woman wants to sue them for making her fat. She claims that if bartenders can be sued for serving alcohol to drunk people bakeries should be liable for selling eclairs to the obese."

"Oh, good Lord," I say.

He rubs my shoulders and soaps my back, washes me with a washcloth.

"Did we spend too much money tonight?" I ask him.

"No," he says. "And it was worth every penny. Elizabeth was so happy. She'll never forget this day. Sometimes you just have to spend some money to gather everyone together, let the photographer take all the pictures, let fathers dance with daughters and mothers with sons. Let little girls wear flowers in their hair. It's worth it. It almost stops time."

I squint up at him trying not to get water in my eyes. "What a beautiful thing to say."

He dries me when I rise from the tub, and though we have known each other's bodies for thirty-six years now, he still likes to look at mine, and I still go soft when I feel his hands on my back, his hardness, when he lifts me, still strong enough to do that, and tells me I am as small as the day we married (a lie) and carries me to the bed.

After we make love, Josh falls asleep, but I am awake. He is snoring softly. There is a half-eaten slice of cake on our bedside table, and I need to get it before it brings in ants. The icing on the cake is running, and the raspberry part looks a little scary, like bright-red blood, so fresh it had to come from a baby. I scrape it into the sink and turn on the disposal. Why do I always feel sad when I throw food away? I wash the plate by hand since the dishwasher is full, dry it, put it in the cupboard.

It would have been nice to have a few other lovers. There must be a million ways for a man to touch a woman. I know that Elizabeth has had at least three lovers, and Ben lost his virginity at sixteen to Laura Lampkin in the comfort of his own bedroom on his narrow twin bed with the baseball-themed comforter. I know this because in their passion they knocked over and broke the lamp with the ceramic baseball player at the base and I heard the noise and found the door locked, heard the sounds inside. When I told my husband about it, he neither smiled nor frowned. He bought Ben a pack of condoms and warned him not to get anyone pregnant.

The teacher in me must share this observation. The calculations of men and women never add up. Even now. Women may have had five, ten lovers; men always claim ten times that amount, and if we are supposed to match one to one, someone has to be lying. Or a handful of women are very busy.

I have been married to my husband for thirty-six years, all of them faithful, and I think faithful for him too, and if this is not so, I don't want to know. The urgency of total honesty fades in the first decade, I think. There are secrets I have kept from my husband and will take to the grave. Little things, like I hate the mole on his left buttock and that Bill Ferguson, the founding partner at his law firm, got drunk at an office Christmas party and put his arm around me, told me Josh was up for partnership but that no one made partner at the firm without his blessing. Then he went in for a kiss. This was not an uncommon event. Of course, we knew people who had affairs, midlife crises, got divorces, bought convertibles, but Josh and I felt sorry for them. We were happy together. I found Bill Ferguson repulsive. I tried to forget the vulgar things he said. I didn't care if Josh got rich. That was never our aspiration. To raise happy children and love each other and be kind to the people in our orbit, not to damage too much of the world, those were our goals. I don't need to spend time at the club with the likes of Chip and Bunny Walton. In fact, I am grateful that we do not spend time at the club with those people. I have never told Josh what Bill Ferguson did. He only knows that I hated Bill Ferguson and was not sad when he died relatively young at fifty-seven — the same age I am now — of liver cancer. Josh would shake his head at Bill's suffering, at his wasted frame, and at the orange-yellow tint that seeped over him into his eyeballs. "'Poor Bill,' he said. 'Dying so young.'" Terminally kind, my husband.

When I said, "He did it to himself," Josh would look at me as if I were stating a fact he wished wasn't true.

When Katie's dog died, he told her, "They don't make a dog that lives as long as we do, sweetheart." He sounded as if he had researched it extensively before coming to this conclusion. After my mother died, Katie asked if she was in heaven. When Josh answered that of course she was, she said, "What's it like in heaven?"

"I don't know," he said truthfully. "I've never been there." Then he told her about the Eiffel Tower and Windsor Castle, places he has been, until she fell asleep, confusing croissants, princesses, and the clouds of heaven into a jumbled mess of perfection.

"Maybe true," he said of Bill Ferguson. "But no one deserves such an ugly death." Here's another secret I have kept from him. I have an angry streak, and I was happy to see Bill Ferguson suffer.

Outside of my marriage, the only kiss that ever meant something to me was that night in our first house when Jack Chandler showed up high on something, skinny and eyes glittering with fear and mystery, clutching his sweat-soaked draft notice. My sweet and devoted husband offered a dozen ways to get him out of it. Josh would have married him if it would have kept Jack out of Vietnam. Neither of us believed in that ridiculous war, though we kept that opinion hidden from the red-blooded Republicans of Josh's law firm and, for that matter, 99 percent of white Atlanta. I don't think Jack really wanted our help; he just wanted to hear us try, the same way my kids would cry when they fell down, not because they were hurt but because it was so reassuring to have me swoop down over them, pick them up, and hold them close. Jack sat at our dining-room table and wolfed down the spaghetti I had made as if it were his last meal. That was something Jack would do—everything with him had the urgency of a last-time-in-life event, even this wedding when he presented that breathtaking painting to my daughter as if she were the Christ child and all the kings would come on bended knee bearing their best gifts instead of blenders and Wedgwood place settings. I am sure Jack has forgotten all about that night. At the wedding, he kissed my cheek with dry lips, and I saw him watching Elizabeth's friends dancing. He has never burdened himself with the stability of middle-class life, no mortgage, no children, and I suppose in some way this allows him to never grow up, to dance with young girls, to bed his students, to lie on the hood of his car and stare up at the stars even as he approaches sixty-one. While everyone else wonders if they have saved enough for retirement, Jack Chandler is still dreaming about falling in love and getting famous, dreams that expired for the rest of us by age thirty.

The memory of that kiss, late at night while my husband slept, his audacity, my audacity, my nakedness in a white cotton nightgown, a double dose of hormones with a child growing inside me. If Jack had pushed, I would have lain down beside him. I would have pulled the nightgown over my head and offered myself up to him under the cold November moon. He loved Josh more than he loved me. I pushed his hand away, and he let me. He stepped back, and we came to our senses. The picture he had drawn of me, the only time I have ever looked at an image of myself and seen someone beautiful, he tore it up. My whole body was burning. The feel of his tongue against mine in that moment was as intimate as if we had made love. He *had* been inside me. I am sure he has forgotten about it. Jack, no doubt, has had a thousand urgent kisses; I, only the one. I love my husband, but our lives, so scripted, so correctly lived, the biggest horror a speeding ticket and a fine, have never mustered the passion of that kiss. Warmth, tenderness, devotion, sacrifice. I would do anything for Josh. If he needs me to, I would give him a kidney. I will spoon-feed him in old age; I want to die when he dies, holding hands in our hospital beds in the nursing home, but that kiss with Jack, that was the passion the Indian women feel when their beloved dies, that was a bury-me-alive, set-me-on-fire moment, the only one in my life.

What does my husband dream about while I drink this chamomile tea and watch the darkening sky over the detritus of all our accomplishments, this lovely house, that married daughter? Someone trampled the flower bed; there are daffodils with broken necks, bruised tulips. One of the bridesmaids tossed her bouquet up on the roof of the garage. I have carefully gone through the wedding site as if it were a crime scene looking for stray envelopes and gifts, earrings trampled into the lawn, a forgotten pocketbook. The panicked calls will come — did you by any chance find a wallet? A ring? A soul? A dream? A reason to live? I can hear the television. Josh must have left it on. Jack Chandler's painting is propped up against a wall in our living room, too big for Elizabeth and Hank's small apartment, and too much for this house that I have decorated in shades of blue and gray.

In the den, I find the remote and turn off the TV. There is an empty glass etched white with milk sitting on the side table. My husband drinks milk before bed, he wears pajamas, he checks with me before he sets the alarm so I know when to expect that clanging call of another day. I don't have to get up anymore. The children are gone, and he knows that I could fall back onto the pillow and sleep until noon, not rise with him and brush my teeth, get dressed, start the day. In truth, the world does not care about the order we have imposed on it. It gives us light and dark; we are the ones who feel the need to chop the hours up into little pieces. Maybe it's just a habit for the two of us; we drink coffee together, and I rinse the dishes and put them away before he leaves. Monday through Friday, we walk out of the house together, Josh in a tie and I in a tracksuit, though I don't run. I walk three houses down and pick up Esther Tobin; then we go around the block and down to the river, greeting the other ladies like me who are trying hard to keep their figures.

Elizabeth's generation will be different. Isn't this what all those girls burned their bras for? A purpose beyond the care and comfort of husbands and children. They will give things up for this. We, born before 1950, the last generation of women to be bound to home and hearth, know that, even with help, a home empty of its occupants saddens, springs leaks that left unattended for minutes or hours grow from trickles to rivers, same for the sprouting cobwebs and the thin layer of dust; unattended, the cobwebs turn to rope, the dust to an unbreakable shell. We were there all day, beating back this entropy, stacking the papers of math problems and vocabulary into neat piles, collecting the half-empty glasses before the skin of the milk could harden, before the water marks formed on the table. We were there for the children, for the whimpers, the first words, the steps and the falls, for the husbands, for the double bogeys and the missed promotions and the poorly packed suitcases left on the bed after business trips. We didn't imagine that these things needed doing; they needed doing, and left unwatched, the garden will change; tamed things will become wild again. For husbands, maybe this is not a bad thing, but for the children, I wonder. It isn't just the milestones, the first words and steps, the first day of kindergarten, the birthdays, the holidays, it's the sound of a small throat swallowing, the sweat on the neck after an afternoon nap, the discarded blanket picked up and folded, these are the things that make a life, that add up to love and complete a child.

Every generation has a rule or two that it thinks it will break and change the world. Showing ankles, smoking cigarettes, baring arms, wearing pants, getting divorced. Then we realize the rules had advantages, and breaking them didn't change the world the way we thought it would. Now that there are veins on my legs and my stomach will never be flat again, I think it would be nice to cover myself in layers and wear a dress that sweeps the floor. More than a few of our friends from college had affairs, got divorced. The happy ones remarried, usually to someone just like the person they'd left, for the men, maybe a few years younger. Elizabeth has married a boy from another world, raised Episcopalian though apparently his mother's mother is Jewish, a fact that came out after they announced their engagement. The grandmother willingly shed her Judaism for the safety of the last name of Burke — not Berkowitz — and children who could claim descent from English farmers and maybe a famous philosopher.

Christmas trees and Easter bunnies filled her house, she said, but at the ceremony, I saw her mouth moving through all the prayers. Elizabeth doesn't think it will matter that Hank's not Jewish. It's all the same God, she told me, as if the deaths of tens of millions of people throughout history isn't proof enough to her that kings and armies, false prophets and pharaohs, do not agree with her. She says they'll celebrate all the holidays, Rosh Hashanah and Yom Kippur, Good Friday and Easter, and when the kids are older, they can make a choice between jelly beans and matzo, she said, laughing. A choice between the prayers I said — that my mother said, my grandmother, her mother, going back five thousand years — and some candy. I wasn't going to argue with her. There's no arguing with Elizabeth. She'll find out later how difficult you can make your life. Or how you can keep it simple.

When my mother died, Jeanine and I, the oldest and the youngest, cleaned out her house, and I found a notebook of poems I wrote. The ones about love were pretty awful, but there were a few that were not terrible. I also found several letters I had written to Jack Chandler when he was in Vietnam and after he came back. They weren't love letters. I had no intention of having an affair with him, and I never mentioned the kiss. I told myself that I was writing to him because he needed to receive letters. Josh said that Jack was estranged from his family: his mother was dead; he had had the world's shortest marriage, had no children. His brothers were farmers, and something he had done had angered them or vice versa. Either way, they did not speak. Jack had been living in New York, but after the war, there were many holidays, Thanksgiving and Christmas — which we do not celebrate

—when he would show up on our doorstep unannounced, hungry but exalted, as if he had been sentenced to exile on a deserted island and miraculously made his way back to us, crossing the vast ocean in a raft. By the time of the letters, I had Ben, then Katie, and there was no question of passion. When I became a mother, Jack looked at me differently. He admired me, honored me, but when he called me lovely, it was in the way someone calls the very young or the very old lovely, with no imagination of their naked body.

I don't know why I used my parents' home address rather than ours. There was nothing shameful in the letters. I just told him the details of my daily life. How Katie slept curled up, like a fuzzy insect, hand under her chin, lips pressed together. Ben turned four years old. We put a pointy hat on his head and he blew out four candles, and I wondered why no one questioned this ritual, blowing away the years, extinguishing the fire. It seemed all wrong. I watched my children sleep and felt in the stillness the movement of time, the stretching of their bones, the expansion of their hearts, the knitting together of thoughts that would one day form words and sentences and the memories that would define them. Sometimes I felt so sad, watching my babies rush forward through time to adolescence. Ben would grow a dark fuzz on his lip, his voice would change from a squeak to a growl, Katie would sprout breasts and hide her secret loves from me, my parents would die and be forgotten, the children would marry and move away, Josh and I would die one day and also be forgotten. While nothing happened, while they breathed in the quiet way that babies and young children breathe, with small sighs and twitches, everything happened. And then I apologized, because Jack was in a place where everything was happening, where people were dying and bombs were exploding, and here I was, obsessing over the fact that I was already putting away the newborn clothes and taking out the next size up and that the last three months were just a blur. That letter didn't get to Jack. It was returned to sender. Others got through, musings on the magnolia tree in the front yard, whose tender white leaves I crushed for their too-sweet smell; on an ice storm that coated the bare branches of the trees as if they had been outlined with a thick black pen; on a burned pot roast that looked like the remains of some extinct animal; on the protests in Washington and the women who invited me to lunch and didn't want to talk about the protests in Washington; and then on another pregnancy, turning my body over to the unending universe for the perpetuation of the species, the movement inside me, the creation.

I kept writing even after Jack got home from the war. I wrote to him in New York and San Francisco, New Hampshire and Indiana, college towns where he got teaching jobs, artists' colonies. As the children got bigger, I wrote things I would never say out loud. I confessed that I hated going to Ben's interminable baseball games even though he was the star pitcher. I found the adulation of a boy throwing a ball ridiculous. Externally, I was a perfect baseball mom. Pitchers of lemonade, homemade cookies, and PB&J sandwiches packed and wrapped in wax paper for away games. I cheered. I drove around town in my station wagon, sweaty boys laughing and farting in the backseat, kicking one another, coarse and stupid, and just when I was about to give up, just when the sky was darkening in the late afternoon and I was wondering how far I could get on a tank of gas and the loose change in my purse, a boy, my boy, in a mud-stained baseball uniform, would bow his head, concentrating, I am sure, on a spitball or a double play or what he wanted for dinner, but he would look in that moment like a supplicant bowing to the oracle, accepting his fate and the fate of all boys everywhere, to only get so far, to lose in the quarterfinals, to grow too old for playing games, and when he looked up with his pale face and dark eyes, I would want to run to him, and say, It's fine. It's fine. Whatever you need, I will give you. I have no needs or desires beyond your happiness. I would not say that, of course. I would pour lemonade into Styrofoam cups and give them to the boys waiting their turn to bat, pick up the dropped wax paper and cupcake wrappers, smooth them flat and throw them away, giving order to the universe. That's what I did. That's what I wrote to Jack Chandler.

I confessed to him that I loved Katie the most. First she lisped and couldn't pronounce her *r*'s. Thilly wabbit. Thee how she wuns. Then she started to stutter. Th-th-thee h-h-h-how she w-w-w-wuns. No one called her for playdates. The few kids that came over did so out of the kindness of their mothers, bribed with offers of ice cream and new toys. I bribed them myself — come with us to the zoo! Ice-skating! To McDonald's! We're the house with Little Debbies and ice cream sandwiches and homemade chocolate chip cookies. Katie wasn't fooled. When the kids came over, she sulked and then cried when they left. She sat in a corner at birthday parties. She didn't have any friends until high school, and then I knew she had cast her lot with the losers, the pot smokers and the nerds. She didn't get asked to dances; she spent prom night at *The Rocky Horror Picture Show* dressed in torn stockings and a purple wig. The more the world rejected her, the more I favored her. What could I do? Each child is entitled to an equal amount of love. Ben got his from us, from his teammates, from girls, an order that reversed itself in high school and has stayed reversed. Elizabeth from us, from strangers, from teachers, from other children, from boys, from men, and now I assume from her husband. So little love was given to Katie by the world that it was incumbent on me to make up for it.

Once she started kindergarten, Elizabeth was the belle of the ball. Her teacher told me that children fought to lay their nap mats next to hers. The teacher, Mrs. Mallory, had to assign seats at snack time or a melee broke out with children pushing to be at the same table as Elizabeth. I asked if she was cruel, but she was not. Children recognize beauty, the teacher said, and Elizabeth was an astonishingly beautiful child. Other mothers, I am sure, would bask in that reflected glory. Instead, I felt for the little girls who just wanted to be near her. They would have to fight for their place in the world, whereas Josh and I had miraculously made a child whose path was laid in stardust and jewels. I felt like the goose that lays a golden egg and stands up on her webbed feet, looks at her nest, and thinks, What in the world is that?

All of these thoughts I poured into letters to Jack Chandler, most of which apparently never reached him since I found them tied with string in a shoe box in my mother's pantry. Looking at the envelopes, I could track the many times he picked up and moved, the letters coming back stamped RE-TURN TO SENDER until a new address emerged. That would explain why Jack so seldom responded, and when he did, it was usually with a short "Thank you for your letter. It's awfully nice to receive mail." But then it really wasn't about Jack.

In retrospect, I was lonely. Josh was working long hours, trying to become a partner. He asked me about my day, but there was nothing specific to say about my day, so we talked about his, about the cases he was working on and his coworkers. His secretary was pregnant and due around the same time as I was due with Katie. He dreaded her leaving; he relied on her so much, but he knew she would leave and not come back. "That's what we do," I wrote to Jack. "When the children come, we leave whatever we are doing, and we do not go back."

Not this generation. They intend to have it all, careers, families, creativity, at least for the lucky few who can afford it. They intend to travel the world, children in tow, and write books, shoot off into space, leaving their tidy houses and the dog and the cat behind, return and find it all just so, the dog well fed, the grass trimmed, the cat purring, the windows clean and clear with a view of the pond and the wildflowers. I have my doubts that it will work, and I worry that this generation has torn an unwitting hole in the order of the universe. Katie would call me reactionary. I want them to be happy, but when you attend to one thing, you have to neglect another. To say that everything we did was worthless and that this new way of life promises infinite happiness, I know that to be false. There were good things about the choices we made, and although it was limiting, it evolved that way for a reason.

I have tried to make this family something that will endure even after we are no longer under the same roof, but Katie and Elizabeth have so little in common, and Ben will no doubt find a woman to love and follow. There isn't a law that sisters have to love each other, but there is a law about mothers and children. Josh and I will be gone someday; I hope before our children go. At that point, only the three of them will be able to bear witness to the people that Ben, Katie, and Elizabeth Gottlieb were before they learned how to control their image, before they tore up the pictures of themselves they didn't like and retold the stories of their childhood to exclude the parts where they were less than kind. Maybe that's the reason to have children. To know someone before they have really learned to lie. Children are expert liars about the little things, who ate the cookie, who spilled the water; but they are completely transparent about the big things, how openly you love, how big you dream, your moral compass. I know these things about my children. As we grow up, that honesty fades. The mother is the last person a child learns to lie to, but eventually they start to hide their failings and lie even to us. Despite our reassurances that we will love them, warts and all, despite the mothers visiting murderers on death row and weeping at the graves of serial killers, they start to lie to us. It may be true that it is not possible to both fully know and truly love another human being, and that none of us, not in America, not in China, not anywhere on this planet, can bear to believe this truth, and that it is this lack of belief that turns us all into liars. I suppose it is more important to be loved than to be known, though for a short time early in life, a child can have both.

Someone has rung the doorbell. Maybe Katie or Ben forgot their key. Everyone else is staying in a hotel. This house with its five bedrooms has felt too big for us for a long time, but when either Josh or I suggest moving, we say we will wait for grandchildren. Grandchildren will fill the house again, and Elizabeth doesn't want us to change her room. We made Ben's room into a library. I took down the posters in Katie's room, all the unpleasant pictures of rock bands and fallen guerrilla leaders, and underneath I found the wallpaper of clouds and rainbows that she picked out when she was seven years old and we first moved to this house. One day she and Elizabeth had colored along the edges in a corner where they thought I wouldn't notice. I should have congratulated myself on not being angry when I found it, though the wallpaper was discontinued and the pictures of dogs and hearts and unicorns (I think they are unicorns, my children are not artists) could not be erased. They are still there, and there they will remain until the house is sold and another family will come and leave their mark, and then the house will be sold again or torn down, which is happening to so many houses in this neighborhood. The persistence of memory. I think that is a title of a painting Jack Chandler showed me once when he took Elizabeth and me on a tour of the Museum of Modern Art in New York. I can't remember the painting, but I know now, looking at Elizabeth's wedding dress — what am I supposed to do with this wedding dress? — that the title was wrong. It's the persistence of things, of wedding dresses that will never be worn again, of forks and spoons trampled into the dirt, of this planet once all the people and their dogs have died, things maybe, but not memory. Memories die with us.

I go to open the door, but there is no one there, just the dark night, the white tent, the wind, and the stars.

True love

IT WAS SO HOT. There was so much noise. I couldn't remember whose wedding this was, and I couldn't find Julius to tell me. Why I always had to go with him to these weddings I will never know. He loved his patients, his other family he used to call them, and brought home the postcards they sent from summer camp, the pictures of them in cap and gown, graduating from high school, from college, even from medical school. Sometimes I secretly thought he gave himself too much credit. Their parents were proud; they wanted to brag, and Dr. Rosenblatt would listen, but if we really needed them, if we were down to our last crumb and they were down to their last loaf of bread, would they break us off a piece? No. No, they would not. I never said it to Julius, but I knew they weren't family, and I knew he knew it too. In the Bronx, in New York City, in America, we were all alone, he and I and our two children we were so unprepared to defend. He could imagine that the wife of a city councilman was telling the truth when she said, If there's anything you need, you call me. My husband knows people who can help you. That was after her baby had meningitis, and Julius knew what it was and saved him, even called the emergency room when they wanted to send him home, and said, That baby is sick. Don't you dare send that baby home. My Julius went there and did whatever a doctor has to do to save a baby's life, and the city councilman owed us, but Julius and I both know that gratitude has its limits; gratitude is not as strong as fear.

I underestimated these woods. While I sat there in the heat wondering what had become of Julius, watching the young girls laugh and the boys pretend to be men, I studied these woods. They are young and thin, unsuitable for hiding anything bigger than a mouse. I doubted anything lived there; they seemed too shallow and dry for mushrooms or wild boar or deer. Pheasants? Certainly not. Stags, peacocks, wolves, bears — impossible. No one could weave a fairy tale out of these sticks and dried leaves. Still, it looked cooler there than here, quieter, safer. So I left just for a moment. Julius must have been congratulating the parents, kissing the bride. He felt one should never miss a chance to kiss a bride. He would never admit to superstition. He was a scientist, he would say. There is no evil eye; there is no bad luck, no good luck, no charms or curses. For better or for worse, we make the world, he would say. But then he would also say that you should never miss a chance to kiss a bride; he touched the children's foreheads before he put the thermometer in their mouths; he forbade me to even speak their names before they were born; old beliefs die hard because they are old beliefs.

It was hazy in the woods, partly because the sun is so strong in America. I know the world is round, but the rays of the sun seem to have decided to concentrate their glare here. It is colder and hotter. The sun turns away, crosses her arms, won't even consider a glance until summer when she pivots back, slit eyes and furrowed brow, and concentrates on nothing but this part of the world. Or that's how it feels to the foreigner. Some of the haze was due to the growing moonstones in my eyes. Don't make it pretty, Rachel, my husband would say. They are cataracts. When the doctor told me, I couldn't understand what he said, but it is rude to keep asking someone to repeat themselves, so I asked Annette to write it down. I have a dictionary. It was my Simon's when he was in high school. It has a red binder, and inside I found a valentine there once, from a girl who said she loved him, and I wondered if he loved her back. Susan was her name, and I never heard that name before, so was it a secret he kept from me or maybe he didn't care for her. I looked up the word *cataract*, and the book said it was a waterfall, a cascade. I have a waterfall in my eye? It sounded rather nice, a waterfall in my eye, a cascade in my ear, blocking out all the terrible things I have seen and heard.

As I walked away, away, the trees grew thicker, the clouds heavier, the sun softer so there was a blur between earth and sky, and it seemed to me that if I wanted to I could walk up the sides of the edges of the universe, a little bit of a steep climb, but one I might be able to do if I could find a walking stick. I saw the sides of the Earth slope upward, and it seemed to me that the top of that slope was my destination, though now I am too old, too frail, to get there even with a walking stick. I would need someone to help me, and there was no one. Still, I focused on the edge of the world and decided to walk there. What else did I have to do? It grew silent. I could not even hear my own footsteps. Again, the soft leaf floor might have been sucking in the sound, but my antiquity was also to blame. I had left my hearing aids back in the nursing home. Nursing home was a terrible name for that place. It had nothing to do with nursing. English is a language of meshuga people where nursing can mean the baby at the breast, the lady in white who tends to the wounded, and a place to hide the half dead and forgotten, where they light the halls with a blazing light that screams, You're still here! Don't go anywhere! We've got you!

It was a relief to be in the half darkness of the woods even if it was only a degree or two cooler. What does a breeze in hell get you? Someone asked that question once. I can't remember the context, although I can imagine quite a few, a crumb for the starving, a piece of cotton on a gaping wound, a kiss for the dying, a breeze in hell. Julius and I, we knew what it meant to be offered too little, but the people at this wedding — whose wedding was it? — they did not know that. They would say thank you to be polite and toss the breeze, the cotton, the kiss, over their shoulders, smile conspiratorially, acknowledging the effort as if it were charming.

It never really got hot in Hesse. I didn't know heat until I came to America and burned my skin one day at the beach in New Jersey. In Hesse, there was a river outside of town with a rocky beach and tiny purple snail shells where we used to go to for swimming. The goyim ate snails, not the Jews, but these snails were too tiny to be eaten by anything but the hungriest and most desperate birds. The water was cold. *Ai* was it cold! It never bothered my brothers, but Eva made a great show of dashing in and running out. David coaxed us in, his arm outstretched; he held Eva with one hand and Levi with the other, because Levi was deaf and my mother assumed this made other things difficult for him. In fact, once he was in, Levi was a great swimmer. A regular fish, the one word of English I spoke when I came to America because it is the same in Yiddish. *Fisch.* Fish.

Once at dinner in a Chinese restaurant in New York, I saw a little boy tapping on a tank full of orange fish. He tapped and tapped and tapped and made faces, and Julius finally had to get up and stop him. I asked him, Why, was it bothering him? And he said, No, it was bothering the fish. How would it bother the fish? I asked. They're deaf. Fish are not deaf, Rachel. They hear things we can't hear, movement and the shift of waves, and that boy's fingers on the glass were probably like an earthquake to them. I was embarrassed; I stopped going to school when the war started when I was eight years old, so what do I know from books? I did go to some classes here and there in the displaced persons camp after the war, but by then, I was a teenager and — like when I rode a bicycle, something else I learned too late in life — I was never very comfortable with reading and writing, especially in English, which was my fifth language after Yiddish, Polish, Hebrew, and German. If I had gone to school, I would have known that fish could hear. I would have known that Bach was a German but Mendelssohn was a Jew. I would have known that the heart does not actually control our emotions and that when we feel it breaking that's the brain telling the heart to ache because we are knowing sadness.

Levi was a fish. He swam strongly, and Eva, once in the water, bobbed and danced there, but it was too cold for me, as small and skinny as I was. The water cut into me, and the stones were sharp on my feet. I hurried out, and the air was

like a cold cage because it never got that hot in Hesse even
in July under a cloudless sky with the sun as yellow as an egg
yolk. It was hot now, though, and I found a little stream, not a
river, not even a creek. It was a gash in my path to the end of
the world, but it seemed to have been put there just for me,
a chance to rest and cool off before I continued on my journey. It was down a gully, but someone had been kind enough
to put steps here, made of stone, with a railing of a twisted
green vine. I held on and lowered myself down. The water
was clear, but at the bottom, despite the waterfall in my eye,
I could see mud and bubbles so I knew something was living
there, deep and buried. I took my shoes off and stepped in,
watched the cool water make eddies around my ankles. The
bottom of the stream was sandy and it glittered in the weak
sun. The woods were absolutely silent. When I looked up, I
could still see my destination, the end of the world, sloping
upward, not down over a horizon but up to a white sky that
would lead me, not to heaven, there is no heaven, but to rest.
Standing in the stream with my feet sinking deeper so now I
felt the sand around my ankles, I could have been anywhere:
America where airplanes soar overhead and cars honk, or in
the north of Israel where the desert turns to mountains and
forest, or in Germany where the tree trunks are so thick that
Eva, Levi, and I would have to link hands and stretch out our
arms to get around one. This was a trap. I knew it. Something
was pulling me down, deeper than my ankles, almost past my
calves. The hem of my dress was wet. It was a pink dress. I
found it in my closet one day. I would never buy myself such
a dress. When I was a little girl, I always wanted a pink dress,
or a red one, or a yellow one, but it was not practical. My

mother bought me dresses in navy blue and gray, and when I said they were ugly, my mother said, The dress should be ugly because the girl is so pretty. She tied my hair back, and said, Maybe I will buy you a beautiful dress, like a princess would wear, but then I would have to cut off your hair because too much beauty brings the evil eye. Too much beauty brings the evil eye. It's too lovely here to be real.

There was music coming from somewhere. Bach or the Jew Mendelssohn who wrote the "Wedding March." I looked up through the trees to see black birds crawling across the white sky. Their talons shredded the sky. The sky is paper. The earth is nothing but sand and water, stone and salt, as are we humans. Julius once told me that the body is almost all water; throw in a little salt, some minerals and electricity, and that's all it takes to make a human being. God made us from the water, dirt, and salt of the earth, and we go back to the earth. In these trees and leaves and animals are the souls of the dead. If I wait long enough, they will pull their roots from the ground and come for me. Come to me dancing. I am going to wait here for that moment. Julius will find me here. So will my mother and my sister, my father and my brothers. Find me here, please. I have been waiting for so long.

I abandoned my quest for the highway. It was too hard. The streets all had the same name. River Place, River Edge, River Drive, the place of rivers, the edge of rivers, the drive of rivers. I kept making wrong turns, kept reaching dead ends, cul-de-sacs, coal-de-sacs, sacks of coal. I found myself walking in circles under the blazing hot sun while a sprinkler made fun of me: fool, fool, fool, fooooooool. I screamed, and two kids ran inside the house, banged the door shut so loudly that the mailboxes shook. My shirt was soaked with sweat. I took off my coat, threw it into someone's yard, then the tie, a new blue tie my mom gave me to wear to Elizabeth's wedding. My feet were sloshing in my shoes. I had to take them off too. I stuffed them into a mailbox that stood at the end of a long driveway leading up to a redbrick house. I wondered what the people who lived there would think when they found the shoes — because they were nice shoes, expensive, Johnston & Murphy. They'd have to think that whoever wore these shoes was a lucky guy. Someone loved him enough to buy him expensive shoes, or maybe that the son of a bitch was just plain rich, not the type who has to worry when he hands over his credit card. Rich enough that when he gets a scuff on these shoes or steps in dog shit he can just throw them away and buy another pair. There wasn't any dog shit on the shoes when I stuffed them in the mailbox. I'm not that big of an asshole.

People were staring at me. Cars slowed down to check me out. A black Mercedes followed me for several minutes, then pretended to turn into a driveway. The windows were tinted. I couldn't look in, but I knew they were watching me. I heard a siren far away. The Mercedes guy must have called the police. They would never believe I was innocent. The sirens were far away. How stupid were the cops to turn on their sirens and let me know they were coming! I ducked into the woods. I knew those woods. I used to go there when I was a kid. The other boys in the neighborhood and I used to take off our shirts, paint stripes on our chests and faces with red clay, and whoop like warriors. We would divide up, stalk each other, tackle from behind, roll down over the dead leaves and pinecones, and crash into trees and mud puddles and anthills. War was our default game. When did it stop being war? Never, really. The boys were men, but we were all still locked in battle, fighting for the pretty girl, the house, the car, the home, to say I've got the biggest dick and the hottest chick. If you didn't want to fight, you'd get tackled unless you ran home and locked the door or found a really, really good hiding place and stayed there until dusk, when the streetlights came on and the warriors had been called home and scrubbed clean.

Then you could come out. Then you could watch the fireflies float in the inky blue sky, higher and higher until they blended in with the stars. Someone told me once that stars were made of fireflies. I was a little boy. I think it was one of my babysitters, one of those pretty girls who used to tuck me in at night, and then I would sneak out and watch her brush her hair and talk on the phone. Not every firefly became a star, but there were anointed ones, chosen ones, whose tiny phosphorescent wings could ascend high enough, past the clouds into the darkness of space, through the millions and millions of miles into the galaxy, until they came across a sticky piece of the velvety sky, and there they stayed, beaming down at us for what might as well be eternity for human beings but was not eternity because every fucking thing dies, the sun, the stars, and the world as we know it.

I took girls into the woods. We all did. The basement worked sometimes, but your mom or your sister could come home anytime. Your sister could come downstairs and tell you she wanted to watch TV with her friend Elizabeth, and you and Jenna Cook would have to snap to attention. You'd have to take your hands out of her pants and resist the sensation that *everyone* could tell your fingers smelled like Jenna's pussy, and your mom was pretty good. She smiled as if she were happy you had gotten to third base, and she smiled sweetly, but she knew; she had to know because everyone could see the shame, read your mind, know that your dick was so hard it hurt. Still, Mom smiled because she just wanted her little boy to be happy, so she backed away hoping that Jenna would at least give you a hand job. Your sister. She wasn't so nice. She looked the girl you were with up and down, sized her up. Laughed. Crinkled her nose at the smell on your fingers. Then she and her friend sat down on the sofa, took out nail polish and lipstick, and started putting on clown faces, smacking their lips, batting their eyelashes. And then, of course, Jenna or Suzanne or Lori weren't in the mood anymore. Her shirt was buttoned. She'd scooped up her schoolbooks and was headed for the door. So we made a fort in the woods at a spot where the rocks came together. We laid down some Astroturf we stole when the high school was renovating the gym, then ringed it with stones and painted one stone red. If the red stone was sitting on the tree stump, the fort was taken. When we graduated and went to college, Stan Hammond willed the spot to his younger brother. Some friend of Stan's brother must have passed on the favor, and so it was likely, almost certain, that the fort was still there, and I was pretty sure that if I could find the creek and follow it I would be able to find it.

I knew there wouldn't be a girl there waiting for me. I'd be thrown in jail if some high school girl was there, some girl half my age, waiting to do it with her seventeen-year-old boyfriend or left there, passed out and half-dressed, splayed out on a rock, and offering to the gods what you might have the hubris to take and for which you would be eternally punished. But maybe I'd get lucky, maybe some fantasy of a girl, half fairy, half sorority sister in a diaphanous gown, would be lying on a bed of rose petals. I'm not crazy. I knew there wouldn't be any princesses or fairies, but I figured it would be a good place to rest, maybe even live like those hermits in ancient times. Despite all the pollution and the fact that sometimes the river bubbled orange with sewage, I still saw people fishing there once in a while. They caught tiny bass, probably three-eyed bass and finless trout, but who wants to live forever? I could live on radioactive fish and berries for a while, and maybe one day a girl would appear, a fairy, to save me. A beautiful fairy in a white gown would carry me up on the wings of some giant mutant firefly. A fairy with huge tits and no underwear — it's a known fact that fairies don't wear underwear. Under those gowns, there was nothing, and if you were ever to see one — you never would, asshole, fairies don't exist — but if they did and you came across one in the woods and she flew high enough, you could look right up her dress, and if you survived the act of seeing a fairy's pussy, you'd probably be changed forever, and in a good way. The world would suddenly make sense.

I found a trickle of water that had to be the beginning of the creek. It wasn't much, but everything starts small and gets big, or the other way around, right? Maybe this was all that was left of the creek; by thirty, I had come to realize that everything was shallow and shrunken now compared to my memory of it. Barefoot, I stepped into the water. It barely covered my hairy feet, but it cooled me, and I watched my sweat blend into the water and drift away in a spiral. There were snakes in the creek, or there used to be, water moccasins and cottonmouths. I saw one once with Jenna, and I threw a stick at it, and she jumped closer to me, though actually at the time I was scared shitless myself. Standing in the trickle of water that passed for a creek, I wasn't scared of the snakes. If a water moccasin bit me, or a copperhead, or even a rattlesnake, and I died here, that would be God's plan. That would be the way things were supposed to be, my punishment for taking what wasn't mine, the naked girl on the rock, the half-dressed girl on the dorm-room bed. I was not supposed to find a fairy; I was supposed to get poison injected into my foot that would travel to my heart and brain; I was supposed to die a very painful death alone.

Elias Auerbach was running toward me. Splashing water as he ran, Eva's lover had his arms stretched out to me. Handsome Elias, truly the most handsome young man in our village, who loved the prettiest girl. The picture of him I saw after the war did not do him justice. I showed it to Julius, and said, Elias was more beautiful than a movie star, tall and thin, a little like Gregory Peck but with skin the color of strong tea. What was he doing here? No one ever knew exactly what happened to Elias. We left Hesse; he stayed. When the SS came, he ran into the woods and was never seen again. His sister told me that she thought he joined the partisans, but others said a peasant kept him as slave labor and turned him in for money after he had worked him nearly to death.

Others said wild animals had killed him. Nothing was confirmed, but I never imagined he had come to America. How had he stayed so young? Was it true, what my Simon said, that there were tiny, tiny slits in the universe, holes in time — What did he call them? Bug holes, worm holes? — and you could take yourself out for a minute and a lifetime would pass on Earth and you could return only one minute older? That's what happened to Elias! He had done it. I called Simon my little heder boy, *nezer* in the *bikhl* he was, nose in the book always. Full of meshuga ideas, maybe not so meshuga. Here was Elias Auerbach, who should have been dead, and if not dead, then old, as old as I was, running toward me, toward Rachel Rosenblatt. Did he think I was Eva? No, you couldn't confuse dark-haired skinny Rachel with graceful blond Eva, Eva with her full lips and full breasts and eyes so big and soft that it was said half the village was in love with her, including the German boys who were taught there was no such thing as a pretty Jew, who were taught that under her clothes she was covered in sharp silver scales. He must see Eva somewhere. He is calling to her — Hey, he shouts. Don't move! When did Elias learn English? Where has he been all these years? Has he been in hiding, and only just now, when he heard the music, the "Wedding March" written by a Jew, did he realize that it was safe to come out? The birds tore the paper of the sky open, and Elias came through. I understood now. He must have saved Eva too. He was running toward her, not me. I looked all around for my sister, tried to see past the trees up into the paper sky, all the way to the edge of the world where the Earth turned upward like the lip of a bowl. Nothing would focus, but it was Levi and Michael that needed glasses, not me. Thank God, my mother said. A boy in glasses looks like a scholar, but a girl — no.

"I don't know where she is!" I had to tell him. Wherever he had been, he could not have known what happened. He was running toward me with such joy; I feared the disappointment would kill him. He had survived, but his beloved had not. "I think she died," I shouted. "Eva. A long time ago."

It was as if he didn't hear me. He just kept shouting, "Don't move. Don't be scared. I just want to see you. I won't hurt you!"

"I know you won't," I said. "I know you're a Jew." He was close enough for me to really see him now. Elias was changed; of course, he would have changed. Sixty years had passed. He looked a little older but still young, not nearly as old as I. He'd gotten fatter, but hadn't we all wanted to be fat after the war; after we had nearly starved, hadn't we wanted to never have an empty cupboard again, to always have a refrigerator full of meat and cheese and milk. Hadn't Julius laughed at me the first time we went out to dinner in America when I ordered two of everything and tried to wrap up the steak in a napkin to put in my purse. When they brought me coffee and a little silver pitcher of milk, I looked around for something to pour the milk into, and then asked Julius if we could take the silver pitcher — there was one on every table, so I was sure the hotel wouldn't miss it. Julius had said that would be stealing, and I had said, Is that such a crime? My husband examined the pitcher of milk, and told me, If you want a silver pitcher, I will buy you one. I don't want the pitcher, I said. I want the milk.

We stood face-to-face now. Elias had survived, but he

was different, and I barely recognized him. He was no longer handsome, but he wouldn't be, of course. His beauty had been tied up with his innocence and his courage, loving a girl when the world was about to end but not having experienced its end.

"We thought you were lost, but you were here all along."

"Where?"

"Here."

"You're old."

I said, "I know. Why aren't you?"

"I am."

"Not as old as I am. At least you don't look it."

"I feel it."

"Eva is dead. Michael found a man in a refugee camp who saw her killed. She died in Bergen-Belsen," I said. "And I thought you were dead too. All these years I thought you were dead. Your sister found me after the war and she was certain of it. Where have you been?"

"I've been in terrible places," he told me. "Where the rivers boil with blood and doctors kill people instead of saving them. Men in white stomp through the halls carrying sharp knives, and people lie in beds with their arms outstretched getting poison pumped in their veins, begging for more life. The lights are so bright there that everyone looks old, even the newborn babies. That's why babies cry when they're born. They see their death. Where I was, everything that looks pretty is ugly, and that means everything that's ugly should be pretty, but it's not. Or if it was, I couldn't see it."

"I was there too."

"I thought you'd be younger. And prettier."

"I think you're thinking of my sister. She was the beauty of the family."

"Can you fly?"

What a thing to say! But maybe that was not an unreasonable question in whatever place he had been. "No." I shook my head. "Not yet, at least. Can you?"

"No, of course not. You're the one who should be able to fly. But you should be younger, prettier . . ." He looked up to the sky. "Nothing is ever the way it's supposed to be for me. I always get the wrong side of the coin. Old, not new; ugly, not pretty. Stupid, not smart. Dead, not living. Tails, not heads."

He reached out for me and held me by the shoulders, held me strong, hurt me a little, but I didn't pull away. I was afraid of losing him.

"Will you fix what's wrong with me?" he asked.

"I don't think I can," I said. "Too much time has passed." I was sad for him. He wanted Eva, but he got me. Perhaps it was not a better fate to survive that way. I think he was realizing it too, and we both blinked at each other. I didn't cry though. I had a talent for not crying, not crying when I got on the train that took me away from my mother, not crying when I saw Levi killed, not crying when I learned that my mother and my father were dead, not crying when Julius died. If you want the milk, Julius said, drink it now. I told him that I wasn't thirsty or hungry, so he called the waiter over and asked if we could buy the silver pitcher. The waiter didn't know what to do. No one had ever asked to buy the silver pitcher before. He got his manager. Julius reached for his wallet, and the manager saw the tattoo on his wrist, and said, "Sir, you may have the pitcher. Compliments of the Plaza."

"You have to," Elias insisted. "Please," he begged. "I can't stay this way."

The water was swirling around our ankles. The hem of my dress was wet, and the young man's trousers were wet. I hadn't noticed before, but there were tiny silver fish in the water. And bits of gold and maybe diamonds.

I reached up to Elias and placed my hands, my old bony hands, on either side of his face. "Everything is fine now," I told him. "I can't remember the last time I was hungry. Everything will be fine. You did what you had to do. All is forgiven. All is forgiven."

I leaned my head against his chest and heard his heartbeat. The sound of life, of all life, so fast in a baby, then slower as we age until there is one last clap and we're done. Seeing Elias, my heart was happy. People talk of heartbreak, the pain you feel there, but there is also joy there, a quicksilver lightening, a skip, a song in my heart. I know, I know, Julius, it all comes from the brain, but you feel it in your heart, and it is your heart that makes things final. You have a thought, you speak your last words, but it isn't over until the heart stops beating. I counted out his heartbeats. My own heart is so slow that the doctor wanted to put in a thing to make it keep working, a pacemaker. Annette was mad at me, but I said, No, it's slowing down, thank God; I should be so lucky that one day it will just come to a stop.

Of course I would get an old wrinkled fairy, tired and sad and maybe a little crazy. She wasn't making any sense. Who was this Eva she kept talking about? Was that supposed to be my fairy? She kept saying how beautiful she was — figures, there was some last-minute switch, and I don't get the fairy, I get the witch. They're probably the same thing anyway, fairies, good witches, bad witches, bitches. My girlfriend, my love, Serena, that bitch was beautiful and evil, so I am probably better off with hideous and good. This fairy didn't seem very powerful though, no wings, a pink dress and jacket that looked like something my mother would put in the pile to be taken to the Salvation Army, but I had no choice but to believe her when she said everything would be fine. She got the part about being hungry all the time, how the meds do that to me, fucking with the satiety center in the hypothalamus so a stack of pizzas reaching the moon couldn't fill me up. I'd puke before my brain said to stop already.

I was trying to remember what was supposed to happen now. She kept talking about my taking her away, but I thought she was supposed to take me away, link her arm through mine so we could float up to heaven. I was pretty sure I was supposed to kiss her. Jesus fucking Christ, I didn't know if I could. She had brown splatters all over her face, her skin was papery and crinkled as if some little kid had wadded it and then tried to stretch it out again like a hundred times. It was weird when she touched me, though, because her hands were soft, and for a minute, I felt safe and happy. The last time I felt that happy, my mom was pushing me on a swing. How high do you want to go? she asked me. Would you like your feet to touch the clouds? Yes! Yes! I wanted my feet to touch the clouds. There was music coming from somewhere, classical, and there should be classical music, right, because fairies were old like Mozart and Beethoven. Your fairy isn't going to come floating down to AC/DC or the Rolling Stones. She's going to arrive with violins and a little flute, a harp maybe.

"Something's wrong with my brain," I told her. "And I really need help. The doctors can't fix me. My mom and dad are giving up. I am pretty sure no one is ever going to love me."

"Don't say those things," she said. "Eva loved you so much. Someone will love you. I used to think the same thing. Worse even. I thought the world was a terrible place; how could anyone ever love someone after seeing what people could do to one another? But I found Julius. He had suffered even more than I did, and he loved me. Children he lost, and then I gave him children, and he loved them too. Could you see any of this from where you were? No." She searched my eyes. "No. It seems you don't know all the terrible things that happened. Eva was killed. Levi was shot dead. My mother and father, your mother and father. Your sister survived, but I am sorry. I don't know if she's still alive. We lost touch a long time ago."

"My sister's alive," I said. "In a way, she's lucky. She only wants what the world can give her, and she's really, really good at not seeing all the shitty things that happen. The world's more shit than good. But don't tell my sister that. She thinks there's redemption in a shopping bag."

My fairy's eyes were gray and glassy. They looked a little watery, loose in the sockets. I had the sudden thought that they were going to pop out and I would have to catch them because they were actually precious gemstones that would hold the secret to something, the answer to a question so important that I didn't even know how to ask it.

"A shopping bag," she said. "Redemption in a shopping bag."

She laughed, and it was a really beautiful laugh, a laugh in a foreign language if there is such a thing. It definitely wasn't an American laugh, not even one in English. It was a laugh I'd never heard before. "Redemption in a shopping bag," she said again. "Elias" — she squeezed my face — "let's go back to where you were. It's probably better there. The bug hole, the worm hole, the cut in the sky, let's go through it. I'm ready. Eva's not here. There isn't anything for you here. Let's go back there. I'm never going to die. That's obvious now. But everyone has to leave somehow. Isn't that why you are here? To take me away?"

"I think it's the other way around. You're supposed to save me. You're the one with all the magic."

She closed her eyes tightly. I could see the veins bulging around her eyes. She clutched her hands to her chest. "My heart is breaking," she said. "Seeing you and remembering Eva. I know the heart doesn't really break. Julius taught me that. You feel sad in your brain, and the brain tells the heart to hurt and makes you feel pain here — in the chest — but it hurts, Elias. It hurts so much." Her face was flushed red; she reached for my hands. "I don't think we have a lot of time, Elias. We need to go now." She stumbled a bit, falling into me.

"I'm not Elias."

"Of course you are. Who else would you be?"

Who else would I be? That was a good question. "Can you make me someone else?" I asked. "Is that something you can do?"

She shook her head against my shirt. "I'm not the magical one. You are." She dropped my hands and held her arms out. "Look at me. I'm old and tired. Yes, I survived the war, but that wasn't magic. It was luck. You're the magical one. You survived. You survived and stayed young."

The music stopped. Suddenly, like in a game of musical chairs. There were shouts now, of joy or fear, I couldn't tell. Shouts but no sirens. I listened for them. Then the sky fell apart, crumbled, and let in so much light that it seemed like all the stars were being drawn to us, an uncountable number of suns bearing down on us. We had only a moment, the smallest fraction of time, before we'd burn to death. I looked up to where the shouts were and now I could see them all, see all the fairies dancing, tossing flowers in the air, shouting with delight at the end of the world. There were flowers everywhere.

"We have to go now," I said. I scooped her up in my arms. She put her arms around my neck. Someone would come to rescue the fairies. They'd never be allowed to die. We had to find a way to get to them.

"Thank you, Elias," she said. She let her head fall back, and her eyes darted back and forth, following the leaves and branches as I rushed us toward safety. Her eyes were moving, moving so quickly. There was a name for it, a name I'd learned in medical school. Nostradamus? No, nystagmus.

The music started again. This old fairy was heavier than she looked. She was probably centuries old, and after so long, her body must have become denser so inside of her, rather than carbon and calcium, I would find lead and mercury. I got closer and saw all the fairies dancing, the young ones, the pretty ones, the ones who were not meant for me. My fairy's eyes were closed, and I thought I heard her humming. The circle opened, and in the center was a woman in white.

Veiled and illuminated, her arms lifted to heaven, the queen of the fairies. She looked squarely at me. I had seen her before. I suddenly realized I had seen her before, and I had done something terrible to her, something for which there was no atoning. She looked through my skin, through my skull to the tangle of my brain. It was her fault, I realized. She had cursed me, and no one could fix me.

Then I knew why I had been sent this ancient fairy. She was the only one who could undo the curse. In all the stories I ever read, the oldest witch, the oldest king, the oldest wizard, they were always the strongest, and even though she didn't look like much, given her unworldly weight and her wisdom, she had to be more powerful, able to stir the seas with a twitch of her finger. And she was mine. She had said it. All was forgiven. Now I understood. If the queen of the fairies, who looked so beautiful, so lovely all in white, enchanting, my mother would say, as if it were a compliment, when what it really meant was that your beauty could cast a spell, an evil spell — most spells are evil — and curse the brain of the young doctor so he could no longer cure the sick, so he would become fat and ugly and stupid; if she had cursed me, it would take a strong fairy to break the curse, an ancient one with potions and powers unknown even to the queen.

"You did nothing wrong," my fairy murmured. "All is forgiven." Her eyelids were as thin as crushed flower petals, veined and lilac in color.

"I need you to help me," I said. She was getting heavier by the minute as all the power of the universe was condensed into her small ancient body. I was determined not to drop her. I knew I was being tested. The circle closed. Confetti in the air.

The crowd rushed away from us like water down a drain, leaving the castle suddenly empty, the glasses still full of wine, flowers in the vases, cake on the plates. I staggered up the hill. I thought we were going to be burned up or left alone in a wasteland, but there we stood, a fat, stupid hero carrying a leaden, tired fairy, and it was cool and quiet and very still. Where had they all gone? And in such a hurry. Balloons bobbed in a man-made breeze from slow-turning fans in the tent. We had our choice of tables.

"Lay me down," she said. "I'm so tired." Someone had left a sparkly gold shoe on the dance floor, Cinderella's shoe maybe; there could, of course, be more than one story at a time. I was not the only one suffering in the world. Some poor mistreated princess who had lost her throne might have come here seeking the assistance of the fairies. I lay her down on the floor. There were three silver fans turning overhead and a string of bright lights, rose petals and confetti on the floor, a half-eaten giant white cake on the center table. Her eyes were still closed. She moaned and turned her face to the side. My God, my God, I realized, she had to die to save me. It had taken so much out of her, every last scrap of energy; she had used all of it to expel them, all of them who had wished me unwell.

Cake! Maybe the cake was magical — why else would it be here? I sprang up and sank my hand into the cake. "Here," I said urgently. "Here." I had a fistful of the stuff, too much cake, too much icing. I nipped a piece off, opened her mouth to put it in. The icing smeared on her lips, the cake sat on her tongue. She didn't swallow it, but she smiled. She tried to sit up, beckoned for me to come closer. She said, cake falling out of her mouth, "I can't believe you found me. Eva would be so happy you survived. That's true love, you know. Wanting someone to live even after you die." She touched a bony finger to her lips and examined it, the white and pink icing. She lay back down, turned her head away from me. The veins in her neck bulged.

I felt the curse lifting, the doctor in me returning, like blood through an arm after the tourniquet is removed. Heart failure! She was in heart failure. I looked down to her feet, fallen apart in the shape of a V, and saw her swollen legs, doughy and sodden. If I had my stethoscope, I would listen to her lungs and hear the telltale sloshing of extra water, the drowning that comes when the blood returns to a weakened heart, a heart that can't push forward anymore and, exhausted, keeps the blood waiting but can't stop it from returning, returning, even though this is the end of the line. Fairies have hearts, I realized. So do hummingbirds and armadillos, rhinoceroses and sorority sisters. Dinosaurs had hearts too. Dragons must. And unicorns. Everything that breathes. Hearts that fail. Hearts that stop.

I dragged a chair over and propped her legs up, then sat Indian-style with her head in my lap. Her neck was damp with sweat, her breath shallow. I smoothed the gray hair off her face; even the lightest touch of my hand left a bruise. I watched it blossom under my thumb, a lilac flower on her cheek. "Elias," she sighed.

I started to tell her that I am not Elias, but then I thought maybe I was. Maybe there was a mix-up all along, and I should just be whoever this worn-out fairy wanted me to be. It had to be better than being Steven Shapiro. "Yes?"

"Thank you for coming to get me. We can go now."

"You can go," I said. "If you want to. *Shh.*" I smoothed her hair. "Go." The cake now had a giant gash in its side. It hadn't saved her. Cinderella's shoe was still lying there. There didn't seem to be a prince coming back for it. Maybe I was the prince. You don't really know who you are until the end of the story. I picked up the shoe, tried to put it on her foot, but her feet were massively swollen. It would never fit. I crossed her arms over her abdomen and tucked the shoe in her hands. "You go find the prince," I said. "I think I have to stay here for a while longer."

Acknowledgments

Thank you to agent extraordinaire Rayhané Sanders, who believed in this book before anyone else, to my wise editor, Lauren Wein, who saw the humor and the sorrow in these stories, and to David Hough for his careful and incisive copy-editing, as well as all the staff at Houghton Mifflin Harcourt who valiantly kept me on task. I am eternally grateful to my parents, Evan and Nancy Weisman, who taught me a love of literature and bought me endless books and paid library fines when I was growing up. Thank you to Tiffany Lorente for reminding that I am a writer and to Marie Edwards for running my practice so well that I can find time to work. Jonathan Weisman and Jennifer Steinhauer helped fine-tune Carla and Steven. My daughters, Shira and Isabelle Balaban, inspire me to greater compassion and bigger dreams. To the moon and back, my darlings. Finally, this book, like everything I write, is a collaborative effort with my husband, Victor Balaban, my Maxwell Perkins. Till China and Africa meet, *mi amor.*

Questions for Discussion

1. *We Are Gathered* gives voice to the guests at a wedding — not, as one might expect, the bride and groom. Do you feel like you have a sense of who the bride and groom are after hearing from their guests?

2. "We are supposed to be hardwired to decide what is beautiful and what is ugly" (33). Constructs of beauty and ugliness have shaped Carla's life. Discuss her relationship to her appearance and the ways in which that relationship evolves, or doesn't, by the end of her chapter. What has her port wine stain taught her about herself? And, importantly, about others and their values?

3. In "To be a king, you have to be born a prince," Albert, wheelchair-bound after his stroke, reflects on who he was a person and what he will leave behind: "I used to dream of stores bearing my name far into the future, when men traveled highways in the air and Mars was a vacation spot. It is clear that this is not going to happen, but then, most of the things that we predict for the fu-

ture do not come to pass" (52–53). Where do you think this desire to have a legacy — to leave an imprint on the world — comes from?

4. "We are neither heroic nor condemned . . . God's world, including Jeffrey, especially Jeffrey, is beautiful exactly the way it is" (91). Discuss what Jeffrey's mother means by this. Do her feelings toward Jeffrey, and how others see him, differ from her husband's? If so, how?

5. "Inside some people there is a block of rage, a hidden organ that you cannot see with a CT scan or exploratory surgery, but it is there, solid, pulsating, bloody, and inoperable, and it has a life of its own. It is passed from generation to generation. At times, I have consoled myself with the idea that it is in everyone" (130). What fills Jack with rage? What has he repressed; what in his life has gone unacknowledged?

6. In "The fucked-up nipple," Steven meets Elizabeth's great-aunt Rachel in the woods and says of her, "This lady is crazy, I think, and then I start to laugh, because so am I, and neither of us belongs here with all the people who are managing to live normal lives" (179). What do you make of their meeting? What is each looking for? Do they find it?

7. On page 214, Rachel recounts a conversation she had with Julius about souls. He tells her "human beings are so much more than the workings of the body. There is a

soul, Rachel." Discuss the idea of souls and why this conversation has stuck with Rachel for so long. Does this idea offer her hope? Release? Comfort?

8. By the time Annette's section arrives toward the end of the book, "A slice of leftover cake (with raspberry filling)," we have met her through many other characters. Is her voice as you expected? One page 249, she concludes that memory isn't persistent, things are: "It's the persistence of things, of wedding dresses that will never be worn again, of forks and spoons trampled into the dirt, of this planet once all the people and their dogs have died, things maybe, but not memory." What leads her to this realization? Are memories and things separate?

9. On the last page of the book, Steven thinks, "You don't really know who you are until the end of the story". Discuss what he means by this. Do the characters in the book who are approaching the end of their lives see themselves differently than the characters who aren't?

10. *We Are Gathered* is filled with both sorrow and happiness. Does one beget the other? Can one exist without the other?

A Conversation with Jamie Weisman

What inspired you to write *We Are Gathered*?

The very first section of this book was written ten years ago at a friend's wedding where her grandfather, a once very powerful man, was confined to a wheelchair. I was a medical student and just learning the details of how a stroke could alter the function of the brain so dramatically, and watching this man, whom I had known — and somewhat feared — most of my life, wondering what had become of his soul now that his body was so damaged, led me to put pen to paper. Every writer will tell you that what happens from that moment is a mystery, a communing with unconscious memories, rhythms, and thoughts that leads to a story. I did want to represent archetypes since a Wedding (capital W) is such an archetypal event, to have a balance of the powerful and the weak, the brave and the cowardly, the beautiful and the ugly, and finally, I hope, with this mix of characters to make you see that these opposing forces are in fact contained within each of us. After writing the book I wove back in the observations, where one character would relate to another through his or her personal pain or desires. While the voices vary greatly, if you read carefully, you might see that there is one overarching voice imagining it all.

Were the characters inspired by real people in your life?

Every character has a kernel of someone I have known. There are people in this book who correspond to people in my life, and I am sure that there will be a game locally trying to figure out who's who, but as Jack Chandler, the painter, says, once you start creating, once the image starts to form on the paper, "It isn't her anymore. It's partly me and partly a dream and partly a story, but it isn't ever the physically and morally flawed person who breathes in oxygen and breathes out carbon dioxide."

We Are Gathered **is set at a wedding, but we never hear from the bride and groom. Why did you choose not to tell their stories?**

I think at every major life event the participants reflect on who they are, what brought them to this point and where they are going. Days melt away, but weddings and funerals, bar mitzvahs and christenings divide up our lives into sections that allow us to measure not only ourselves and our place in the world but the overall order of the universe in some sense. The great pain of life is its time limits, but it is also the primary source of meaning. You have a limited amount of time to find love, to create or accomplish something, before you are nudged along, from your wedding to the wedding of your children to the end of your life.

Tolstoy's famous adage that happy people are all happy in the same way really holds true for fiction. Characters and stories need conflict. The mother of the bride, without knowing the Tolstoy quote, actually paraphrases it when she says, "Still, happy families must exist. It's just that no one gossips about them. What is there to say?" In fact, the good fortune of the bride and groom is a touch point for the guests who often measure their lives against them.

The wedding at the center of *We Are Gathered* in an interfaith Jewish wedding. What role—if any—does religion play in the book and in the lives of the characters?

Religions in all cultures have chosen weddings as an event in which ritual and authority must be imposed. What in some ways is the most intimate of choices — the person you are supposed to have sex with for the rest of your life — turns into a public spectacle. The village is invited, witnesses are needed, vows are read. Judaism has defined many of these characters — even Jack who is Pentecostal — both politically and emotionally. For Rachel, a Holocaust survivor, the fact of her Jewishness has been the defining point of her life, everything she has suffered and endured is a result of this identity, but even for characters that don't see religion as central to their lives, like Annette, the mother of the bride, the restrictions of religion have shaped her life, in terms of whom she would consider in marriage and the legacy of her parents. There are obvious political reasons why religion should play a role in marriage, control of dynasties and power, but because marriage also centers on love — even arranged marriages invoke love — it is natural that religion, as defined by humanity's grappling with the divine and inexplicable, would be central to the custom. Love is the closest we come to the divine in our life. In both the Old and New Testaments as well as the Koran, we are instructed not just to worship but to love God. In Hinduism love is a sacrament, an act of selflessness. Love is not something we can explain in Darwinian terms, and anything beyond the fully explicable and comprehensible evokes the divine.

You are a doctor and a writer. Are those two roles difficult to reconcile?

The function of the human body, the need for food, water and air are defining plot points. The body has to function, fear of disease and danger, in order for the character to have thoughts, memories, and aspirations. It's ultimately the limitation of the human body, the built-in expiration date, that inspires literature, philosophy, and religion. Doctors have an understanding of how things break down and go wrong, whether from genetic flaws or spasms of blood vessels or biochemical misfires. Every day we see suffering because of the limits of the human body, and all this suffering, since it occurs in a human being, is a story, but to be a doctor you have to separate yourself from that story in order to deliver consistent, dispassionate care. Yes, we strive to see each of our patients as individuals, but thankfully the workings of the human body are roughly the same for all of us. The writer in me takes over when I start imagining the effects of disease on the individual.

People who help shape my writing often have to check me when I get too medical. It can be hard to separate my knowledge from the knowledge that other people might have, so I am grateful to my wise early readers who help dissect the doctor from the story. I want to leave in enough science to be intriguing — science is cool! — without losing the compassion and emotion that make fiction so satisfying.

The soul is housed in the body, just like art is housed in a museum. And if there is a storm and the paintings are soaked are pocked with hailstones, they're changed. The body is mortal and vulnerable. This fact unites all of humanity, defines us and in the end is both a terrible deal and the reason great works of art have been created.